KRACKERS

By

Quill Stark

Quill Stark

Dedication

Michael Paul Bennier – May you rest in peace. With out you there would be no Krackers.

Ilene Daniel – Thanks from a large sheep.

Thomas Fairly – None of this would have been done without your jocularity and your chats.

Amy Elizabeth Fiscus – Without your help and encouragement, I would never have finished.

Eddie Hall – Thank you for your friendship.

John Breiner – Thank you for the 10 plus years I have known you.

Mr. English – Ashcroft High School English teacher –1974 - 1979. Without your guidance, this novel would never have been written.

Table of Content

Krackers

One.

Arrival

A naked body lay on a stainless-steel table in an air-conditioned room. He shivered slightly but didn't seem to notice the arctic blast. He was over-secured with fifteen restraints. He had given up struggling half an hour earlier.

He looked unusual, to say the least. His most striking feature was his shoulder-length, wispy platinum-blonde hair. Each strand shot out at different angles. Another curious feature of his hair was, well, it seemed to move by itself. In his present condition, his hair was in a highly agitated state. The hair lashed out at the frigid air, flicking it with savage ferocity.

"Look, Hair," the naked man shouted in the same agitated tone. "Stop it! I'm doing the best I can!" After his outburst, his hair became sullen and flopped about his head.

He started mumbling incoherently to himself. He suddenly stopped his babbling and looked around the room as though seeing it for the first time. He decided to struggle against his restraints again… his hair lashed out annoyingly in disapproval…

"Well, viewers, it's not looking that great for Krackers," he muttered to himself.

A clank brought the man back to the present.

"Hark…" he tried to look at the metal door. "Medication time," he smirked. "It must be a new mission."

The door hissed open; the darkness beyond enticed him.

"Nursie," he whispered seductively. The mere mention of her name released such pleasure.

She sauntered into the room; her barely-there uniform fought to cover her modesty. Her booted legs swam into view, they seemed to go on forever. She reached behind her head and coaxed her auburn-red hair forward. She fondled and caressed it, letting it flow through her hands repeatedly. She let it lift into the air then suddenly let it fall, breaking the moment.

"Hello, lover," she licked her lips. She drifted toward the secured man. "It's medication time…" As she reached the bed she looked up at the not-so-hidden camera jutting from the ceiling. She looked up and blew it a kiss. She wiggled across to the table, obscuring the view of the man.

"Medication time, lover," she leaned into the secured man and raised a gloved hand that held a syringe. She brought it down hard. Nursie giggled as she removed the syringe from his arm. She winked at him.

"Night-night, sweetie," she whispered. Nursie turned to the camera and blew another kiss. She straightened her uniform and sauntered out of the room. The camera whirred closer, then followed her to the door and lingered as Nursie bent to straighten her stockings. She slowly rose and smiled at the camera. She sauntered to the edge of the room and placed a hand into a pocket.

In a darkened control room, the vision of a voluptuous nurse blew a kiss toward the camera then wiggled toward the door. She reached into a small pocket and pressed a button on a remote. The video feed of the man and his hair interrupted for a brief moment, then returned as a doctored feed. The security guard leant back in his chair; lust splashed across his face as he watched Nursie leave.

With the feed now running, Nursie wandered back through the door, carrying a bundle of clothes.

"All clear, my love." She strolled over to the bed and released the security restraints, they echoed loudly in the large room. She dropped the clothing on the floor and stepped back. She leant against a wall, crossed her arms, and a smile spread across her face.

"Stop it… turn around, please…" the man asked.

"Since when have you ever been embarrassed?" she shrugged and turned around. After a moment she turned back and stared at his well-built body. The only thing that halted the nude figure was the well-proportioned form. She sighed, chuckled and turned back around.

"You know I don't need clothing," Krackers muttered.

"I'm sorry, darling," Nursie cooed, "I just love watching you change into your stealth outfit." Her voice trailed off. "But I've never really liked that thing." She pointed at his head.

"I thought you liked him?" Krackers feigned indignation.

A man lay on a table, tubes snaked from him into various machines. In a large container floated a mass of something. It shivered, forming various shapes.

"Are you sure you want to do this?" a masked doctor asked.

"I'm sure," the bald man answered.

"This is the Mark Three Hybrid. Artificial. Intelligence. Retaliator," the doctor stated. "Once the symbiont is attached, there is no going back."

"I understand," the bald man said.

The doctor moved to the container. With long tongs he lifted the mass and moved toward the man. The mass reached out with tendril-like fingers toward him. The doctor began to wrestle the mass, then finally released the Hair. It jumped, landed on the man's skull and surrounded the bald head. That was the point the man screamed.

"It burns!" The man tried to move away but the restraints that bound him halted him. His eyes rolled back into his head. He babbled incoherently; his mouth began to froth.

The Hair flicked, seemingly very agitated.

"Something's gone wrong," the doctor yelled.

With that, the man flat-lined.

The doctor rushed in to revive him, but the Hair tried to protect the man, attacking the doctor. After a minute, the man arched his back and took a deep breath.

"Hair, stealth mode!" It was like watching an excited child. Hair quivered and danced about Krackers's head. After a moment it slithered around Krackers's neck, moved quickly down and surrounded his whole body. It finally detached from his head, becoming a separate entity. Hair formed around Krackers's body, accentuating his features. Hair's colour dimmed, becoming a black hue…

"You have one day," Nursie said, "to complete your mission. After that you will be far too psychotic to continue… Also, the security video will end. Are you ready for the mission?" Her voluptuous figure caught the guard's attention; he seemed preoccupied with the monitor.

"Just popping out to buy a packet of smokes," she said, a rasp in her voice. The security guard jumped and switched the monitor to another corridor.

"I have some if you'd like, Nurse," the guard spluttered.

"No, it's okay," Nursie rasped. "I need some fresh air." She waited a moment. "The door, please?"

"I know I am."

"Oh, I am so ready," Krackers smiled, "give it to me, baby."

Nursie leaned forward, her mouth opened slightly; Krackers did the same. They leant in toward each other. Finally, the coupling began. When the 'Kiss', or the formal version, 'Knowledge in Saliva Sample', commenced, a micro-message was passed from the host to the victim. The time to administer the message was relatively short, but the Kiss itself could last much longer.

Krackers was the first to move away. He tried to slow his breathing. Nursie stood there, eyes closed, her chest heaving, and her breaths sharp and fast.

"Did you receive the mission specs?" Nursie whispered.

"Oh yeah." Krackers had to clear his throat. "Would you consider trying again?"

"I'd love to, lover," Nursie smiled, "but time's a wasting. I have to get back to my station before I'm missed."

Krackers leant forward and kissed Nursie hard.

"Mission accepted," Krackers muffled as the kiss concluded.

Nursie sighed, then straightened her uniform. After a moment she smiled and blew a kiss to Krackers. She wiggled toward the door, then turned.

"You have twenty-four hours to complete the mission before, well, 'you know what' will happen. Good luck, lover." She stepped through the door, leaving Krackers to his thoughts.

"Krackers is on the case." He stood on the spot, hands on his hips. He waited a while. "Hair, cape." Suddenly, from his stealth suit, a cape shot out. It started to waft and wave, although the air in the room was dead calm. After standing there for a moment, he looked around and, seeing nothing, said, "Lose the cape." He raised his head and strode bravely out through the door.

He leaned out of his door and looked both ways…

'Damn,' he thought, 'the hall camera. I need to get past it!' He paused, then inspiration dawned. 'Nursie! You can help me yet again.'

Nursie sauntered down a corridor toward the exit. Her wiggle was captured by one of the cameras. She reached the security station and noticed one of the monitors was showing her rear.

The guard stopped gazing at her and pressed the button to open the door. He watched her leave and sighed. After a moment, he turned his attention back to the monitors.

As Nursie walked down the stairs outside the hospital and along a darkened street, an overhead light flickered. She noticed a man appearing out of the shadows; a moment later, three more men emerged.

"What's a pretty young thing like you doing out here this late?" one mugger's gravelly voice asked.

"So," Nursie mumbled, "the Shrink is attacking early tonight." She smiled at the lead mugger. "I think he should have waited till later, but if you insist."

"Let's see what you can offer," the mugger licked his lips while the others laughed.

Nursie bent down, straightened her stockings, then slowly stood up. "I'll show you something you've seen before… but you must give a message to your boss, the Shrink…" she cooed seductively.

"I'll do that," the mugger grinned, licking his lips again. Abruptly he thought about what she'd said and stopped. "What the..?"

She reached down to the hem of her uniform and began to lift it. "Check this out." Suddenly there was a ruffle of hair starting at her feet. It travelled up her legs, turning them to dark armour. It moved rapidly up her body, changing it into something darker. Before them stood an armoured man, head raised and hands on hips. The main mugger was about to speak, but the armoured man raised a finger to his lips…

"Hair…" the armoured man whispered, "you know what I want, I want it now…" He lowered his hand and placed it on his hip. He turned his head. "I can wait all night!" He tapped his foot in annoyance.

Finally, a cape oozed out of the armour. It flopped across his chest…

"What are you doing?" Krackers asked, frustration in his voice.

"Can we continue?" the mugger asked.

"Just one moment," Krackers said, raising a finger. "Hair," he looked down at the fluttering cape. "You know it doesn't go there?" The cape retracted slowly into his chest. "Now, where does it go?" The cape shot out the back, fluttering madly. "Now, where was I?"

"You were dealing with me." The mugger raised his hand.

"Arh," Krackers said, "the Shrink's minions!"

Krackers dove at the main mugger, beating him senseless. Hair attacked the other two. It grabbed one in a headlock, shook him, then slammed him to the ground with a bone-crushing thud. The last mugger realised his mistake and tried to run. Hair, however, released the unconscious one and lunged at the other. A wave of Hair crashed over him. When it retracted, it left the mugger semi-conscious. Krackers walked over and looked at him.

"You can tell your boss that I will stop him, no matter what," Krackers declared. He put his hands on his hips and stood there, heroic.

"What?" the mugger muttered, "which boss was that?"

"Your boss, the Shrink!"

"You're crazy!" the mugger spat.

"You're probably right," Krackers nodded thoughtfully. "You tell the Shrink, I'm on to him!"

The muggers stood, turned, and staggered off.

"You make sure you tell him!" Krackers yelled. He patted his armour. "Well, what a good boy you are… who wants ice cream?"

After some time, Krackers came across an all-night ice cream shop. He muttered quietly to himself, "They seem to be where they are not, how strange?"

Making Hair behave could be such a task, but with the threat of 'no ice cream', Hair obeyed. Krackers walked into the shop and ordered two cones. After taking them, he wandered into an alleyway and Hair went wild. It shot out of Krackers' skull and hovered above him, leaving only the smallest of strands attached. The mass flickered, agitated. Krackers raised one cone and Hair swooped upon it, engulfing the iced treat. It made 'slurping' sounds as it floated above him.

"I don't feel like mine," Krackers smirked, "do you want it?" Hair quivered and attacked the second cone, making more 'slurping' noises. When finished, it curled around Krackers' neck and purred. He ruffled his sidekick.

"It's getting late, Hair," Krackers said, "let's get the Shrink!" Krackers and his cohort strode into the night after his arch-nemesis. His footfall echoed in the dark.

"Morning, sunshine," a gruff voice said. Rough hands shook Krackers.

"Mmmm, Nursie?" Krackers muttered, still half asleep. "Did I get him?"

"Get who?" the gruff voice asked.

"What the..?" Krackers opened a sleepy eye. Reality crashed down upon him as he looked at a huge man. "Doesn't matter." He opened the other eye. "You're not Nursie."

"And you're not Miss Universe," the huge man replied. "I am your wardsman. My name is Tristan."

"Tristan?" Krackers tried to suppress a laugh, then failed. "HAHAHA!!!"

"You shouldn't laugh," Tristan leant centimetres from Krackers' face, "at the person who has the keys to your restraints."

"I'm sorry," Krackers stopped giggling, "I had a hamster named that."

"What happened to him?" the wardsman asked.

"Bernard, my snake, ate him." Krackers giggled at the memory. "Watching Tristan's little eyes bulging as Bernard devoured him."

"You really shouldn't antagonise," Tristan leant in and yelled, spittle spraying Krackers' face, "the person who has the keys to your f#$*en restraints!" After a moment, Tristan composed himself. He stood up and unlocked the restraints. As he walked to the door, he added, "I wouldn't talk, Michael. Breakfast is being served." Tristan chuckled as he left.

"Krackers," Michael screamed after him, anger in his voice. "My name is Krackers!" After a brief pause, his eyes brightened. "Ooh, I wonder what's for breakfast?" He jumped out of bed and skipped to the door, yodelling brightly, "I wonder if they have ice cream? Gotta love ice cream." His voice trailed into the distance.

Two.

The Chase

'Later that afternoon.'

"Nursie gave me my mission briefing 'smooch' a little earlier than normal," Krackers muttered to himself, a smirk tugging at his lips. "Must prowl the streets, attack bad guys and save the innocents, whether they want to be or not." He paused for a moment, then added, "and more importantly, find the Shrink!"

He strode through the afternoon city. Crowds pushed and jostled for position along the streets. At a bus stop, an elderly woman sat, totally engrossed in a book. He marched up to her.

"Forgive me, dear lady," Krackers said. "I'm Krackers!"

"That's sad, dearie," the old lady replied. "Have you been that for long?"

"What the—?" Krackers was stopped in his tracks.

"How long have you been crackers for?" the old woman asked.

"I'm not crackers…" Krackers spluttered, "well, I am…" He tried to order his thoughts. "Although I am crazy, my name is Krackers!"

"Pleased to meet you, young man," the elderly woman smiled. "Would you care to sit down for a while?"

"No thank you, Ma'am," Krackers said politely. "Have you seen a man, about my size, wearing a white coat that looks like this?" He rubbed his coat. "Hair, if you please."

From Krackers' clothing, Hair feathered out and spilled. Around him, Hair swirled into a new person. The person was just as Krackers had described, except for one detail he had omitted. The man's face… it was darkened to the point of being featureless.

"Oh dear," the old woman gasped, raising a hand to her mouth.

"Why do people always do that?" Krackers muttered. "Enough, Hair. She doesn't know anything." He started to walk away, then stopped. "Or maybe that's the way the Shrink wants her to act!" He turned, about to ask her again, less politely this time, when he halted.

Beyond her, through the crowds, he noticed a shadowy figure near the corner of a building. Hair had just finished knitting itself back into his stealth suit.

"Halt, you!" he yelled, charging down the road.

The old woman looked where Krackers was shouting but saw nothing. She shook her head.

"Krackers by name, Krackers by nature!"

After running five blocks, Krackers was no closer to capturing his nemesis. The Shrink was always one step ahead. He entered a busier part of the city.

"Hair, 'homeless man outfit', and hurry up about it!" While Hair knitted the latest costume, Krackers flopped to the pavement. He looked at the passing crowds; no one seemed to notice him. From out of the throng, a young woman stopped in front of him. She smiled sweetly and handed him some cash.

"God bless."

He rose, keeping the homeless costume on. Looking down at his hand, he saw fifty dollars. He walked into an alleyway and emerged as a 'businessman.' Straightening his tie, he continued with the crowd. A homeless man sat in a doorway. Krackers stopped and gave him the money. He shook the man's hand, opened his mouth to say something, then walked off anyway.

At a cross street, he spotted his foe again.

"Stop, Shrink!"

He shoved through the crowd, which seemed to resist him. "Move!" Krackers bellowed. "Resist the Shrink!"

The crowd seemed to respond, parting for him. Krackers dashed through the newly opened path. He saw the shadowy figure dart into a building. At the entrance, he strode up to the security station.

"Did you see the Shrink come in here?"

"You'll have to be more specific," the overweight security guard grunted, pointing at the building's listings. "There are at least twenty of them in this building alone."

"Once again," Krackers muttered, "you have foiled me!" He shook his fist. As he turned, he spotted the shadowy figure slipping into a lift. "I have you now!"

Krackers darted toward it, his outfit shifting back to the stealth suit. He reached the doors just as they closed and watched the display: the lift was headed for the roof.

"I have you now!" he chuckled, stabbing the roof button in another lift.

You're a little crazy... played softly in the background.

"Hey, I know that song," Krackers said. "La de do!" He sang to himself. "I really love that song, la de do."

The lift stopped and he burst onto the roof. Above, a black helicopter circled, then veered away.

"Damn, he's done it again!" Krackers shook his head, scanning for somewhere to sit.

"Don't come any closer," a voice called out. "I'll jump!"

"I might join you," Krackers said despondently, turning to see a chubby man perched on the edge. Krackers flopped down beside him.

"Don't come any closer," the man repeated. "I'll jump!"

"I heard you the first time."

"So you won't stop me?"

"I've got my own problems, Citizen," Krackers replied.

"I've had enough of cleaning up other people's problems," the man blubbered.

Krackers sighed, looking down as a crowd gathered on the pavement below, watching the drama unfold.

"I just want to end it all."

"Would ending it all fix your problem?" Krackers asked.

"Yes," the man sobbed.

"Okay then," Krackers said, and shoved him off the ledge.

"Nooo!" the man screamed. "Help me!"

"People should decide," Krackers said, "whether they do or don't want to die!"

He leapt after the falling man.

"Hair," Krackers commanded, "grab that sobbing heap." From his head, Hair shot forth, wrapping around the flailing man's ample girth. Hair retracted, pulling him back into Krackers' embrace. Just as they hit the ground, Hair engulfed them both, cushioning the impact with a muffled *pffft*.

The crowd erupted in cheers.

Hair retracted, revealing Krackers, now dressed as a fireman, and the shaken chubby man, pale as a ghost and trembling.

Another cheer rose from the crowd.

"No need for that," Krackers said. "I mean it, no need for that." The people surged forward, congratulating him, patting his back.

"Please, don't touch me!" Krackers cringed. "I have to go, I've left the stove on at home."

With that, he looked skyward, then bolted toward the direction of the black helicopter. As he ran, the fireman's uniform faded back into his stealth suit.

"I think I need some altitude."

After some time running, he came upon one of the tallest buildings in the city. As he entered the foyer, his attire shifted back into the businessman. He ran up to the security station. Krackers stopped, bending over to catch his breath, he was not in good shape. The security guard leant forward but was met with a finger raised in the air, motioning him to wait. After catching his breath, Krackers straightened and smiled at the guard.

"Hi," Krackers said, "I'm Krackers. Would there be a psychiatrist in this fine building?"

"Are you?" the guard replied. "That's sad."

"Well?" Krackers sounded annoyingly.

"There is," the guard said. "Top floor." As Krackers passed the security station, the guard stopped him. "Do you have an appointment?"

Krackers paused, looking forlornly at the row of elevators. He was about to answer when a shadowy figure began exiting one of the lifts. The figure saw Krackers and darted through the stairwell door.

"I don't have time for this!" Krackers started to push past the guard. Hair stretched out, grabbed the guard by the head, and slammed it onto the station desk. "Sorry, but, as I said, I haven't got time for this! He's getting away!"

"No use trying to run, I have you!" Krackers raced around the desk and dashed for the stairwell. Inside, he looked up and saw a hand on the handrail three floors above.

That was how it continued for 130 floors. His nemesis always stayed three floors ahead. No matter how fast Krackers ran, his foe maintained the gap. Finally, the door to the top floor opened and closed.

"Now," Krackers panted, "you have nowhere to go…" He opened the door and staggered onto the top floor, hands on his hips. The only businesses there were a high-end beauty salon, a real estate agent, and a psychiatrist's office.

"Finally, a name to my nemesis!" Krackers looked at the title on the closing door. "Dr Delooz'nl," he scoffed. "I have you now!" Krackers stormed into the office, where a receptionist waited behind a desk.

"Can I help you?" the pert woman asked.

"I doubt it," Krackers replied, "but many have tried."

He walked past her and opened the inner door. Behind a huge desk was the back of an equally large chair.

"Turn around," Krackers said slowly, "I have you now. There's nowhere to go!"

The chair slowly turned.

"What the?" Krackers spat. "Who the hell are you?"

"I am Dr Delooz'nl," the female psychiatrist stated. "Can I help you?"

"Where is he?" Krackers was dumbfounded. "I followed him in here. He's got to be here!"

"I'm sorry," the female doctor said, "there's only me here. Are you okay?"

"He's done it again!" Krackers turned slowly and walked out of the office. "But I followed him in here." He went to the elevator and pressed the button. "I think I should go back to my ward, report to Nursie, and have a little lie down."

The trip down in the lift was excruciatingly long, each second dragging. Finally, it reached the foyer. He walked over to the security station. The guard was slumped in a chair, blood still dripping from his nose.

"You'll be alright," Krackers said, walking past. "Better put some ice on that." He made his way to the entrance. "I need a drink!"

Outside, the crowds were starting to thin. He wandered aimlessly until he came upon a bar. Krackers entered and approached the counter.

"What'll you have?" the barman asked.

"Have you ever," Krackers said, "wanted something so much, only to have it slip through your fingers?"

"Yeah, I did," the barman replied. "And I never saw her again." Sadness lingered, a tear welling in his eye. He wiped it away and pulled himself together. "What'll you have?"

"Something strong! Something that reacts poorly with multiple medications!" Krackers muttered. His gaze fell on a jukebox.

"Ooooh, a jukebox," a smile spread across his face. He walked over and scanned the music. "My favourite song," Krackers cooed. It started, and he began to sing.

"You're a little crazy," he belted out, "doo de for doo." He returned to the bar, the song still on his lips.

"Karaoke is on Friday night," the barman said sternly. "No singing till then!" He pointed to a sign above:

'No singing outside of Karaoke times. Offenders will be removed, with extreme prejudice!'

Krackers stopped mid 'doo.'

"Good choice," the barman said.

"Anyway, I'm Krackers," he extended a hand.

"You certainly are… a bit," the barman shook it.

"Why do people keep saying that?" Krackers muttered, reaching for his drink. After finishing it, he had another, and another, and another. After ten or so drinks, he left the bar, or more like poured himself out and into a cab.

"The Peter Adams Memorial Psychiatric Hospital, if you please, driver," Krackers slurred, laying his head back. "Do you know who I am?"

"I think the question should be," the driver replied, "do you know who I am?"

Krackers tried to focus in the rear-view mirror. He couldn't see the cab driver's face clearly, but the voice seemed familiar. He looked at the licence, was the photo blurry, or was it just his drunken state?

The taxi pulled up outside the psychiatric hospital. The driver got out, his back to Krackers.

"You should know me," the driver said. "You've been trying to catch me all day." He ran toward the darkened hospital.

"What the?" It finally dawned on Krackers. "The Shrink!"

He fumbled with the door handle and finally got it open. He ran inside, Hair transforming him into Nursie. Realising he was running, he slowed down.

"Hair," Krackers muttered, "get ready to change my look again. We don't want two Nursies…"

Hair modified the disguise, transforming the voluptuous Nursie into a muscle-bound Wardsman. He walked along a dark corridor to the nurse's station. Nursie sat, watching a video screen. On it was a 'sleeping Krackers.' The Wardsman stood next to her, smiling. A blank smile was plastered on Nursie's face.

"How is our patient?" Krackers asked, trying not to smile.

"He's been quiet," Nursie said.

"Could I have a word in private?" the Wardsman asked.

"Okay," Nursie looked perplexed at the request. They walked into a darkened office, Nursie first. She switched on the light and turned to speak to him.

"Surprise!" The Wardsman's face shifted back into his own. "Did you see the Shrink come through here?"

"You can't do that!" Nursie raced to the closed door, opening it slightly to peer through. "Someone could've seen you change."

"The Shrink was disguised as a taxi driver!" Krackers muttered. "I've been all over the place." He paced back and forth, his mutterings becoming increasingly incoherent.

"Okay, my love," Nursie said, "I think it's time for your bed." She went to the office door. "I'll just get you a gurney. Will you be alright, Michael?" She returned and stroked his hair, it purred. She kissed him on the cheek.

She left and came back with the gurney.

"I am Krackers," he muttered. "I am the undiagnosed people's choice." His voice rose, and his pacing grew more frantic.

"Medication time, my sweet," Nursie whispered, retrieving a syringe from her pocket.

"Medication time." Krackers repeated the phrase, then spiralled into a psychotic rant about cheese.

Nursie guided the disturbed man onto the gurney. He lay down momentarily, then sat up. She laid him down again, only for him to sit back up.

"Good night, sweet prince," she said, injecting him.

"Good night," Krackers muttered. His eyes glazed over, then closed as he finally lay down.

"Hair," she said, "a nondescript male disguise. Activation code N.U.R.S.6.9."

Hair feathered out around Krackers, transforming him into a forty-year-old man. When Hair finished, Nursie pushed the gurney out of the office and down the corridor, back to Krackers' ward. After securing him in his bed, she turned and blew a kiss to the security camera, reactivating it. The feed switched back to live action.

The camera followed Nursie, wiggling across the room as she switched off the light and left.

Three.

Misplacement

"Night had fallen on The Peter Adams Memorial Psychiatric Hospital, and all was well… or so it seems, Viewers," Krackers muttered to himself. "The clock has struck nine bells, and nothing to report." He struggled, trying to reposition himself. "The restraints are starting to chafe, and there's no sign of Nursie."

As thoughts of the sexy nurse swirled in his mind, other areas began to react. Before he could dwell further, there was a 'clank' and all thoughts of Nursie exploded.

"Mmmm, medication time, my love," he whispered, closing his eyes. "I thought you'd never come."

"So did I, my love," a deep new voice shattered the moment. "Nine p.m. is changeover time. I am your nurse for the evening. My name is Gertrude."

"Where is Nursie?" Krackers asked, opening one eye. What he saw made him shut it immediately again. Gertrude was a short man in a nurse's uniform, the image burned onto Krackers' cornea.

"Nurse Bre Bwee has some days off," Nurse Gertrude replied. "Orders from Admin."

"Admin!" he spat. "A constant thorn in my side!"

"Do you need anything else, Michael?" Gertrude asked.

"Krackers, damn you! My name is Krackers!" Krackers screamed. "Look, why don't you have a shave? You've got a five o'clock shadow!" That was the last thing Krackers said as Gertrude cocked his fist and cracked Krackers on the chin. Nighty night, lights out.

"Good night, sweet Prince," Nurse Gertrude smirked, tapping Krackers on the cheek and leaving the room, where he soon fell into snoring la-la land.

Light finally filtered into Krackers' psyche. Eyes still closed, he did an internal check. His chin hurt, but after wiggling it, he decided it was unbroken. It was six a.m. He considered returning the favour when he next saw Nurse Gertrude.

"I really have to find Nursie, Viewers," Krackers muttered. "It's not like her to take holidays. Hair, I have a plan, though you're not going to like it."

"Hair," Krackers whispered, "convince the camera that everything is hunky-dory." A small strand shot out, hitting the base of the camera. Like a caterpillar, it crept to the input port and slid in. At the security station, the monitor flickered as the vision rewound.

Krackers stood beside his bed, looking down at a slumbering copy of himself. Strands of Hair trailed up into his head. He gently removed them; they flinched slightly, then retracted into the sleeping form. The remainder of Hair swirled around Krackers. After a moment, Nursie slipped out of the room and out of the hospital.

Once clear of the hospital, Hair changed him from the voluptuous nurse back into stealthy, 'man on a mission' Krackers. He stopped outside the gates, trying to order his racing thoughts.

"If Admin had a hand in this," Krackers muttered, "then the Shrink certainly had to be party to it!" He paced back and forth. "How do I find out where Nursie is? Think, damn you, think!" He looked around, shrugged. "I have to order my thoughts. I think beating something into a pulp might help! Where's a bad guy when you need one!" He paced again, frustration clear. "Look, I'll have to go to plan B. Okay, Hair, let's do it."

A pudgy policeman waddled up to the front desk of Admin, clipboard at his side. He flashed a strained smile.

"I haven't had much sleep, gastric reflux, you know," he rasped, patting his gut and belching loudly. "I'm here to talk to Nursie, I mean

Nurse Bre Bwee. Here are my credentials." He flashed a badge. The receptionist squinted; the image was a blur.

"She's a popular girl," a young blonde said, shaking her head. "You're the second person to ask about her this morning." She fluffed her hair.

"May I enquire as to whom the other person was?" The pudgy officer asked, trying to appear nonchalant.

"It was one of the Psychiatrists," she tapped the keyboard. "Doctor Peter Adams. She's not rostered on for the next two days."

"Is there any way to contact her?" The officer forced a smile, hiding his frustration. "I seem to have misplaced her info."

"Who did you say you were?" the receptionist asked.

"I'm Officer D'Turbed," he said, flashing his badge again.

The receptionist shrugged, tapped the keyboard, and a moment later handed him a printout of Nursie's details.

Officer D'Turbed walked out of Admin, now back in stealthy Krackers form, though feeling somewhat lost. He looked down at the printout.

"Looks like a road trip, Viewers," he smirked, skipping across the road. "Hair, I need some transport." He spotted an ice cream truck approaching and stepped in front of it, waving it down.

"I'm sorry, mate, but I've finished my shift," the man said, somewhat angrily.

Krackers stood his ground, hands on hips.

"Come on, man," the ice cream man added, "I just want to go home."

"I'm Krackers," Krackers said.

"You know," the man replied, "you don't look it… but after dealing with you, I think you are."

"Why do people keep saying that?" Krackers asked. "Anyway, I need this van. I don't have time for this! Hair, help this man out of his van, with extreme prejudice."

Hair didn't need to be asked twice. It shot from Krackers' head like a wave, grabbed the ice cream man, dragged him out, then lofted him into the air and slammed him to the ground. The mighty 'thwack' and 'oof' signified the man's agreement to let Krackers use the vehicle.

"Thank you for the use of your vehicle, Citizen," Krackers said as he climbed in. "The streets will be a little safer with your help."

"You are crackers!" the ice cream man muttered groggily, rubbing his bruised face.

"Yes, I am," Krackers laughed. The van skidded off toward Nursie's address, ice cream music blaring, Krackers yodelling along.

After an hour, he'd driven around the block fifteen times, almost killed five people, and made fifteen dollars in ice cream sales. Still, he was no closer to finding Nursie. No matter, he'd never give up. He scanned for a way to reach her address. Suddenly, he spied a possible solution.

"Ooh, look," Krackers exclaimed, a 'G.P.S.' He reached over and began typing.

"It is 12,791.43 kilometres," the female G.P.S. voice stated, "to get to the North Pole!"

"Hahaha!" Krackers threw his head back and laughed. He typed again.

"Ice cream," the female voice said, "is an unknown word."

Krackers finally lost it. He fell off the seat, wriggling in the footwell, tears of joy streaming from his eyes. After composing himself, he sat back, studied the printout, and punched the address into the G.P.S. He started the van and was about to move.

"Your destination," the G.P.S. announced, "is on your left."

"Wow," Krackers said, turning off the van. "That didn't take long, thank you, G.P.S." He climbed out and stretched, then suddenly stopped, scratching his head. "What was I doing again, Hair?"

Hair was incensed. It flapped and slapped Krackers' face. He tried to ignore it and returned to the ice cream truck. As he prepared to climb in, he caught his reflection in the side mirror.

"What the…?" Krackers exclaimed. His stealth suit had changed into a pink nurse's uniform, with a ridiculously huge beehive hairdo, big purple bows, and matching makeup.

"Okay, okay," Krackers said, "stop yelling at me and calm down. You know I can never understand you when you're like this. What are you saying about Nursie?"

After a moment, a spark of memory hit him. "What are you doing, Hair! I have no time for your yelling, we have to find Nursie."

If Hair could have sighed, it would have. Instead, it reverted Krackers to the stealth suit and flopped down in frustration.

"Okay," Krackers said loudly, "this is Nursie's address!" Hair whipped around his face and muffled him. After a moment, Hair released him.

"Good call, Hair. It's late, and we don't want to draw undue attention to ourselves."

As Krackers approached Nursie's house, a shadowy figure seemed to be lurking at the front door. He froze mid-step. The figure looked like it was breaking into Nursie's place! Krackers took another step, then leapt, grabbing the figure and wrestling it to the ground. A security light splashed on, brilliantly illuminating the area.

"After all this time, I have you now! There is no escape," Krackers yelled at a large plant he was sitting on, trying to strangle. "Hey, you're not the Shrink!"

Just then, the front door opened, revealing an elderly woman with curlers in her hair. She looked down at Krackers and screamed. Krackers looked up and screamed back. Then they looked at each other and screamed again in unison.

"Hi, I'm Krackers," Krackers said, smiling his biggest smile. Hair fanned out.

The elderly lady did something Krackers definitely wasn't expecting. She jumped up and threw a roundhouse kick, connecting with his chin and sending him flying off the porch onto the front lawn. She started screaming for the police.

"Why do people react that way?" Krackers muttered as he picked himself up and staggered back to the ice cream truck. He climbed in, checked the G.P.S., and it seemed like the right address. He looked back at the printout, everything seemed correct. So what went wrong? He turned the paper over.

"Crap!" Sheepishly, he looked around to see if anyone had noticed, then tapped in the correct address. He started the van and tried to drive away quietly. That didn't seem on the cards. The ice cream music blared, the tyres squealed, and the entire street woke up.

After an hour of aimless driving, the G.P.S. still didn't seem to understand the address. Krackers yawned, found a park, and put his head down for a moment.

Children's noises filtered into his psyche. He raised his head, it was morning. A mob of sugar-craving kids assaulted him. He lowered his head, trying 'not to be there,' and raised a 'hold on a moment' finger, but it didn't seem to work either.

"We want ice cream!" the children cried. An adult pushed through the collection of rug rats.

"Excuse me, sir," a female voice said, soothingly. "These children have been waiting quite a while." Her voice bounced around his head, and finally it registered.

"Nursie?" Krackers, still with his head down, tried to filter out the commotion. He raised his head and focused on the 'possible target' he had been searching for. His eyes were still closed.

"Who…?" Her voice had to be Nursie.

"I need my medication and my mission kiss," Krackers said, slowly opening his eyes, his lips starting to pucker.

When he opened his eyes fully and saw the 'possible' Nursie, he widened in surprise. The woman was definitely not Nursie. To prove it, she let out an ungodly scream. Hair reacted, shooting out in a vicious appearance, looming large. The woman froze, eyes rolling back, and fainted, dropping to the ground.

The children stood silent, eyes wide at the enormous monster hair. Suddenly, they cheered and 'wooed,' pumping their little fists in the air.

Krackers did what any brave superhero would do: he shut the counter window. It would have worked, but the window was clear. So he did the next best thing, he ducked. Crawling to the driver's seat, he started the truck and floored it. It squealed sideways out of the park. The van music spewed forth. Krackers fiddled with the dashboard knobs, to no avail. He did the next best thing, he started to yodel.

After a panic-filled episode, Krackers noticed someone seemed to be following him. He finally found the button to the music and turned on the radio.

"Once again," the radio said, "there is an escaped mental patient on the loose."

"That sounds serious, Viewers," Krackers said. "I must help!"

"He is considered extremely dangerous," the radio continued. "His name is Michael Ness. Citizens are advised to avoid him and stay indoors."

"My name is Krackers, damn you!" He kicked the radio. Sparks flew, the faceplate hung down, trailing wires. It bounced with the van.

"You know, Michael," the broken radio said, "this is your fault, it's always your fault!" Krackers did a double take.

"Don't call me that!" he screamed at the defunct radio. He tore it from the dashboard and threw it to the floor.

"And as for Hair," the radio continued, "without it, you're just a man, a pathetic little man."

"Hair and I are a crime-fighting duo!" Krackers shouted, shaking his fist at the broken radio.

"You don't deserve Hair," the radio berated him. "It's always saving your sorry arse. When they 'mated' the two of you, you should have died!"

Something flicked at Krackers' face.

"It would have been better for all of us," the radio added. "You're in a van, driving extremely fast. It would be easy to crash and kill yourself. No one would blame you."

The radio continued, increasingly irritating.

"Do it!" it cajoled. "You know you want to. Everybody would blame Hair."

Suddenly, something covered Krackers' face, cutting off his air supply. He began to blackout. The last thing he saw was Hair steering the ice cream truck, and then nothing.

"Hair," Krackers said, his voice gravelly and weak, "what happened?"

"I may be able to explain," a familiar voice cooed.

"Nursie?"

"Yes, Krackers," she smiled. "It's me."

"What happened?"

"I found you outside," Nursie explained, "in an ice cream truck, of all things."

"I can explain," Krackers said sheepishly.

"You were lucky," Nursie said, holding back a tear. "You hadn't taken your medication in twenty-four hours. You could have died."

"Shhh," Krackers whispered, reaching up and holding her close. "I made it back here."

"It seems Hair managed to deliver you back to the hospital," Nursie said, changing the subject. "Luckily, I got to you first and back to your room. I guess you were suffering hallucinations?"

"You might say that," Krackers chuckled.

"I have to go," Nursie rose, smoothing her uniform. "I'll check in later."

Krackers watched her wiggle away, leaving his room. She stopped outside, leaning on a wall. Tears exploded as she sobbed uncontrollably. A beep sounded from her ear. After a moment, she composed herself.

"Yes," she answered. "I understand, Doctor Adams. I'll get the 'asset' onto it at once." She nodded and walked down the darkened corridor toward another mission.

Four.

Crime Thwarted!

The city of Karma was a huge city of four million people. The citizens carried on with their lives, oblivious to the seedier side of life. Alleys were the lifeblood of the underworld. A quick dollar could be made through muggings. The foolhardy, traversing the darkness, would be tolled a pretty penny, whether it be credit cards, jewellery, or other trinkets.

Word filtered through the world of crime of a crazy man with 'living' Hair. His name was Krackers, and he was deadly. The best men had gone up against him and failed miserably. Criminal In Misdeed Enterprise Engagements, or CRIME for short, was the go-to for anything unlawful. The head of CRIME was a shadowy figure, although no one had ever seen him. He was rumoured to have been a disgraced psychiatrist with a severe hatred for the Peter Adams Memorial Psychiatric Hospital.

An order had come down from the top: 'kill Krackers.' The reward was one hundred million dollars to the person who delivered his body intact.

The Peter Adams Memorial Psychiatric Hospital was a massive institution, first built five hundred years ago. Extremely fortified, it was originally used as a warlord fortress. C.R.A.P.I. owned it, although none of the citizens knew. They maintained the upkeep, continuing to strengthen its defences. It covered fifty hectares — forty-nine football pitches of extreme fortification — and stood in the dead centre of Karma.

Krackers was going stir-crazy, and poor Hair took the brunt of it. At present, Krackers was trying to give Hair a perm, but that was no mean feat. He was attempting to bundle Hair into a ponytail.

"So, have you got any juicy gossip?" Krackers said with a lisp. "After the perm, you'll need a Brazilian."

Hair had had enough!

It exploded everywhere, forming a huge wave that dwarfed Krackers. Arcs of electricity rippled across it. As Hair moved, thunder rolled through it.

"Oh crap!" Krackers said, closing his eyes as Hair came crashing down. The room was filled to the rafters with Hair. Muffled cries came through and, after the appropriate time, Hair retracted back into Krackers' skull.

"Point taken," Krackers smirked. "You win this one. This proves one thing, we need a mission, stat! Call Nursie now!" Hair reached up and started vibrating. Within moments, the familiar 'clank', and Nursie swam into the room. Her 'barely there' uniform just covered her modesty as she moved towards Krackers.

"This mission doesn't exist as far as C.R.A.P.I. is concerned," Nursie said. "It's personal." She ran over and buried her head in Krackers' chest. "They have my father." Her body was racked with sobs.

"Who has your father?"

Nursie looked up at Krackers. She reached up and guided him to her lips. They met, kissing deeply. The mission was transferred successfully, yet they continued to kiss. After some time, they parted, breathing heavily. As they calmed, Krackers hugged Nursie.

"I'm so sorry," Krackers whispered. "I won't stop until I find him! C.R.I.M.E. will pay for this, I promise you that!" He suddenly released Nursie, and she fell to the floor. Krackers put his hands on his hips, head raised back as he tried to look courageous.

"Okay, Hair," Krackers started, "it's show time!" He strode to the door as Hair feathered him into a doctor.

After going through several checkpoints, Krackers walked into the night. He inhaled 'freedom', and it was good to meet his 'mistress' again. He bumped into several passers-by. There were too many people. He needed to see the mission from a different perspective. Krackers did a handstand. He held the position for five minutes. People kept walking by, somewhat oblivious to such strangeness.

"Oh dear." Krackers started to wobble. "Blood rushing to my head. Oh crap!" He crumpled to the ground. The crowd parted around him, ignoring the strange man. He picked himself up and gazed skyward. He needed some height.

On the roof of the tallest building in Karma, Krackers sat on the edge, rocking his legs back and forth.

"Two hundred floors," Krackers mused. "That's a long way to fall." He leant forward. "And you wouldn't even feel the 'splat!'" He leant further still. Hair suddenly shot out, anchoring Krackers. Hair winched itself back from the edge. Krackers lay on his back and stared at the darkening sky, Hair trailing from his head to the anchor points.

Hair, without warning, exploded around Krackers. It smacked and vibrated; some wisps berated him while others pointed at the possible 'bad idea' near the edge of the roof.

"I know, Hair," Krackers said, numbness in his voice. "It was a dumb idea. You, of all people, know what's going on in my head." Hair abruptly stopped the abuse. Instead, it cocooned around him, rocking him softly. After some time, Krackers slowly climbed out of Hair.

"Enough feeling sorry for yourself, Hair," Krackers jumped to his feet. "We have a father to save and gratefulness from a daughter. Bring up the mission briefing, if you'd be so kind."

Superimposed over Krackers' eyesight, the mission briefing slowly scrolled by.

"Okay," Krackers muttered to himself. "Doctor Thaddaeus Bwee," he tried to suppress a chuckle. "Thaddaeus," *snigger*. "He was last seen near the north exit of the Department of Health and Wellbeing building. He had an appointment yesterday at three, but the Department said he didn't attend, and they haven't heard a thing from him."

Krackers considered this as he scratched Hair thoughtfully. Hair smacked his hand away.

"Well, that's a good place to start," Krackers chirped. His brow furrowed. "But first, ice cream!"

Krackers walked over to some thick pipes. Hair ribboned out from his skull, wrapping itself around the pipes. Krackers turned and ran to the edge.

"Going down!" Krackers screamed with joy. He leapt off the two-hundred-storey building, arms outstretched and a smile on his face. He freestyled down, the air whistling past him. Just before hitting the ground, Hair slowed the fall dramatically. As his feet softly touched the pavement, Hair retracted into his cranium.

"That was great!" Krackers jumped up and down. "Can we do that again?" His brow furrowed. "What were we doing again?" Hair fanned out in front of him, forming an ice cream cone. "That's right, dear Hair!"

He walked out from beside the building and into the masses. The crowd parted, walking around him. They ignored him, and he liked that. He activated his internal GPS and found the nearest ice cream shop: *I Scream U Scream, Ice Cream Parlour.*

Krackers walked out of the shop, holding two ice cream cones. Hair could hardly contain itself, vibrating and barely suppressing excitement. Krackers ducked into an alley, away from the crowds. The moment he did, Hair launched itself at the cone. It devoured it with one slurp, vibrating with enjoyment as it hovered just above Krackers.

"Since you've been a good boy," Krackers smiled, "you can have mine." Hair made smacking noises as Krackers threw the cone into the air. Hair tracked it, plucking it out of the air and slurping it down. It flowed back into Krackers' head.

"Frivolity aside," Krackers began, "we have to find Nursie's father, Doctor Thaddaeus Bwee." He snickered again. "Thaddaeus." Krackers couldn't hold it in and exploded into laughter, slapping his thigh with glee. Even Hair found it amusing. After a moment, the two of them calmed down. Hair wiped the tears from Krackers' eyes.

"Okay," Krackers said, "what were we doing? That's right, Doctor Bwee needs our help. Hair, show me the way to go." Krackers traversed the city and made it across the road from the northern entrance of the Department of Health and Wellbeing. He faded into the scenery with Hair's help.

"You've got to love a stakeout."

Krackers waited and waited. He started to fidget; Hair tightened its grip on him. "Okay Hair, you shouldn't move around too much," Krackers hissed. He was about to call it a day when something caught his attention. A figure got out of a car, although he couldn't make out any features. He had to get closer. Hair released him, swirling into a Department of Health and Wellbeing uniform. He watched as the figure looked directly at him, then laughed and ran into the building. Krackers dashed across the road to the entrance. As he watched the figure vanish into the dimness, he reached the checkpoint.

"I. D.," the guard ordered. Krackers reached back as Hair fashioned an I.D. card. It cleared, and the guard handed it back.

"I'm new here," Krackers said. "Was that the new boss?"

"Yeah," the guard replied. "That's Doctor Bwee. He's a hard-arse and very weird. He's one of the new psychiatrists here, doing psych evaluations for the whole Department."

"Thanks for the warning." Krackers walked into the building. After a few turns, he found a bathroom. Once he had closed the door, Hair transformed Krackers into a doctor. His nametag read: 'Doctor Delooz'nl.'

Krackers walked out of the bathroom and into a corridor. On one of the walls, a digital directory showed the different sub-departments.

"Hair," Krackers said, "find out which department the psychiatrists are supposed to be in." Krackers raised his hand and touched the screen.

From behind him, a Department of Health and Wellbeing worker tapped him on the shoulder.

"Are you lost?"

"I'm Doctor Delooz'nl," Krackers turned, "and, yes, I'm lost."

"Yes, Doctor Delooz'nl," the worker said. "Go straight down the corridor, then take the elevator to sub-basement thirteen. You can check in there." The worker nodded and went on his way.

"Now that was a very polite employee," Krackers muttered. "Don't you think, Viewers?" He wandered down the corridor and, as the worker had directed, found the elevator. On the wall, there was a card reader. He swiped the 'Hair' I.D. card, summoning the lift. After a moment, the elevator chimed and the doors slid open. Krackers walked in and scanned the interior. Beneath the floor buttons was another card reader.

"They certainly like their security, Viewers." Krackers swiped the card again. After pressing the button, the elevator descended swiftly.

"Weee," Krackers squealed as he arrived at the floor. It clanged loudly and the doors opened, revealing—

"Oh my god," Krackers gasped. "So many shrinks!"

The crowd of doctors were seated and turned as one, staring at Krackers. After a moment, they turned back as he walked tentatively into the room. Krackers found a chair near the back and sat down. At the front of the large room was a huge display. On the screen, a silhouetted figure appeared.

"Once again," the figure said, "I thank you all. Some of you will be assisting in creating a specialised team to help with the mental health and wellness of the employees."

"We have to find Nursie's dad," Krackers whispered.

The figure started naming the psychiatrists that would be joining the team. Some of the doctors rose and stood in front of the screen.

"Finally, Doctor Thaddaeus Bwee," the figure said, "and Doctor Michael Delooz'nl."

"What the..?" Krackers started to pay attention, although Hair had to give him an internal nudge. "Oh, right." He rose and walked to the front. "How the hell did you get me on the team?" he muttered. "There's a double helping of ice cream for you when we've finished." He reached the front and stood with the other psychiatrists—about ten in total.

"The rest of you may leave," the figure stated. "And thank you for your time." The room slowly cleared, leaving the team waiting until it was empty.

"Ladies and gentlemen, if you would kindly move to the door behind the screen." The team made their way to the door. It slid open, revealing beds and med stations. There were a lot of them—enough to treat at least a quarter of Karma's citizens.

Hundreds of technicians scurried about, tending to the med stations, supplying patients with medicines and other equipment. As the team entered, an alert sounded. The techs stopped what they were doing and stood by their stations. Half the beds were already filled with 'patients.'

"This seems like a large endeavour," Krackers whispered to Doctor Bwee.

"It's a glorious undertaking," Doctor Bwee whispered back. "You did read the associated material that was supplied, didn't you?"

"I skimmed it," Krackers replied, "but I didn't realise it would be so big."

Above the room, a huge screen was suspended from the ceiling. The same silhouetted figure appeared on it.

"Greetings, ladies and gentlemen," the figure boomed. "Welcome to *Conditioning. Research. Initiated. Medical. Endeavour.*" The team applauded. "If you would follow your allotted technicians, they will take you to your station." The figure was replaced with a rotating C.R.I.M.E. logo.

"Doesn't that logo seem somewhat strange?" Krackers leant towards Doctor Bwee.

"Not really," the doctor replied. "It seems apt for the service we're supplying. Plus, the wages C.R.I.M.E. is paying me—well, it's more money than I could make in a lifetime!"

Krackers excused himself as a technician came over and escorted him to his workstation. The 'station' was a desk with three monitors, a keyboard, and a panel with a series of buttons.

"Hey, Hair," Krackers whispered, "do you know what the buttons do?" He waited for a response.

"Press one?" Krackers questioned. "Do you think that's a wise idea?" He listened intently, then exploded: "Why not, good idea Hair!"

Krackers stabbed wildly at the panel. On one of the monitors, a beep sounded, and a file came up: *PROJECT TRANSMOGRIFICATION.* A red flashing warning appeared: *Security Clearance Alpha.*

"Hair," Krackers said, "see what you can do." He moved his hand close to the input port. Hair snaked out and slid into it. Krackers closed his eyes and, after a moment, opened them wide in shock. Hair retracted abruptly, vibrating excitedly. The monitor went blank.

"Slow down," Krackers whispered. "I can't understand you. What are you saying, 'he's here, he's here!'?"

"Doctor Delooz'nl," the figure returned to the overhead screen, "could you come to my office? I need to speak to you." A technician walked over and waited behind Krackers.

"Doctor Delooz'nl," the tech said, waiting.

"Before we go," Krackers said, "I need to use the bathroom." The tech nodded and showed him the way. Krackers walked in while the tech waited outside.

"Hair," Krackers whispered, "apprise Nursie of the situation. Send her all the relevant information and tell her I have been in contact with her father." Hair flowed up from Krackers' head and started vibrating. The door began to open, and Hair retracted, smoothing itself back into Krackers.

"Doctor Delooz'nl?"

"Sorry," Krackers apologised, "it must be something I ate."

Krackers followed the technician through the gigantic hall. As he walked, he noticed some of the beds were occupied. He tried to slow down so he could see more. The tech noticed and moved a hand to Krackers' elbow and motioned him forward. They finally came to a door marked 'Private.' The tech knocked once, then opened the door; light splashed out. Krackers entered, and the light was so bright. The silhouetted figure could just be made out.

"Wow," Krackers stated, "your power bill must be astronomical."

"Welcome, Krackers," the figure said, "so good to see you again. How goes the crazy?"

"I don't know what you're talking about?"

"Please," the figure said smugly, "don't insult my intelligence!"

"Hair," Krackers started, "if you would be so kind."

Hair didn't need to be prompted. It shot out, spearing at the figure, only to go through the swimming hologram and into the back wall.

"HAHAHA! You've failed. Again!"

"No, you've failed," Krackers uttered. "You'd better start looking behind you, because I will be there!" Krackers smiled. "Right now, there are crack C.R.A.P.I. agents about to storm this place!"

"What an unfortunate name for a security agency."

The figure waved, fading into nothingness. The lights faded to a more comfortable level. Krackers stormed to the door, kicking it. The door exploded into pieces. He strode into the hall, weariness creeping in. He walked by C.R.A.P.I. agents who were tending to the patients. At the other end of the hall was the familiar sight of Nursie. She hugged her dad, then she walked to her loving agent.

"Hey, you," Nursie cooed, "thanks for finding my dad. I have something for you." Hair fanned out, teaming over the two of them, and she looked behind her back. It vibrated excitedly. She brought her hands around, holding two ice cream cones. "Well done."

Hair didn't wait to be asked; it attacked one of the cones. The 'smacking' noises were amusing. Hair hovered again and waited impatiently.

"Yes, Hair, you can have mine, buddy," Krackers smiled weakly. "I think I need a lie-down, I'm not feeling the best."

Five.

Holly Roller, Heaven Sent.

Krackers was feeling low. Low enough not to care. He was so low that he didn't even want to play with Hair. But more horrifying, he didn't even want ice cream. He sighed loudly, rolled over, and flopped dramatically onto the mattress.

Hair was really concerned. It had seen Krackers' 'feeling sad' moods before, but this was far worse. Hair flowed out, cocooning Krackers and gently rocking him to and fro.

"Hair," Krackers said pensively, "have you ever thought about life and stuff?" Hair unfurled itself. It felt for Krackers, but it didn't know how to help.

Krackers hadn't had a mission in a while, and it was definitely showing.

"Enough of this, Hair," said Krackers, cartwheeling to his feet. "Contact Nursie—she must have a mission!" Hair rose from Krackers' skull and started vibrating.

After ten minutes, there was the familiar 'clank' as the door opened. Nursie sauntered in and up to Krackers. Her 'barely there' uniform adhered to her form. She embraced him, holding him tightly. She brought her lips to his and kissed him deeply. Both closed their eyes and enjoyed it. After some time, they released each other's embrace.

"The mission didn't transfer," Krackers muttered, his eyes still closed, the experience still fresh in his mind.

"I haven't transferred it yet," Nursie smiled. "I'll download it now."

She grabbed Krackers' face and kissed him fiercely. Krackers closed his eyes again. This time, he *saw* the data transfer. Mission stats, profiles, and secondary details flowed into his psyche—although there was something odd about the mission. The transference was intense, even more than the previous kiss. This was the part of the mission he hungered for; the sensation was intoxicating.

"There hasn't been much chatter regarding C.R.I.M.E. lately," Nursie explained. "But there has been a rise in criminal incidences." Nursie suddenly seemed a little sheepish.

"I know that look," Krackers said with a curious eye. "What's wrong? Out with it!"

"C.R.A.P.I. has a request, but you might not like it," Nursie continued coyly. "Well, they want me to accompany you on a mission."

"No, no, no," Krackers backed up, hands outstretched. "I already have a partner, and Hair's a good one." He crossed his arms.

Hair flowed out and started vibrating furiously at Krackers, then at Nursie.

"Stop it," Krackers snapped. "I don't care what you say—it's too dangerous." He pointed at Nursie and was about to continue the argument when Hair vibrated at him again. "There is no way I'm taking a civilian out on a mission. That's final!"

Later that night.

In a darkened alley, Krackers hid on a second-storey fire escape. He kept low, peeking down, trying to stay in the shadows.

"I don't like this, Hair," Krackers whispered. Hair vibrated, and Krackers shook his head. "What do you mean 'bait'? This whole operation is wrong!" Hair vibrated again. "I appreciate what C.R.A.P.I. has done for us, but there has got to be a better way."

Memories can sometimes be a painful thing, although they shape the present.

It was Krackers' first solo assignment. The mission was simple: follow a high-risk subject, keeping them under surveillance and protecting the individual at all costs.

Simple enough.

Krackers peered out from a darkened escape, watching the subject walk into an alleyway. The subject stopped to light a cigarette. That was when all hell broke loose. From out of the darkness, three assailants appeared, moving quickly towards the subject.

Krackers charged in. Hair flowed out and attacked the first assailant, fatally stabbing him. Krackers leapt, kicking the second one and bringing him to the ground. With a deft move, Krackers broke his neck. Hair shot out, grabbing the final one by the head, then flicked him up before slamming him down onto the alleyway floor.

The subject dropped the cigarette and stepped into a beam of light. She reached into her bag and retrieved a small handgun. She levelled it at Krackers. He called out to her, but she fired, nicking him on the arm. Hair shot out and reared up, stabbing her multiple times.

Her questioning eyes met his horrified gaze. She dropped to the ground and crawled towards the entrance before collapsing lifelessly onto the pavement. There were screams, then moments later, police sirens could be heard.

He moved further down the alley, turning to see her 'accusing' look. The image burnt itself into his mind.

Memories can appear forever, while in the present, just a moment.

From the entrance of the alley, a young woman wandered down. She was dressed provocatively, her outfit showing enough to melt the eyes of mortal men. She reached into her bag. Fumbling, she dropped it.

"Damn!" She bent down to pick up the spilled contents. She gathered up a lipstick, a compact, and a rather large, ominous black gun.

Around her, figures materialised from the shadows. She turned to the entrance, but more muggers were blocking her escape.

"Hello, boys," she smirked, steadying herself. She counted eight burly men. "You want some of this?" She smoothed down her mini skirt. That was Krackers' cue.

Krackers jumped into the air. Hair splashed out, dwarfing his partner. It rained down over three of the men, squashing them and breaking bones. Krackers grabbed one of the men, lifting him up. Hair shot straight through him, blood exploding and partially covering Krackers.

"You took your time," Nursie giggled as she dispatched another mugger with a roundhouse kick to the head. His head leant at an unnatural angle. The remaining three assailants turned tail and ran for the entrance. Hair flowed out, creating a wall and blocking their escape.

Nursie smiled a cruel smile as she drew her gun and fired twice, killing two of the three remaining men. The surviving thug cringed, pressing himself against Hair's wall.

"You can tell your boss, the Shrink," Krackers fumed, murder in his eyes, "this is what will happen to you and your cronies when I catch up with you!" Krackers waved away Hair, and it flowed back into his head. The henchman bolted out of the alleyway.

"We should check them," Nursie said as she searched one of the fallen muggers. "We might be able to find some clues we can use." After a gruesome, bloody time of it, they gathered the items. Krackers glanced around and found a filthy hessian sack. He placed the 'tell-tale' items inside.

Nursie looked at Krackers and wrinkled her nose.

"What's that face for?"

Nursie rummaged through her bag and retrieved a compact. She opened it and held the mirror up to Krackers.

"Oh dear," Krackers exclaimed as he looked in the mirror. He glanced around, searching for water to rinse away the blood. As if by divine intervention, the heavens opened. The rain poured down, beginning to wash the blood away.

Nursie, on the other hand, looked even hotter, if that was possible.

"We should get these clues back to the hospital," Nursie said. After Krackers reined in his tongue, he nodded, and they made their way back.

Nursie walked into The Peter Adams Memorial Psychiatric Hospital. She flashed her I.D. card, and a pudgy doctor trailed after her, copying her movements. They headed back to Krackers' room. Hair retracted, peeling away the doctor disguise.

"I'll just go and change," Nursie excused herself. "While I'm gone, sort through the items." She turned and walked out. Krackers watched her sway, sighed, and went to the hessian sack, emptying its contents onto his bed. He started sifting through the items. There wasn't much.

A mobile phone, a torn piece of paper, a piece of candy with pocket lint, a set of keys, and several wallets.

"There wasn't much, Viewers," Krackers muttered. "I have to see this from a different perspective." He shook his head and stepped back. He did a handstand and squinted at the bed. He tried different angles, but nothing worked. He stretched out a hand, balancing on it, but still no result. Nursie sauntered in. She was dressed in her 'barely there' uniform. She giggled at the sight of an upside-down Krackers.

"Oh, look, Viewers," Krackers grinned, "an upside-down Nursie!" He laughed at the hidden meaning. He overbalanced and tumbled into a giggling heap. He looked up to see Nursie standing over him.

"If you're quite finished," Nursie smiled, "we need to sort through those items." Nursie helped a chuckling Krackers up, and together they walked over to his bed.

"I suppose the mobile phone," Krackers said, picking it up, "would be the obvious choice." He gazed at it, turning it over. He tapped the screen and the mobile activated. On the display was a rotating logo of 'C.R.I.M.E.' He tapped again. 'Please enter an 8-digit security code.' Krackers hovered his finger over the keypad. He typed 69696969 and chuckled as he was about to press the 'enter' key.

"No," Nursie shouted as Krackers stabbed the screen. It flashed 'incorrect security code.'

"Oops," Krackers muttered. The phone began to flash and vibrate. A high-pitched whine grew louder and louder. Hair suddenly shot out and swallowed the mobile. A moment later, there was a muffled explosion. Hair opened, revealing a smouldering mess.

"Now that was," Krackers said, "a definite wrong number. Thanks Hair."

"Okay," Nursie said, "that was unfortunate. What else do we have?" She picked up the paper and examined it. While she did, Krackers suddenly rolled on the floor.

"I'm a ball, rolling to and fro. Wee!"

"When was the last time," Nursie asked, concern in her tone, "you had your meds?"

"I'm a hummingbird," Krackers buzzed, "flitting from flower to flower!" He flapped his arms and darted around the room.

"Well, that answers my question," Nursie murmured. She set the paper back on the bed and rose, leaving the room. When she returned, she carried a syringe. She found Krackers curled up in a ball, rocking softly, muttering incoherently. She injected his meds and sat on the bed. While she waited for them to work, she went through the wallets. She discovered seven blank key cards and not much else. After some time, Krackers drifted back into reality, or some semblance of it. He stood on unsteady legs.

"I 'wigged out,' didn't I?"

"Something like that," Nursie said softly. "If you're feeling up to it, we need to sort through these items."

"Yep," Krackers nodded. "What did you find out while I was out?"

"In the wallets, I found some key cards." She handed one to Krackers. He looked it over, then bit down on it. "It's definitely not a piece of fruit." He handed the card back to Nursie.

"I wonder if this tastes more like fruit?" Krackers picked up the fluff covered candy. He raised it to his mouth, licking his lips. Hair flicked it from his fingers. He watched it fly across the room, bounce off a wall, then hit the floor, cracking open. An earbud sat inside one half of the candy.

"And I was going to eat that," Krackers pulled a 'yuck' face.

Nursie walked over and picked up the earbud. She turned it over, examining it. "What do you make of this?" She tossed it to Krackers, who caught it nimbly.

"I think," Krackers said, placing the earbud into his ear, "I'll put it in my ear." He did just that. Suddenly, horror filled his face. He toppled backwards, clutching his ear.

"Michael!" Nursie screamed, running over to him.

"I got you," Krackers laughed loudly. Then he snapped serious. "And my name is Krackers. Krackers, if you please." Nursie playfully shoved him away.

"So," Nursie asked, "what can you hear?"

Krackers tapped the bud, and it came to life.

"Calling the individual who has taken my equipment, do you read me?"

"I am Krackers, receiving," Krackers replied.

"You don't sound like it."

"Why do people always say that?" Krackers asked.

"I want my equipment now, Michael!"

"Wait, what?" Krackers did a double take. "My name is Krackers! Hang on, I know your voice. You're the Shrink!"

"Yes, Michael, and you've ruined a particular hit."

"You attacked a friend of mine," Krackers said, danger in his voice. "If you surrender now, I won't kill you. But honestly, I hope you don't!"

"Hahaha! You know the truth. You're a dead man. I'll bring forth all my resources."

"Bring it on, bitch!" Krackers shouted, ripping the earbud out and throwing it down. He raised a booted foot, about to stomp it, when Nursie stopped him. She picked it up and pressed the power button, cutting the transmission.

"We can use this against him," Nursie said. "Let's check the other items." She placed the earbud on the bed, then picked up the torn paper. "What do you think? And don't put it in your mouth!"

"I won't," Krackers said indignantly. He turned his head, sneaking the paper towards his lips.

"Krackers!"

"I was only going to smell it," Krackers said, holding the paper to his nose. After sniffing, he shrugged. "It smells like paper. What do you think, Hair?"

Hair plucked the paper from Krackers and flowed over it. A moment later, Hair floated back, handing it to Nursie while ignoring Krackers' reaching hand. Hair began to vibrate.

"Hair accessed the C.R.A.P.I. database," Krackers reported. "It says the paper came from a small offset printing company. Oddly enough, that company burnt down six months ago."

"Anything else?" Nursie asked. Hair vibrated again.

"Really?" Krackers tilted his head. "Now that's interesting. Hair says it's a partial letterhead and, wait for it, it's from the Department of Consciousness!" Krackers paused. "One question, what is the Department of Consciousness?"

"I haven't heard of that department. It's possibly new. Anyway, good work, Hair!" Nursie praised.

"What about me?" Krackers complained. "I translated what Hair was saying." Hair vibrated again. "I am not! You are!"

"So?" Nursie asked, "what did Hair say?"

"Hair said, 'I'm a baby,'" Krackers muttered, cheeks red, "and that I should 'suck it up.'"

Nursie tried to hold it back but it didn't work, and she exploded in laughter. Hair buzzed along with her.

"When you two are quite finished," Krackers said, irritation creeping into his voice, "what about the keys? What do you think they're for?"

"They could be for any electronic lock," Nursie mused. "So, what's our next move?"

"What's the word from C.R.A.P.I.?" Krackers asked.

Nursie tapped her ear, muttered softly, and waited. After a pause, she nodded.

"C.R.A.P.I. has sanctioned the mission," Nursie stated. "With the information we've got, I'll coordinate the operation from here."

"And I'll stride boldly," Krackers declared, "to defeat C.R.I.M.E. and the dreaded Shrink!"

"I'll get things set up," Nursie said. She leaned in, kissed him deeply, and whispered, "Come back safely."

Surprised by the 'non-mission' kiss, Krackers watched her wiggle away before steadying himself for the upcoming assignment.

The Peter Adams Memorial Psychiatric Hospital was a fully functioning mental health institution. Beneath its façade, the organisation known as C.R.A.P.I., Controlled. Response. And. Police. Intervention., worked tirelessly to keep Karma's citizens safe. The hospital itself knew nothing of C.R.A.P.I., and that's the way they liked it.

Nurse Bre Bwee was a competent nurse, but she was an even better liaison with Agent Krackers 'Michael' Krackers. He was an exemplary agent, partnered with his Hybrid. Artificial. Intelligence. Retaliator., or as he called it, Hair. Together they had an outstanding record, though sometime she didn't have a clue.

"Are you ready?" Nursie asked as she entered Krackers' room. He was busy playing with his toes.

Krackers

"This little piggy went to market," he said, grabbing one. "This little piggy stayed home. This little piggy had roast beef. This little piggy had none. And this little piggy cried 'ice cream' all the way home." Krackers rolled around on the bed, laughing gleefully.

She waited until his laughter faded, then took his face in her hands and kissed him firmly. This time, he absorbed the mission briefing. He smiled at her.

"I liked the 'non-mission' kisses better," Krackers blinked.

"So," Nursie said seriously, "do you need anything else? Remember, the Shrink is extremely dangerous, be careful." Then, as an afterthought, she added, "come back to me safely. I'd hate to have to train a new partner." She kissed his forehead gently.

Krackers stood as Hair feathered around him, forming his Doctor Delooz'nl disguise. "I'll let you know when I find something." The pudgy doctor winked and left the room.

Krackers had never been inside the Department of Consciousness before, in fact, he'd never even heard of it.

The pudgy doctor exited the Peter Adams Memorial Psychiatric Hospital and slipped into the streets of Karma. The disguise feathered away, leaving the stealth-ready Krackers.

"Hair," he asked, "pull up all available information on the Department of Consciousness, please." Hair vibrated, and moments revealed it to Krackers.

Superimposed over his eyes were the details of the Department of Consciousness. "Interesting," Krackers murmured. "Up until six months ago, it didn't exist. It's registered as a church. The brochure says it's 'a refuge from everyday life and the loose morals of society. With a strict regimen, designed to cleanse the soul and uphold uncompromising order.'"

Hair buzzed, and Krackers nodded.

"I agree," Krackers said. "Looks like it's time to cleanse my soul."

The first thing he did was a walk-by. The building stood five storeys tall, though Krackers suspected it went at least twenty storeys underground. Security was intense: one entrance. Two guards with weapons were stationed outside. There were, scanners, cameras, key card swipes, and who knows what else waiting inside.

"Hair," Krackers said, "tell Nursie to upload anything about Consciousness' security. Tell her this is far too heavy for a church.

Ask if she has any further updates." Hair vibrated with the answers.

It seemed the Department of Consciousness, in six short months, had become the top 'church' in Karma. It drew in all the outcasts, the downtrodden and the mentally ill from the city, and that was a lot.

Nursie had uploaded security clearances and possible disguise algorithms. Krackers sat in a quaint café opposite the Department, nursing a quadruple-shot cappuccino while watching the entrance. There was heavy traffic into the building; each person was frisked and scanned. It seemed the perfect chance to join the 'flock,' so to speak.

Krackers rose and walked toward the lengthening line. As he moved, Hair feathered out into a dishevelled man with wild hair and an even wilder beard. He stood in line and waited, then turned to a gaunt woman swaddled in rags.

"Are you as excited as I am?"

"I really am," she said, eyes wide. "Finally, I'll be rid of the voices in my head!"

"I know what you mean," Krackers replied. "Can't keep mine from bickering away!" He looked into the woman's eyes and saw a painful nothingness.

Abruptly the woman screamed, dropped to the ground and writhed. She pointed an accusing finger at Krackers.

"Blasphemer!" she shrieked. "Bringer of injustice! You will bring down great institutions!"

Krackers

Two guards emerged from the entrance, scooped her up and dragged her inside. Those in line started to grumble, then muttered among themselves about how unfair it was, 'line jumper, you'll burn in hell!' After an hour, Krackers was at the head of the line.

'I hope Nursie's intel is up to date, this could be embarrassing!'

Krackers reached into his clothing. Hair fashioned the key card and Krackers produced it, clutching the card. He swiped; a red light flashed.

"I think it's dirty," Krackers said nervously, forcing a laugh at the guard. He rubbed the card on his robes and tried again. After a few tense seconds the green light glowed. One guard scanned him with a flat paddle. After that, he was allowed through. Inside was a retinal scanner; he placed his chin on the cradle as the camera whirred and took a series of photos. After the all clear, he was led into a huge chamber, where he waited with what looked like half the citizens of Karma.

The turkey effect happens when large groups muttered together, a sudden loud noise would spike the muttering before it settled back to quiet mumbling.

As if to hone it home, a sudden screech echoed from the centre and the effect rippled outward

A massive screen at one end of the chamber descended slowly. A silhouetted figure materialised on the display.

"Greetings, my children," the voice boomed, reverberating around the chamber. The crowd cheered as one, a deafening hurrah.

"Welcome to the Department of Consciousness! My Acolytes will come amongst you and guide you to salvation!" Flowery music washed over the throng, calming them.

"Hair," Krackers whispered, "check the music, it's calming them far too much and I can feel it working on me. Tell me what you find." Hair vibrated, and after a minute or so it buzzed again.

"So, there's a calmative effect laced in the music. Make sure you've negated it for me."

Men and women in white flowing robes moved through the crowd, selecting people and ushering them through a gilded door. Shining light spilled out; those who passed through were bathed in brilliance.

"Welcome, sinner," a large robed man said as he approached Krackers. "If you would come with me, we will start you on the road to salvation." Krackers recognised him as the thug from the mugging. They walked toward the door and into the light.

The next room was brilliantly white, about the same size as the previous chamber and filled with curtained beds. The robe-clad thug guided Krackers to a bed, slid open the curtain, then guided him to lie down. Beside it sat a small panelled machine and an odd pair of headphones.

The robed man fitted the headphones on Krackers and punched at a keyboard. A small readout flashed letters, numbers and more letters. Finally, the readout read 'begin when ready.'

"This won't hurt a bit," the man said. "Just relax and everything will be fine." He leant over and pressed 'enter.' In an instant everything flipped from zero to abnormal, far stranger than Krackers' own mind. His eyes went blank and he began to drool.

Krackers found himself on a grassy plain, a cool breeze brushing his face. The plain stretched out in all directions.

"Welcome, my son," a voice boomed above him. "I know your thoughts and your fears." Suddenly something began to solidify overhead. As Krackers looked up he saw Hair form, but altered. It landed with a wet splat and slithered toward him. With one fluid movement it lunged, flying through the air and whipping wisps across Krackers' face.

"Nooo!" Krackers screamed. "Hair, what are you doing?!" A silhouetted figure appeared.

"Let go, my son! Once you do, you will be mine!"

Krackers snapped back with a start, horror still in his eyes. Hair was slapping his face.

"Okay, mate," Krackers said weakly, peeling off the headphones. "I'm awake."

Hair vibrated.

"Yeah, I agree, that wasn't pleasant." Hair continued to buzz.

"Yes, this is definitely not what it seems. "Did you monitor what I was experiencing?"

Hair shuddered.

"I agree," Krackers said. "It's an immensely powerful and dangerous tool to use on someone seeking help and redemption," Krackers said. "Contact Nursie and brief her on the situation."

He shook the last of the grogginess away, rose and studied the machine.

"Hair," Krackers asked, "can you disable this without letting 'them' know?"

Hair buzzed angrily.

"Calm down," Krackers backpedalled. "Of course, I have faith in you."

Wisps of Hair flowed out from Krackers' head, snaking over the panel and into the machine. A second later, Hair retracted and vibrated again.

"That's good, she's ready with C.R.A.P.I. to storm this place," Krackers nodded. "Tell her to wait for my signal." Hair hummed.

"Let's change out of these dirty clothes," Krackers began, "and into some white flowing robes. I think we should use the thug's face as a template." Hair didn't waste a second, feathering away the rags into an Acolyte's robes and a face to match. "Any chance of disabling the whole system?"

Hair vibrated.

"Okay," Krackers muttered, "that's unfortunate. Is there any way of tracking down the main system?"

Hair shot into the machine again and, after a moment, retracted and oscillated. It superimposed an image of the Department of Consciousness, then turned it into a three-dimensional plan. The place was a rabbit warren of corridors, rooms and chambers. On subbasement ten, the main computer system lay.

Krackers made his way down to the far wall where an elevator waited. After jabbing the button several times, he stood impatiently. At last, the doors opened. Two Acolytes stepped out with a curt nod; Krackers nodded back. He studied the panel; the sub-basement ten button had a security lock. Hair didn't wait to be asked. It shot out and on to the panel and, within a moment, unlocked the button.

"While you're there," Krackers added, "make sure we go express, so we don't run into any other wrongdoers. The elevator seemed to answer with a 'click' and it descended at a gut-wrenching rate. Within a minute, it reached its destination and the doors slid open to a handful of Acolytes

"Excuse me," Krackers asked the nearest one, "could you direct me to the Supervisor?"

"Did you forget something?" The Acolyte scratched his head.

"Arh, yeah, I forgot why I came down here in the first place, then I went back upstairs and remembered why I was here," Krackers said smoothly. "I need to ask the Supervisor a question from the big boss."

"Alright. Go to the end of the servers, turn right, then left and straight on."

"Thank you kindly," Krackers replied, heading off. He followed the directions and stopped outside the Supervisor's office. He knocked, entered, and closed the door behind him. There was a splat, a muffled scream, a thud, then silence. The door opened and the Supervisor walked out. He glanced back, shut the door, leaving a bloody, broken body behind.

Six Acolytes worked across the floor. As the Supervisor passed the first two, Hair struck, breaking their skulls and flinging them down.

"Well viewers," Krackers muttered, "two down, four to go." Hair shot out again, subduing two more. "Wait, two left!" He moved forward.

"Excuse me, Supervisor," one Acolyte said.

"You're excused," Krackers replied as Hair stabbed him in the heart. The Acolyte stared down to see Hair withdraw from his bloodstained chest and returning into the Supervisor. "And then there was one."

"Could you help me with something?" Krackers asked the last Acolyte.

"Certainly, Supervisor."

"Can you play dead?"

"Say what?"

Hair reared up and fanned out. It came crashing down, snapping his neck instantly.

"Hair," Krackers commanded, "find an input port and shut down the system." He watched as Hair snaked into a jack and began the process. Hair vibrated the request.

On a nearby monitor, a familiar silhouette appeared.

"What is going on here?"

"Tell Nursie to begin the attack!" Krackers shouted. He activated the monitor and grinned. The Supervisor's face slowly shifted into his own. "The jig's up, Shrink, the system's shutting down." There were muffled explosions. "It sounds like my friends have arrived!"

"I'll get you, Michael, you and your mutation!" On the monitor, the door behind the Shrink blew open. C.R.A.P.I. agents stormed in, cuffing him instantly. "You haven't heard the last of me!" He was bundled away.

"Good work, partner," Krackers said, ruffling Hair. Hair purred in response. "Let's go find Nursie. I'm starting to feel strange." Krackers made his way quickly back to the surface and saw the Shrink being loaded into a van. He could only glimpse the back of the Shrink's head and he wanted so desperately to see his face. Nursie walked up to Krackers, with ice cream treat for both him and Hair.

"Ready to go back to the ward?" she asked. Hair shot out, snatching the treat and slurping it away.

"For being the best partner ever," Krackers offered the ice cream to Hair. It didn't need to be told twice. Hair 'slurped' at the ice cream. After it finished, it made a 'smacking' noise.

"How are you feeling, Michael?" Nursie asked.

"My name is Krackers," he corrected, "and I feel like crap." They walked to a waiting car, got in, and it pulled away. Nurse's phone rang.

"Agent Bwee here," she answered, putting it on speaker.

"Ma'am, the Shrink's escaped! We found the guards curled in the fetal position, crying. They kept repeating, 'Michael is a dead man!' Who is Michael, ma'am?"

"Keep me updated."

Nursie turned to see Krackers cocooned in Hair's embrace. She leaned back as the car drove toward The Peter Adams Memorial Psychiatric Hospital, and Krackers' home.

Six.

Psychotics Need Love Too.

From the air, the city of Karma was a beautiful jewel at night, glittering brightly. Buildings shot up into the sky, each one trying to stretch further than the other. The tallest place in Karma was the Quillstar Technology building; it rose three hundred storeys high. On the rooftop, Krackers paced. He'd been awake for five days, the same amount of time he'd gone without his meds.

"You're the only one I can really trust, Hair," Krackers muttered to himself. "I don't even know why I bother with them!" he yelled to the skies. "They side with people who would do me harm!"

Hair tried to comfort him, but Krackers brushed his partner off.

"I've become their puppet!" Krackers' pacing quickened. "I'm just a lowly enforcer to them! I've got to stop the pretence and take off my mask!" Krackers raised a fist to the sky. "The jig is up, C.R.A.P.I, for I see all!"

Hair vibrated softly.

"I don't care what Nursie said, Hair!" Krackers spat. "My beautiful handler commands, and I must obey? I think not!"

Krackers dropped to his knees, leaned back, raised both fists, and screamed. It was a guttural screech that echoed through the night. He continued until his breath gave out, then fell forward, pounding the roof.

Hair quivered.

"I don't care, Hair," Krackers whispered. "She only wants me back to do her bidding. I don't think I can do this anymore."

Krackers rose and walked toward the edge, resolve in his eyes. He stopped at the edge and gazed down. Karma bustled and buzzed with life below.

"This has to end now, Viewers!" he cried. He stepped off the edge and into oblivion. The building rushed by as Krackers closed his eyes and waited for the end.

Hair was incensed; it had had enough of Krackers' shenanigans. It flowed out and around its partner. Krackers tried to fend off its help but gave in, numbness filling his being. Just before they hit the ground, strands shot out, embedding into the building. Furrows streamed away as glass rained down into the street. Passers-by scattered as Hair landed softly with a hiss. A crowd formed around the man-sized ball of hair.

Hair unfurled and flowed back into Krackers' skull. He jumped to his feet as if nothing had happened.

"Welcome, Viewers," Krackers said in his 'official' voice. "This is just one of the wonders you can expect from the Sykotic Circus, coming soon." He did a cartwheel, then ran off, leaving amazed faces behind.

Hair buzzed.

"I don't care that I haven't taken my meds," Krackers said. "I haven't felt this clear in years."

Hair whirred more urgently.

"Tell her I quit!" he snapped. "I can't do this bullshit anymore. I'm just too tired."

He turned into an alley. The feeling of being watched crept up on him. He turned his head abruptly but saw nothing. The further he went, the stronger his paranoia grew.

Demonic images flickered around him. He pointed at a large one.

"Hair," Krackers commanded, hysteria in his voice, "attack it, it's going to charge!" Hair flowed out, unsure of where the enemy was. "There!" Hair circled over Krackers' head.

Hair buzzed angrily.

"Don't you dare!" Krackers growled. "I don't want to speak to her, is that clear?!"

Hair quivered.

"No, Hair," Krackers whispered. "I'm not angry with you. Why do you ask?"

Hair fell silent.

"Hair," Krackers said suspiciously, "what have you done?"

Still, Hair stayed quiet.

"Hair!"

Hair fluttered.

"You did what?" Krackers spluttered. "You contacted Nursie and activated my G.P.S.?"

Hair fluttered again.

"I don't care if you did it for my own good!" Krackers spat. "Fine, then I'm doing this for *your* good! H.A.I.R., DISENGAGE A.I. KRACKERS. THREE. THREE. NINE. ALPHA. ONE."

Hair went limp, flowing down onto the ground before retracting into Krackers' head.

Krackers felt utterly alone. He wandered aimlessly through Karma. Subtly, the edges of his vision began to blur. He shook his head, and it seemed to fade. He continued down the street, then sat at a bus stop. Hanging his head, he tried to order his thoughts, but they tumbled and shattered as evil voices snarled. He looked up at the sound of a 'whoosh.'

High above, a dragon appeared. It dove, releasing a ball of fire. Krackers leapt aside as it smashed into the bus seat. A sizzling, flaming net engulfed the area.

"Attack!" Krackers pointed. Hair shot forth, wrapping around the dragon and bringing it down. It crashed and spewed forth troll-like demons that began firing green spikes at him. Krackers ran up the side of a building and flipped, the spikes narrowly missing their marks.

From the street ahead, more demons appeared, riding metallic beasts as they trundled forward. From the beasts' mouths, more green spikes shot out.

"Attack Delta point Epsilon!" Krackers screamed as he dodged, weaved, and cartwheeled through the assault. Hair shot out in bizarre angles, striking down demons, but more poured in. By sheer numbers, they surrounded Krackers.

"Spiral assault!" Krackers dropped and spun on one knee. Hair flowed out, slicing the inner circle off at the kneecaps. They fell, only to be replaced by more. Spikes whizzed by, but none found their mark. Krackers realised that without Hair's thinking, he was done for.

"H.A.I.R. RE-ENGAGE A.I. KRACKERS. THREE. THREE. NINE. ALPHA. ONE!" Krackers yelled. Hair instantly wrapped around him. "Good to see you, buddy."

Hair convulsed in tremors.

"Slow down," Krackers said. "I can't understand you."

Hair tightened around him and continued to shake.

"I know I shut you down," Krackers said, gasping. "Cut it out! Can we talk about this once we've killed the demons?"

Hair buzzed.

"What do you mean?" Krackers asked, shocked. "What demons? Look around you, they're everywhere!"

Suddenly, the onslaught ceased as the demons retreated to a safe distance.

"Good work, Buddy," Krackers smirked. "They saw you activate, and they were so terrified they ran away."

"Michael," a demon cried out. It walked out from the masses and stood before Krackers.

"Krackers," Krackers spat, "Wait, what the... Nursie?"

Before Krackers' eyes, the demon changed into the voluptuous nurse. Behind her, the other demons turned into C.R.A.P.I. forces, and the metal beasts shifted into vehicles.

"What the...?" Krackers was befuddled, his head lowered in thought. Hair slowly unfurled itself around him.

Nursie stepped up to Krackers and embraced him.

"I'm so sorry," Nursie whispered as she stepped to him and stabbed him with a syringe. Krackers' eyes widened as he pushed her away.

"Traitor!" Krackers screamed, murder in his eyes. "Hair, attack her, kill her!"

As the contents of the syringe started to work, Krackers staggered, looking into Nursie's eyes.

"Why?" With that, he crumpled to the ground.

Back at the Peter Adams Memorial Psychiatric Hospital, Krackers lay on his side, his back to the door. He barely spoke to anyone, and when he did, it was only one or two words. Every day, Nursie would sit by his bed, and this went on for a month. Slowly, Krackers' medication had been increased to a therapeutic level.

"I'm so sorry," Nursie whispered, tears in her eyes.

"It's me who's sorry," Krackers said softly. "I believed they were demons. I'm so embarrassed, attacking the very organisation I work for."

"They do understand what happened," Nursie continued softly. "They still want you as an agent. They said they'd reinstate you on one condition."

"What's the condition?"

"They want you to get a procedure," Nursie explained. "They want to put in a med pump."

"A pump, you say?"

"It's only about the size of two fists," Nursie continued, "it consists of a delivery system and a medication receptacle."

"I don't know," Krackers said, rubbing his chin.

"They also said they'd reactivate Hair," Nursie added. "You know I'll be with you all the way." She leant over and kissed him passionately.

"Okay, set it up," Krackers whispered. "My life's in your hands."

Later that day.

Krackers lay on a stainless-steel table, a metal bucket housing Hair. Around him, masked doctors stood. He had been unconscious for an hour. The doctors had implanted the med pump, the medication receptacle, another canister and a small button with a tiny flashing light on top. The doctor went over to a panel and tapped a button. The readout displayed a sequence of words and numbers. He hit the enter key, and it registered green.

"Ready to close, doctor," Nursie said, handing over an instrument. True to her word, she had insisted on being the scrub nurse, silently overseeing the operation.

The operation was a complete success.

It was touch and go for a day or two, there were complications. Nursie was by his side constantly; she never left him. He flatlined a couple of times, but they brought him back. When he fell into a coma, she stayed with him.

C.R.A.P.I., true to their word, reactivated Hair. After Nursie calmed Hair down, it flowed over Krackers, cocooning him. It softly buzzed, and Nursie never left his side.

Two weeks later.

Krackers

Kracker's moaned. As he came to, Hair unfurled and slowly retracted into his skull. Nursie stood and looked down; Krackers slowly opened his eyes, staring into hers. He smiled at her gaze.

"Welcome back," Nursie smiled.

"Did I miss much?" Nursie leant in and kissed him passionately. Then it was Hair's turn, it flowed out and hugged the stuffing out of him.

"I didn't get the mission briefing done," Krackers said weakly.

Hair vibrated wildly.

"Died?" Krackers scoffed. "I'd never die on you, Hair. What would you do without me?"

Nursie filled Krackers in on what had happened over the past two weeks. He sat quietly, listening. Nursie started to cry.

"I thought I'd lost you."

"I'm sorry I worried you," Krackers said gently, guiding her down. He embraced her, holding her close.

Two days later.

Krackers was back to normal, he did a cartwheel to prove it. Feeling so good, he kept going.

"Well, Viewers," Krackers started, "not even death could stop this warhorse. I'm fighting fit and ready to battle the Shrink!"

"Were you talking to me?" Nursie walked into the room. "Should you be doing those? It's been just over two weeks since the operation."

"It's only been just over two weeks since the *procedure*," Krackers corrected, chuckling as he continued the cartwheels.

"Will you please stop doing that?" Nursie laughed. "I need to talk to you." Krackers finished the cartwheels with a couple of backflips, the last one landing him sitting on the bed.

"I'm all ears," Krackers said.

"It's about the procedure." Nursie was about to continue when a buzz sounded in her ear. "I'll be back." She turned and walked out.

"Well, that was suspicious, Viewers," Krackers said. He waited and waited, then jumped out of bed, dropped to the floor, and started doing push-ups. Soon he moved to one-handed push-ups and kept going. After some time, Nursie returned.

"If you're up to it," Nursie said, "they have a mission for you."

"What were you going to say about the procedure before?"

"It doesn't matter," Nursie shook her head. "Are you up to it?" Krackers let the question go for now.

"I'm good to go," Krackers smiled.

"Okay," Nursie smirked, "come here." Krackers jumped up; Nursie moved in and kissed him passionately. Krackers closed his eyes, enjoying the rush of mission stats.

"Hair," Krackers said, "if you please." Superimposed on his sight, the mission spread out before him.

"The mission is simple," Nursie explained. "It's a snatch and grab. A high-ranking official's daughter has been taken. We believe it's the Shrink."

"Him again!" Krackers punched a wall, the concrete exploding around his fist. After a moment, Nursie continued.

"She's been fitted with a tracker since childhood. Your job is to follow the tracker, grab her, and bring her back safely. Any questions?"

"About the end game?" Krackers asked sheepishly.

"Yes, Krackers," Nursie smiled, "there will be ice cream."

Hair shot up and vibrated excitedly.

"Don't get too excited, Bud," Krackers laughed. "We have to finish the mission first."

"Are you sure you're okay?" Nursie cupped his face and kissed him again.

"You know me," Krackers smirked.

"I do," Nursie said softly, "and that's what scares me." She stepped back. "There was an extra item added to the medication pump. It's an adrenaline booster. If you need an extra hit during a fight or to get out of a situation, Hair has full access to it."

"Come on, Hair," Krackers declared, "time's a-wasting!"

"Come back safe," Nursie whispered. "Ice cream awaits."

As Krackers left the room, Hair feathered out, changing Krackers' chiselled form into the pudgy Doctor Delooz'nl disguise. He turned and winked at Nursie.

Outside the Peter Adams Memorial Psychiatric Hospital.

Hair feathered again, changing the Doctor back into Krackers' form.

"Arrhh," Krackers stretched, "it's so good to be out. So, how are you doing, Hair, you know, with the previous... unfortunate incident?"

Hair buzzed.

"I know," Krackers said, "I won't let them deactivate you again. I promise."

Hair cooed, then buzzed.

"Activate the girl's tracker," Krackers commanded. "Let's find her." The GPS appeared over Krackers' sight. There was a green blip, she was on the move. Krackers looked along the street for some transport.

An ice cream van was coming up the road. The driver obviously saw Krackers, as the van slammed on its brakes. It started to turn, but Krackers ran up to it. The man inside was terrified. Shaking, he tried to get out of the van but couldn't unbuckle himself. Krackers bounded up and poked his head through the window.

"It's you!" Krackers exclaimed.

"Oh no, it's you!"

"I need to commandeer your fine vehicle again," Krackers said in his official voice.

"Here," the ice cream man said nervously, handing Krackers the key, "take the van."

"I've been through a procedure of late," Krackers said in a serious tone. "You'll have to drive."

"So... your hair won't beat me up again?"

"What's your name, citizen?" Krackers enquired.

"Bob," Bob said nervously.

"If you'll drive us to our destination," Krackers said, "no injury will befall you."

Bob started up the van and moved off. He drove cautiously, which seemed to annoy Krackers.

"Hair," Krackers suggested, "show young Bob how we drive." Hair flowed out, reaching both the accelerator and the wheel. To Bob's horror, the van shot down the road. Krackers stuck his head out the window and started to sing.

"I scream, you scream, we all scream for ice cream!"

The van skidded and slid across the road, breaking all land speed records. At this stage, Bob decided to do the only appropriate thing, he passed out. Krackers noticed the unconscious Bob and pulled his head into the van.

"Oh, goodie," Krackers squealed, "Bob's playing the unconscious game!" With that, Krackers flopped back in his seat, eyes closed, his tongue hanging out limply. After a minute or so, Bob came to. He looked at Hair, still controlling the wheel, then at the 'unconscious' Krackers.

"Wake up!" Bob screamed, panic in his voice. "We're all going to die!"

"Hurrah," Krackers chimed, "I win!"

"You're crackers!" Bob screamed.

"Yes, I am," Krackers laughed. "What a grand adventure we're having, young Bob!"

After a series of near misses, Hair slammed on the brakes and came to a screaming halt at Karma's Docklands. Hair retracted back into Krackers' head.

"Thank you, young Bob," Krackers boomed. "You may have saved a young girl's life. Until next time."

"I hope not," Bob muttered as Krackers got out of the van. He gunned the engine and sped down the road.

"Well, Viewers," Krackers muttered, "with the heroic efforts of young Bob, we'll start the search for the young girl. Hair, have we got a signal?"

Hair rose and started to vibrate. It stopped, then buzzed at Krackers. Superimposed over his eyes, it showed the docks and surrounding warehouses. Among the containers, her signal was strong, situated right in the middle of the ten-hectare container yard.

It was a maze, full of sharp corners. The paths between containers were only two abreast.

Hair buzzed and shook.

"Yes," Krackers said matter-of-factly, "I know it's a trap. That's obvious." He stopped at the edge of the containers. "Activate the radar, three-dimensional, please, Bud." Hair displayed the whole container area: white for structures, red for enemies, and green for the target. The red dots were scattered, but there was a dense cluster in the centre, right where the green one sat.

"Hair," Krackers commanded, "activate camouflage." Hair flowed out and surrounded him. Slowly, Hair and Krackers faded, leaving only a faint distortion in the air. He moved slowly and deliberately. They turned a corner; a guard stood against a container.

"Hair," Krackers whispered, "subdue him, quietly." Krackers crept within centimetres of the guard, and Hair snatched him. The guard dropped his weapon and found himself face to face inside the cocoon.

His eyes widened, about to scream, when Hair tightened and crushed him, breaking every bone in his body. The concealed Krackers laid the guard on the ground and moved on. After dispatching a dozen guards, they moved closer to the centre, and the target.

Realising this was as close as he could get while camouflaged, Hair retracted into Krackers' skull. They stopped around a corner. Before him stood a crowd of guards. In the centre was the girl, more a teenager than a child. She sat quietly, her hands and feet bound to a chair. Around her were several guards with heavy weapons. In front of her stood a shadowy figure, leaning over and speaking softly.

"The Shrink! I think it's time, Hair," Krackers smiled. "Activate the adrenaline boost, now!"

Hair buzzed, then hummed.

"Whoa!" Krackers' eyes widened as suddenly everything slowed. He ran into the nest of guards. Krackers and Hair acted as one, cutting through the group, guards falling one by one. Krackers ran up a container, flipping; they didn't stand a chance.

In reality, a blur was dropping guard after guard, leaving only the girl and the shadowy figure. Hair stopped the adrenaline boost, and the blur ceased, Krackers stood before them.

"Shrink!" Krackers spat with contempt. "Let the girl go and give yourself up!"

"Michael!" The Shrink smirked. "You certainly are a thorn in my side."

"My name is Krackers, Krackers, and I'll be your executioner. Hair!" Hair shot forward toward him and rippled straight through the figure.

"Hahaha," the Shrink laughed, "You've won this one! I'll leave you with a surprise!" The Shrink shimmered away. A beeping started under the chair.

"Adrenaline boost, Hair!" Krackers blurred, and Hair cocooned around him and the girl. The explosion was massive, containers were hurled like rag dolls. A balloon of fire towered into the sky; half the container yard was decimated.

Nursie, with some C.R.A.P.I. agents, arrived on the scene, followed by Emergency Services.

"Michael," Nursie whispered, tears flowing.

It took half an hour to bring the fire under control. They reached the centre of the containers. A huge ball of ash met them, it exploded as Hair retracted into its partner's head. The girl, still bound to the chair, began to cry. Hair cut her bonds, and she ran toward Nursie, then, seeing her father, ran to him. The two embraced.

"That adrenaline boost is *great!*" Krackers walked up to Nursie. Nursie, in turn, ran to him, grabbed him, and held him tightly.

"I thought I'd lost you again." She buried her head against his chest.

"Well, Viewers," Krackers said, "there's only one more thing to do to wrap up the case."

"What's that?" Nursie asked, puzzled.

"There was something about ice cream?"

"Of course," Nursie laughed, "my treat."

As they made their way to their reward, a smacking noise could be heard.

Seven.

In Space, No One Can Hear You Yodel.

The Quillstar Technology building was the tallest structure in the city of Karma, rising some three hundred storeys high. It was steeped in mystery, just as much as C.R.A.P.I. was. On the roof sat a huge space elevator that reached up to a geosynchronous space station, positioned directly in the centre of the building with space to spare. It was the perfect site.

The company, Reality Inc., funded and owned the space station. Yet another mystic and secretive corporation. C.R.A.P.I. only had sketchy intel on the company.

Sitting on the edge of the building, Krackers was playing with his fingers. Hair was draped over the edge, dangling a poor criminal.

"Let's try it again," Krackers asked. "Where is the Shrink?" "Who?" the criminal screamed.

"The Shrink," Krackers said calmly.

"You're crazy!" the man blubbered, and yes, he cried like a baby. "I don't know any Shrink!"

"I'm sure I am," Krackers chuckled. "Are you really sure you don't know?"

"Okay then. Hair."

The man was released from Hair's grip. The criminal shrieked, wet his pants, and dropped like a stone.

"Next!"

Behind Krackers, bound by part of Hair, were four men, equally upset at their predicament. Hair flowed to the men, released its grip momentarily, grabbed another man, then tightened again. It moved the shaking man over the edge, suspending him in mid-air.

Krackers

"You heard what I said?"

"What?!? Wait!" the stumbling man screamed.

"Bzzz, wrong answer."

Hair heard the cue and released the man into gravity's loving embrace.

"Next!"

Hair repeated its actions. Another cry-baby hung over the edge.

"You really should have the right answer," Krackers yawned.

"I know the Shrink!" the criminal cried. "I work for an organisation called C.R.I.M.E. The Shrink is the head of it. Please don't kill me!"

"I was going to ask where the nearest ice cream shop is," Krackers laughed. "Hair, quickly, grab him! He knows about the Shrink!"

Hair shot over the edge, rocketing down to catch the man and bringing him back up onto the roof.

"Hair, put him somewhere safe."

Hair cocooned him and placed him near the space elevator.

"As for the rest of you, I don't really need you, gentlemen. Hair, if you don't mind, take out the trash!"

Hair did as it was told and lofted the three criminals over the edge.

"Going down," Krackers waved.

Hair released them; one man even tried to flap his arms. They plummeted to the ground, smearing the walls with blood and gore.

Krackers walked over to the cocooned lawbreaker and stopped a hand's width from his face. He smirked. The criminal was visibly uncomfortable after seeing his cohorts thrown off the side of the building. Sirens started to wail, faintly filtered from the ground below. Krackers went to the edge and looked over.

"Hey there," he smirked as he walked back. "Damn pity about your friends, I really thought that guy flapping his arms would've flown. Oh well. Now, you were saying about C.R.I.M.E. and the Shrink?"

The crim spilled his guts. He told Krackers how C.R.I.M.E. had become more fluid since C.R.A.P.I. closed their operations. They only stayed in one place for a day or so before moving on. He said that C.R.I.M.E. was now set up in the space station. No one had ever seen the Shrink in the flesh, he was only ever a hologram. As for what they were up to, he said he didn't have clearance, but he did know that something big loomed on the horizon.

"That's good," Krackers said. "Hair, let him go."

Hair did as it was told and tossed the lawbreaker off the building.

"Hair," Krackers remarked, "I meant, let him go inside the building and leave."

Hair vibrated.

"Okay, that's your bad," Krackers chuckled. "We'd better go, the police will be on their way."

As Krackers turned to leave, Hair feathered him into a generic cleaner. He walked to the fire escape, went through the door, and headed down the stairs to the three-hundredth floor. He walked quickly to the bank of elevators. As he reached them, the doors opened and police officers filed out. One of them took Krackers aside.

"Did you see anything unusual?"

"I'd just finished cleaning Doctor Delooz'nl's office," Krackers began, "when I saw four men exit the elevator and make their way to the fire escape."

"Weren't you suspicious?"

"Hey, it's above my pay grade, officer," Krackers said. "My job's to clean, and that's all."

"Thank you for your time, Mister…?"

"Ness," Krackers said, starting to make his way to one of the elevators.

"Thank you, Mister Ness."

Krackers

Krackers made it into one of the lifts. As he entered, Hair feathered him back into his normal form. After the gut-churning drop, Krackers walked out of the foyer and into the street. Hair's handiwork was obvious, the four men had landed in the exact same spot, in an open dumpster. The blood pattern splattered up a nearby wall and across the surrounding area. The police had taped off the scene. Krackers mingled with the growing, ghoulish crowd.

"Nice work, Hair," Krackers whispered. "Ten out of ten for placement."

Hair vibrated.

"I agree," Krackers said under his breath. "Let Nursie know what we've got. Tell her we'll be at the I SCREAM U SCREAM Ice Cream Parlour."

A dozen ice creams later.

Krackers sat in a booth at the back of the ice cream parlour. On the table sat a screen and a virtual keyboard. A live news feed played on the monitor, which also doubled as a video phone. Nursie's official looking face stared out from the screen. Krackers juggled four empty ice cream bowls, enjoying his trick while talking to Nursie.

The bowls clattered to the floor as he let them drop. Luckily, the only other customer was a homeless man lying on a bench seat.

"Thank you for the intel," Nursie said. "We've managed to isolate the C.R.I.M.E. com signal."

"Krackers, cut that out!"

He bent down to retrieve the bowls.

"Michael!"

"I was only stretching," Krackers replied, faking a stretch.

"After scanning it, we cross-referenced the companies that have registered recently," Nursie continued. "We finally found the company that C.R.I.M.E. is trading under, Reality Inc."

"The space elevator company?" Krackers said. "I was just there, throwing out the trash."

"I don't think I want to know what that means," Nursie commented. "I'll get back to you shortly with more info." The connection was severed.

"More ice cream!" Krackers threw up his hands.

Hair rose and buzzed.

One hour later.

The screen lit up and Nursie's beautiful but stern face appeared.

"Nursie," Krackers said, "what's the news?"

"Since you're not here, I'm uploading the mission to Hair, the oldfashioned way."

Hair rose and began to quiver. It lasted a minute, then Hair retracted.

An A.I.'s memories are just as valid.

In deep space, nobody really knows whether you can scream or not. Although it seemed peaceful and calm, flowing silently along.

Before it was Hair, it was the Bar'netpostiche, the closest thing it would approximate to being was an octopus, an extremely intelligent one.

It flowed through the void, using the solar winds as propulsion, exploring the many galaxies. The solar breeze ruffled its hair-like strands. It happened upon the Sol system and slowly moved toward the yellow-white sun.

The Hilda asteroid belt orbited between Mars and Jupiter, and humankind had mined it for a quarter of a century. It was a contentious issue, as a few corporations had been fighting over the mining rights.

C.R.A.P.I. was one of the corporations. It mined at the very edge of the asteroid field near Jupiter. One of the crews reported seeing a strange, hair-like creature. C.R.A.P.I. authorised its capture. With no propulsion of its own, it was easily scooped up and transported to Earth.

The C.R.A.P.I. scientists had a field day with their newest acquisition. One of the first things they did was clone it. The second thing they did was weaponise the original. It was touch and go in the beginning, but they eventually created a working A.I. and grafted it to the Bar'netpostiche. It inhibited its free will but kept its intelligence, and boy, it was intelligent.

And thus, Hair was born.

The past races forward to the present.

"Nursie said it was a simple mission," Krackers scoffed. "But since when have any of our missions been simple, Hair?" Hair buzzed.

"I agree," Krackers nodded. "So, tell me about the mission?" Hair shivered.

The mission briefing seemed simple enough: infiltrate the space station posing as a technician and, when the shift change happened, go up to the station and reconnoitre, taking note of the goings-on, then reporting back. Simple. Yeah, right.

"Okay, Hair," Krackers said confidently, "let's go and tread boldly where no man has gone before." Krackers adopted a hero's stance, hands on hips.

Hair buzzed.

"I know mankind has gone there before," Krackers tried to justify. "It's just a heroic saying."

An hour later.

Krackers hid in the shadows near the entrance to the space elevator and did the one thing he really hated doing, waiting. On cue, the fresh technicians gathered for the shift change. One of them wandered near the edge as he lit a cigarette. Hair flicked out, cocooning him and dragging him back. With horrified eyes, he watched Krackers feather an exact copy of him. Hair picked the tech up and slammed him into a wall, then did it again for good measure.

Krackers walked up to the milling techs. There were at least fifty of them, both men and women, waiting for the lift.

Finally, the elevator door opened and the shift change exited. Krackers moved inside and made his way to the back. The elevator rumbled as the booster rockets ignited. It shot up into the atmosphere and, fifteen seconds later, docked at the space station.

Zero gravity is such a freeing experience, and Krackers loved it. He tumbled on the spot, then a metallic voice sounded.

"Artificial gravity initiated."

Krackers fell to the floor. He picked himself up as the elevator door slid open, revealing a gigantic white room filled with terminals and a panoramic window wrapping around the space. The group of technicians began to disperse, leaving Krackers standing alone.

He walked over to the nearest terminal and sat before it.

"Hair," Krackers whispered, "see what you can find?"

He placed a hand on the input port. Hair snaked into it. On the monitor, file after file appeared, until one file, in particular, caught Krackers' attention.

'Bar'netpostiche'

Hair buzzed excitedly.

"Slow down, Hair," Krackers whispered. "I can't understand you when you get excited." Hair vibrated.

"What do you mean, it's about you?" Krackers muttered. "Try opening the file."

The file flashed 'access level two. Restricted.' Then 'unauthorised access from this terminal.'

"Now, that could be a problem. Keep working on it."

"Supervisor?" a young tech said, waiting for Krackers to answer.

Krackers

"Supervisor?"

"What? Yes?"

"Could you sign this?" The tech handed him a tablet. Krackers scrawled a signature.

"Sir, it might be better if you used the terminal in your office?" The tech looked a little puzzled.

"Yes, my office," Krackers responded, somewhat confused. "Listen lad, I had a week-long bender, could you point me to my office?"

"Of course, Sir," the tech chuckled. "I think we've all had a week like that. This way, Sir."

They walked across the room and up to a door marked 'Supervisor Wan'cer.'

"I can take it from here, lad," Krackers said, patting the technician on the shoulder. "Your name is…?" "I'm Gay," the tech replied.

"You don't look it," Krackers remarked. "Thank you, Technician Gay."

Krackers tried to stifle a laugh. When he entered his office, he couldn't help himself, bursting into hysterics. After composing himself, he locked the door and went to the Supervisor's terminal.

"Okay, Hair," Krackers said, sitting at the computer, "do your thing."

Hair snaked out, found the input port, and entered it. The screen flashed to life and Hair located the 'Bar'netpostiche' file. Hair tried to access it, and Krackers subconsciously held his breath.

The file opened. Sub-files appeared. Hair picked the 'Acquisition' subfile, it opened, and Krackers was genuinely surprised. There was a report from C.R.A.P.I., dated thirteen years ago. It detailed the capture of a strange 'hairy, octopus-like creature.'

Another report described the weaponisation process used to convert the creature into an A.I. killing machine. It went on to mention a volunteer, 'Michael Ness', who had flat-lined three times but successfully integrated with the creature, code-named 'Hybrid. Artificial. Intelligence. Retaliator.'

Upon integration with H.A.I.R., Ness exhibited sociopathic tendencies and, at times, complete psychotic breaks, hallucinations, and grandiose propensities. The handler, Nurse Bre Bwee, was tasked with keeping both Ness and H.A.I.R. under control.

"Hair," Krackers murmured, trying to absorb the information. "Get in touch with Nursie and appraise her of the situation. Let her know there's a mole inside C.R.A.P.I." Hair rose and started to vibrate.

"Check out the 'Exploration' file," Krackers suggested.

The file contained numerous stats and a map of the Solar System. A few red dots blinked across the map, and as it expanded, one large red dot hovered around Alpha Centauri.

"We can't let them do this," Krackers said. "If they capture your species and weaponise them, C.R.I.M.E. would be unstoppable." Hair buzzed.

"I know, Hair," Krackers said quietly. "Any chance we can introduce some kind of virus?"

Hair vibrated, then buzzed.

"So Nursie uploaded a specific virus called 'Retribution,'" Krackers chuckled. "Okay, introduce it into the core, set a timer for ten minutes, then we should really go, now!"

Hair shivered for a moment, then buzzed. "Okay," Krackers said, "ten minutes, you say?" Hair buzzed urgently.

"Ten minutes, what are we waiting for?"

Krackers moved to the door and opened it. Technician Gay stood there, about to knock.

"Sorry, Gay," Krackers said. "I haven't the time right now, I have to get planet-side. I've an errand to run."

"I'm sorry, Supervisor," Gay replied. "The station's on lockdown. There appears to be an intruder."

"An intruder, you say?" Krackers feigned surprise. "Then we must hunt this intruder down and dispatch him into the cold bosom of Lady Death! Is there any way, besides the elevator, to escape the station?" "There are escape pods on the lower level," Gay said.

"Then that would be a good place to start," Krackers suggested. "I'll begin the search down there, you go get security."

"I'd rather go with you," Gay said nervously. "There's safety in numbers."

"Damn," Krackers muttered. Then, "Well, lead the way, young Gay!"

They made their way to an internal elevator. Gay swiped his pass and the door opened. They travelled down to sub-basement thirteen and, after an intolerably long time, reached their destination. The doors opened, and standing in the entrance were two burly guards.

"This level is off-limits to all personnel," one of the guards grunted.

"I haven't got time for this shit," Krackers muttered. "Hair, sort them out!"

Hair reared up. Gay gasped and fainted. Hair shot forward, skewering the two guards, blood gushing everywhere. They dropped like stones. Krackers stepped over the fallen guards and went to one of the escape pods. It was, of course, security locked.

Krackers went back to Gay and relieved him of his security badge. He returned to the pod and swiped the card. A red light flashed, halting his progress.

"We haven't got time for this," Krackers said, frustration in his voice.

"Hair, what can you do?" Hair buzzed.

"What do you mean, watch out?"

Hair shot out, ripping the pod door straight off its hinges. It hurled it over Krackers' head, forcing him to duck.

"Okay, now we've got an escape pod without a door, and no air outside."

Hair buzzed, then vibrated.

"Okay," Krackers said. He entered the pod, sat down, and buckled up.

"Now what?"

Hair flowed out, covering and sealing the vacant doorway.

Hair whirred.

"What do you mean, 'GO'!? Oh, right!" Realisation hit him. He slammed the big red button and the pod released, shooting down from the space station.

The pod glowed as it raced through the atmosphere, then the parachutes deployed, and the pod splashed down just off the coast of Karma.

"How are you doing, Hair?" Krackers asked.

Hair buzzed and hummed.

"A bit singed? Smells like burnt hair. Looks like you're fireproof," Krackers laughed. "Inform Nursie of our situation," he said quietly, the files still swirling in his thoughts.

Hair hummed.

"I agree, bud," Krackers said solemnly. "We've certainly got a number of questions that need answering."

Eight.

Death In The Family.

Krackers lay in a pool of blood; he couldn't work out whether it was his or not. A female body was slumped over him, drenched in blood. With some effort, he managed to push the woman to the side. He recognised the blood-soaked nurse's uniform. Nursie! "Hair," Krackers whispered, "what the hell happened?" Hair stayed quiet.

"What's the last thing I remember?" Krackers tried to sit up; eventually, he succeeded. He looked around, he was in his room. Signs of a struggle were everywhere; the room was overturned. Near the door, three men lay sprawled. Two of them were decapitated.

"Nothing," Krackers muttered, "my mind's so foggy." He tried, he really tried not to think too hard. "Oh well, my mind's not firing on all cylinders, but that's okay. It never worked right in the first place."

Krackers crawled over to Nursie and checked her pulse. It was weak, but it was there.

"Well, viewers," Krackers chuckled weakly, "what do you do when you wake up to this? I have to think… what happened last night?"

Foggy images started to form. They were there, but Krackers couldn't quite grasp them. He calmed himself, breathing steadily. He did an internal check of his body.

"Nothing seems damaged, as far as I can tell," Krackers noticed. His head felt a bit numb.

A feeling of hopelessness washed over him. He felt as though he were being smothered. Thoughts swirled, dragging him down into their cold embrace, when something happened. A memory!

Don't force it, let it form naturally, he thought. The memory slowly solidified, and the fog began to lift.

A day ago.

Krackers was rushing to meet a fellow employee. It was raining, misting, the sort that leaves a fine film of water on you. He hated it; the rain messed with his ice-cream cones.

The memory slowly solidified, revealing a stark and bleak scene.

The night was bright. Sector Thirteen had claustrophobic structures lining the streets, huddled closely together. They rose skywards into the clouds. Light turned night into day. Neon signs covered most of the shop fronts, stretching as far as the eye could see. The light blazed into the darkness, turning the citizens into chaotic porcelain dolls. They never stopped. Reflections from the neon painted the cloud cover overhead into a sickly, chaotic rainbow.

The crowds, always the maddening crush, a sea of people flowing and filling the streets.

There were only two ways to travel in the city of Karma. One was via gravitational manipulation. Cars, vans and trucks were silently suspended thirteen metres above the street. Man's greatest discovery: the conquest of Earth's gravitational forces. From old clunkers and delivery vans to supercars, they were all up there, and road rules didn't apply.

The other way was by train. Anti-grav pylons hugged the train at intervals. It whizzed and snaked through Karma. Circumnavigating the city took four hours, and there was a service every fifteen minutes. Walking was obviously out; Karma was just too big.

Krackers swam through the sea of people, hot and wet, their body odours piercing the senses.

Finally, Krackers reached his destination: a huge café named Wired by Nature! He waded through the crowd to the door. Hair created a card, and after swiping it, it allowed him into a fifteen-storey room. On each level, people sat. At floor level, a huge counter encompassed the room. Krackers couldn't see her; there were too many people.

"Hair," Krackers muttered, "see if you can scan her."

A tap on his back sent him reeling. He spun around, fists at the ready. A shocked female face appeared, Nursie's pretty face swam into view. Krackers was relieved. After a warm, heartfelt hug, she guided Krackers to a small booth filled with a holographic field of nature. It showed a babbling brook, rocks and all. It was so real; it must have cost a fortune. Nursie had always loved water and nature.

They walked into the booth, and the outside world disappeared, replaced with the wondrous scene. All the sights, sounds, and smells of nature were present. The table was set with delicious food and drink, vodka, especially. Krackers sat across from her, and she looked deep into his eyes.

Krackers and Nursie had known each other for many years. She leant forward, a genuine smile on her face, and kissed him deeply. Her smile evaporated, replaced by a serious look.

"I know that look," Krackers said soothingly.

"They've found me," Nursie's face changed to pleading.

"What's happened? Who are they?"

"C.R.I.M.E.! They managed to find me at my address." Her lip started to quiver as the words tumbled out.

"Okay," Krackers said, "calm yourself. Close your eyes, take a deep breath, and tell me what happened." He smiled warmly at her. She smiled back, closed her eyes, took a deep breath, and calmed herself. After a minute, her lips puckered as she exhaled. She opened her beautiful eyes and smiled at him.

"Hey, Bud," Krackers muttered, "check the area for hostiles." Hair rose and hummed, then buzzed.

"Hair says it's all clear."

"I was on the way back to my place. My car's in the shop, so I had a loaner. I was waiting to cross to my exit when another car hovered to a stop behind me. It was a smooth ride."

"Two well-dressed men sat in the car, staring at me. One of the men grabbed for his gun and pointed it at me, so I gunned the car, and now the loaner is in the shop as well." She shrugged.

"Did you follow protocol?"

"Three times round Karma, changing stations every so often. Now I'm here, asking for some help." Tears welled up in her eyes.

"If they've found you there…" Realisation set in. "I think we should go, now."

They raced out of the booth and headlong into the real world. After swimming through the crowd, they made it to the stairs of the train station. They climbed onto the station proper. Krackers checked the timetable: two minutes to go. It was the longest two minutes they'd ever experienced. They casually glanced around, checking for problems, but there was nothing, just a lot of ordinary people waiting for the train.

The train trip seemed agonisingly slow. Nursie moved closer and put her head on Krackers' chest.

"Are we safe?" Nursie whispered.

"Hair has scanned the area. It's safe and secure." The scenery blurred around them.

The train finally stopped in Karma's outer-city sprawl. After disembarking, they checked the area. They had worked together for many years; gestures were minute but understandable.

Nursie glanced at Krackers. The look told him the area seemed secure. They descended the stairs and merged with the flow of people. They made their way to another station. After climbing the stairs, Nursie was in the lead, those booted, shapely legs and that mini skirt. Krackers enjoyed the climb.

After exchanging glances, they relaxed a bit.

They got off at the station and made their way to a C.R.A.P.I. safe house. They stopped and waited for an hour, sitting in some undergrowth surrounding the house. Hair surveyed the property and gave the all-clear. Krackers moved to the side and activated a hidden switch. The ground near him whined quietly, and a hatch opened. Krackers gestured to the hole.

"Welcome to C.R.A.P.I. Safe House Thirteen," he smiled. Nursie descended into the shadows. After navigating the booby traps, she stood near a rock wall and raised a questioning eyebrow at Krackers. He smiled back and tapped a pendant he was wearing. Part of the rock wall faded away, revealing a door, which slid open.

"Let's see what's happening at the other C.R.A.P.I. safe houses."

A monitor lit up. Thirteen panels showed interior and exterior views of the places. One panel showed House Three. Two well-dressed men were hiding, one crouched behind a lounge, the other in the kitchen.

"Crap!" Krackers spat. "I really liked that place. Oh well." He tapped on the keyboard. The view of the house suddenly went blank. A muffled explosion was barely noticeable.

Another panel, House Two, showed an intruder, no, two intruders.

Yet another panel showed multiple intruders. The rest of the panels showed the same.

"Crap!" Krackers leant over the keyboard and typed.

A cascade effect followed as panel after panel went dark. A series of explosions rang out over the city.

Krackers turned to Nursie. As he opened his mouth, more explosions went off just outside the secret entrance.

A trap door in one of the bathrooms slid open. Krackers' adrenaline booster kicked in. He grabbed Nursie and dragged her down the hole. The door to the tunnel was blown to the other side of the room, embedding into the wall, followed by 'flash-bang' grenades.

The escape tunnel ran for a kilometre before ending up under a C.R.A.P.I.-owned shop in the inner sprawl.

"We need some private transportation," Krackers muttered. "Hair, see what you can do about it."

Hair rose and started to vibrate. After a moment, Hair buzzed excitedly.

"No way," Krackers laughed. "Bob, you say? And he's coming this way? How wonderful!" Krackers clapped his hands.

"Who's Bob?"

"Bob's a very special friend," Krackers beamed. "He serves a very important service!"

A van turned the corner, and Krackers stepped in front of it. The van skidded to a stop. The occupant leant forward, shock and horror in his eyes.

"You!" The man tried to turn around, but Krackers deftly opened the driver's side door.

"Bob!" Krackers smiled gleefully. Even Hair rose and hugged the man. "We are in need of your services."

"You're Krackers, aren't you?" Bob was still in shock.

"You know I am," Krackers smiled an evil smile.

"An ice-cream van?" There was amusement in Nursie's voice.

"This is Bob," Krackers said proudly to Nursie. "Purveyor of ice cream and other assorted frozen treats! In the past, he has offered his services for transportation!"

"Wait, what?" Bob coughed.

"Your chariot awaits," Krackers opened the passenger side door. "Okay Bob, please take us to the Peter Adams Memorial Psychiatric Hospital."

Krackers climbed into the back of the van while Nursie took the passenger seat. She turned to Bob. "Hi," Nursie smiled. "I'm Bre."

"I'm Bob," he said, shyly looking away, "but I'm sure you knew that." Bob changed the subject. "So, Krackers, I really don't have much choice in taking you, do I?"

"Not really, young Bob," Krackers laughed. Bob sighed and drove off.

"Bob," Krackers asked, "could you turn the music on?" Bob pressed a button, and the ice-cream van music chimed out. In the back of the van, Hair and Krackers indulged in ice cream treats. Krackers yodeled along to the music. Finally, the van pulled up in front of the hospital, and Krackers and Nursie exited.

"Thank you, young Bob," Krackers smiled. "You've done the city of Karma proud. Till next time."

"I hope not!" Bob screamed and gunned the van. It squealed off down the road.

"Something doesn't feel right," Krackers said uneasily. "Hair, what do you think?"

Hair flickered to life. After it hummed, then buzzed…

"I agree," Krackers whispered. "It doesn't feel right."

As they walked carefully into the hospital, Hair feathered Krackers into a doctor. The place was a ghost town; there was no one at reception. Hair feathered again, changing his partner's outfit into a stealth suit while continuing to scan.

"Keep behind me," Krackers instructed. Nursie agreed.

Hair buzzed angrily.

"Hair said there are unfriendliness but couldn't tell how many." Krackers walked carefully forward. Something whizzed past his ear. He ducked, grabbing Nursie to cover. "I really think there's something wrong!"

Hair instinctively rose and created a shield around the two of them. Krackers stood up as two shots thudded into the shield. With Nursie behind him, they moved down the corridor. More shots hit Hair as they closed on the assailants.

Hair screamed as it flowed out, cutting down one of the foes, spearing him through the heart. The other was sliced to pieces. Hair buzzed.

"Good work, Bud," Krackers said. "Are there any more surprises on this level?"

Hair buzzed an all-clear. It retracted into Krackers' skull.

They made their way to Krackers' room. It was a mess. Someone had gone through the place, searching for something. Three assailants lay in wait. As Krackers entered, Hair flashed into a shield, forming around Krackers and Nursie. Multiple shots were fired; a few missed, ricocheting around the room.

Hair whipped out, instantly decapitating two of the combatants. They fell lifeless to the floor. It reared up, dwarfing the last attacker and poised to strike.

"Hey, Bud," Krackers commanded, "we need this one alive." Hair shot forward, grabbing the combatant by the head and lifting him up. The man reached into his pocket and retrieved a small gadget. He pressed a button and activated it. The force rippled through the room.

Hair suddenly dropped like a stone. The now lifeless Hair was everywhere. The assailant ran at Krackers. Of course, Krackers ran towards him. He leapt, kicking the man in the throat just as the man fired another shot. The bullet whistled past Krackers, missing him by inches. The two collided hard and both dropped to the floor. Concussed, Krackers got to his knee. He was seeing double. That was when he noticed Nursie and crawled to her. He moved to try to pick her up. He succeeded, only to lose consciousness. Nursie slumped over him.

Krackers came to, lying in a pool of blood; he couldn't tell whether it was his or not. A female body was slumped over him. It was covered in blood. With some effort, he managed to push the woman to the side. He recognised the blood-soaked nurse's uniform. Nursie!

"Hair," Krackers whispered, "what the hell happened?" Hair stayed quiet.

Krackers

"What's the last thing I remember?" Krackers tried to sit up; eventually he succeeded. He looked about; he was in his room. Signs of a struggle were everywhere; the room was overturned. Near the door, three men lay. Two of them were decapitated.

Someone came to the door. Krackers didn't have the strength to react, and he slipped back into unconsciousness. After a while he opened his eyes to see more people in the room.

"I'm Doctor Richard Head," the doctor said. "I'm one of the C.R.A.P.I. doctors. You've suffered a severe concussion."

"How is Nursie?" Krackers asked weakly, as he saw Nursie lying on a gurney. She was hooked up to a couple of drips. "Will she be okay?"

"She's lost a lot of blood," the doctor explained. "I think it'll be touch and go."

"What happened here?"

"It's a bit sketchy," the doctor said. "It seems C.R.I.M.E. tried to test

C.R.A.P.I.'s defenses. Many died but the defenses held."

"What about Hair?" Krackers asked. "Is he okay?"

"Hair will be okay," the doctor said. "There was an electromagnetic pulse and Hair took the full force of it."

As two medics lifted Krackers onto a gurney, he drifted back into unconsciousness.

Three days later.

Deep inside the C.R.A.P.I. stronghold, Krackers sat upon his bed. Nursie lay on another; she'd been put into a medical coma. Doctor Head was chatting with Krackers.

"Hair has been repaired," the doctor stated. "You've got the all-clear. We are going to reactivate him." The doctor nodded at a tech. The technician tapped a keyboard. Hair came to life.

Hair buzzed angrily and reared up.

"Calm down, Bud," Krackers said. "Everything is fine."

Hair continued to buzz.

"Nursie will be fine too," Krackers continued. "Nursie is sleeping right now. We're fine." Hair hummed.

"Yes, Hair, C.R.I.M.E. will pay for this dearly!"

Krackers jumped up, did a cartwheel and stormed out of the room, murder in his eyes.

Nine.

Enforcement Personified.

In the outer sprawl of Karma, things weren't so pleasant. Gone were the sparkling skyscrapers, the neon and the cleanliness. They were replaced with low-rise apartments, old crackling fluorescent signage, and grime, lots of grime. Much of the sprawl had fallen into disrepair. There were at least ten shootings a day, sometimes more.

A rolling gun battle was in progress, and Krackers was dispatched to assist local law enforcement to quell the situation. C.R.A.P.I. was often called in when the law was stretched thin or completely overwhelmed.

Bob, the ice-cream van driver, was conscripted by C.R.A.P.I. to transport Krackers whenever needed. Although Krackers horrified Bob, the money C.R.A.P.I. offered was more than enough to counter the fear. In spite of considering Krackers and Hair an abomination, the pay helped quash his stomach-churning feelings.

C.R.A.P.I. took the van, weaponised it and installed advanced weaponry, it was a veritable fortress. They also converted it into an anti-grav vehicle. Bob was overjoyed.

Krackers arrived in the ice-cream van; it hovered above the action. The police were pinned down, losing ground with every passing moment. Krackers leapt out of the van.

"Young Bob," Krackers yelled over the noise of gunfire, "find somewhere safe and wait for my return."

Krackers ran toward the police. Hair flowed up and over him, creating a shield. Bullets thudded into Hair as Krackers skidded to the barricade. Hair flowed back into Krackers' skull as he crouched behind cover.

"You, Krackers?" the police sergeant asked, looking tired and worn out.

"Yes I am, but how did you know?" Krackers asked. "So what's the situation here?"

"We've been pinned down for the last hour," the sergeant said, exhaustion in his voice. "They have far more powerful weapons. It's a losing battle."

"Well, Sergeant," Krackers said, "fear not. Hair and I will change the status quo!"

Hair buzzed.

"Yes, Hair," Krackers chuckled. "Once more unto the breach, dear friends, once more!"

Krackers leapt over the barricade. Hair screamed as it flowed in front of him, creating a shield. Multiple shots slammed into Hair. Krackers moved slowly forward as the number of shots increased.

"Okay, Hair," Krackers yelled, "let's show them why I'm Krackers and you're my partner!"

Strands of Hair shot out from its shield. There were so many of them, wielding so many weapons. It was a bloodbath. As the perps fell, more took their place. Hair started to wear thin as additional strands shot out. Decapitations, stabbings, and bodies being sliced and diced, it was carnage on a grand scale. The perps started to thin out. The police rained down fury.

From high on a building, a sniper lay in wait. He took aim at the valiant Krackers, firing armour-piercing, high-explosive bullets. They shot forth and rocketed toward the psychotic hero. The rounds hit Hair's shielding, passed through it, and struck Krackers' body. Suddenly, everything went black.

Krackers came to in a hospital bed. He tried to sit up, but pain shot through his side, and he quickly lay back down. He turned his head; blinding pain racked his body. Eventually, it subsided to a manageable level. He moved the sheet; a dirty bandage was wrapped around his midsection. A drip stand was set up beside the bed, its tube snaking to his arm. He surveyed the room; the walls were grimy and streaked with dirt. A pain shot through his side, and he passed out.

Krackers regained consciousness to find a woman tending his wound. "Nursie?" Krackers tried to focus.

"No, dear," the woman said. "I'm Sarah. You're extremely sick." She injected something into the drip.

"Where am I?" Krackers drifted back into unconsciousness.

He rolled over, his side still hurting but more manageable. He sat up; his facilities were intact, and he surveyed the room again. He hadn't noticed a huge window set into one of the walls. Outside, it looked like it was snowing. He hung his feet over the bed and tried to stand; his legs felt like jelly. He sat back down.

Half an hour later.

He tried again. This time his legs held him. After a few steps, he walked over to the window using the drip stand as a crutch. The window was filthy, thick with grime. Krackers rubbed it, clearing a small area. The glass didn't feel cold; rather, it was warm to the touch.

What he saw horrified him.

Outside was stark and ruddy. The sun above was huge and shone red. What he first thought was snow turned out to be white ash, softly falling. In the courtyard were mismatched chairs, about thirty of them.

Sarah sat at a table beside a huge drum. A hose hung down, its end taped. From the ash mist, figures began to appear, their clothing streaked with dirt, disheveled and ill-fitting. They shuffled toward Sarah, forming a line in front of the table. Sarah picked up the hose; the first in line took a dirty, food-encrusted bowl. She poured grey goo into it. The man bowed his head and moved to a chair, eating straight from the bowl, leaving nothing behind. This continued until all were fed. Sarah looked up and saw Krackers watching. She waved, filled two more bowls, and came inside. Krackers hobbled back to his bed.

Sarah placed the bowls on the windowsill, walked over to Krackers, and checked his bandage.

"Another few days or so," she said softly, "and you'll be good as new." "Hair?" Krackers reached up and felt his smooth skull. Nothing.

"There were some strands," Sarah said, "when I found you, but they retracted back into your skull."

"Where am I, Sarah?"

She was about to answer when Hair shot out, cocooning Krackers.

Darkness. Sweet darkness.

"Krackers," a disembodied voice sounded.

Hours ticked into seconds, weeks into days.

Finally, Hair released Krackers from the cocoon. Sarah and her windowed room were gone, replaced by a stark, small space. The four walls were puke-light green; the carpet, spongy and moist, was equally disconcerting. There were only two things in the room: a chair and a black-and-white television. On the TV, the C.R.I.M.E. logo slowly turned. A bare bulb flickered overhead. There didn't seem to be a door. "Krackers," a voice echoed.

Suddenly, blinding pain shot up Krackers' side. He dropped to one knee. The grimy bandage showed blood seeping through, turning red.

Abruptly, the walls began to close in, moving the chair and TV toward him.

"Hair!"

Without warning, Hair screamed out, filling the room. Krackers was pressed against a wall as the pressure built, threatening to crush him.

Darkness folded over him.

Reality swirled, ripping at the very fabric of time and space.

Krackers

Unexpectedly, the darkness was filled with blinding light. As Krackers' eyes adjusted, a med-lab came into focus. It was sterile and clean, dazzling white. He tried to sit up but realised he was restrained. Both arms and legs were held down by Hair. Around him, doctors and nurses moved. Some injected themselves, then lay on the floor, staring at the ceiling, playing with their fingers. Others swallowed handfuls of tablets, washing them down with alcohol.

"Hair," Krackers pleaded. "Please!"

"Hair can't help you, Michael," the familiar voice said. "The Retaliator has got its own problems."

Krackers looked down at his bonds. Hair surrounded both his hands and feet.

"There's no one to help you this time!" The man seemed impressed with his own work.

"My name is Krackers! I'd know that voice anywhere," Krackers spat in contempt. "The Shrink!"

"That's right, Michael!" A man in a white nurse's uniform walked up to the bed. He pounced onto Krackers' chest. Krackers 'oofted' as the man pressed closer. They were face to face. Krackers saw the face for the first time.

"It's you!"

"Yes, it is, Michael," the Shrink laughed, throwing his head back. "I have watched you for a long time. Nursie is quite a beauty, isn't she?" "You keep your hands off her!" Anger rang fierce in Krackers' voice. The Shrink jumped off Krackers' body and stood before him.

"Hair, if you would be so kind," the Shrink said. Hair lifted Krackers off the bed, holding him steady a metre above the floor.

"Hair, please?" Krackers begged.

The Shrink outstretched an arm. Nursie appeared, he was holding her by the neck.

"Please, Michael," Nursie pleaded. "Help me?" With a deft squeeze,

97

Nursie went limp. The Shrink tossed her across the room like a ragdoll.

"Nooo!" Krackers cried out. "What do you want from me?"

"I want you to suffer!" The Shrink smiled cruelly. "You're nothing without Hair, just a sad, bald man!"

"Come on, Hair," Krackers pleaded. "I have faith in you."

"Michael, I have faith in you," another disembodied voice spoke.

Hair started to struggle, unravelling slowly at first, then completely. It reared up, and Krackers dropped to the floor, rubbing his wrists.

"Nooo!" It was the Shrink's turn to cry out.

"Good to have you back, Bud," Krackers smiled.

Hair buzzed angrily.

"I agree," Krackers said with a smirk. "Go get 'em, Hair!"

Hair didn't need to be asked twice. It roared as it surged forward, grabbing the Shrink by the head and legs. Blood exploded as Hair tore him apart. Hair threw the two parts to the floor in contempt. The head looked at Krackers with an accusing eye. He ran to it and dropkicked it into the nearest wall. It splattered and burst into gore.

"Nursie!" Krackers cried. "Nooo!" He ran over to her crumpled form, gently cradling her. Her head hung at an unusual angle, her blank eyes staring at him. He reached over, closed her eyes, lifted her head to him, and sobbed.

Hair hummed in sympathy. It flowed out, softly embracing Krackers and the limp Nursie. It gently rocked them.

"Michael, I need you," the disembodied voice spoke.

"I need you too," Krackers whispered, inconsolable.

Hair buzzed and softly unfurled from them both.

"I know, Bud," Krackers said, gently laying Nursie onto the floor. He rose. "She didn't need to die. It's my fault, it was me he wanted, not her!" He ran and kicked the lower torso of the Shrink, spitting on it.

Hair hummed in commiseration.

"You're right," Krackers finally agreed. "Could you wrap up Nursie? We're taking her with us. She deserves a decent burial, not to stay here with that!"

Hair buzzed. It flowed around Nursie, cocooning her, then lifted her onto Krackers' back.

"So, which way is out of here?"

Surveying the room, there were two doors: one closed, the other open.

"I wish we had some ice cream right now," Krackers muttered. "It makes me think more clearly." Hair vibrated in agreement.

Krackers moved toward the open door. Big mistake. The doorway filled with C.R.I.M.E. thugs. They charged, firing randomly. Hair shot out, creating a shield. The rounds thudded into it. Hair created a blade the width of the doorway and fired it, slicing the thugs in twain. The body count grew, forming an unnatural human pile at the doorway.

"Well, viewers, I guess it's door number two," Krackers chimed. He darted across the room and waited at the door. "Whatever you do, Hair, don't drop her."

Hair buzzed, then hummed.

"Good plan," Krackers nodded. "Attack anything that moves! On the count of three… three!" His adrenaline booster kicked in, the rush making him gasp. He charged the door. It splintered, exploding into smithereens. He ran into the darkness and encountered more unfriendlies They didn't stand a chance against the blur of a mourning Krackers, who bulldozed through, leaving the bloody fallen in his wake.

Hair buzzed, cutting the adrenaline boost and slowing the hero down.

"Wow," Krackers shook his head. "What a rush!" He reached the end of the corridor; on either side were two branching corridors. "Which way do you think, Bud?"

"MOVE. RIGHT!" a different voice boomed.

"Hey," Krackers said, "if a big booming voice tells you to go right, you go left!"

Hair buzzed in disagreement.

"Sorry, Bud," Krackers apologised. "How can you trust a voice that appears out of the blue? No body, no way."

Krackers entered the left corridor. Ahead, an explosion sent debris raining down.

"Okay, new plan," he nodded. "We should go with the big booming voice and go right." Krackers, the deceased Nursie, and Hair moved uneasily down the corridor. They met little opposition and stopped at an elevator.

Hair buzzed amusingly.

"Yeah, okay," Krackers whined. "You were right, and the big bad booming voice was right too."

Krackers punched the button and the elevator door opened with a ding. As they entered, the corridor creaked. As the doors started to close, the corridor caved in.

Inside the elevator, hundreds of floor buttons filled the walls and ceiling. There were no labels.

"How do we pick, Hair? It could take years to figure out the right button."

Hair buzzed.

"What do you mean, like this?" A strand of Hair shot out, stabbing a random button. The lift shot upwards, throwing Krackers to the floor. It kept accelerating, pinning him down.

Lightning bolts arced into him; his very being felt on fire. Everything froze, then darkness comforted him. He tried to open his eyes; they seemed wired shut. Something covered his mouth and nose. He tried to move it, but it was battered away.

Abruptly, the elevator floor shattered, debris falling into the abyss. Krackers stared down. Moments later, he was lifted, hands sprawled, and caught part of the floor. He turned so his feet were out of the elevator floor. Hair tried to hold on but the drag increased, dislodging Nursie. Her body dropped into the abyss.

"Nursie," Krackers sighed. With effort, Hair cocooned around him as he gave up. Another bolt of lightning struck, and he let go. He and Hair dropped into the blackness.

Reality has more than one master.

"Clear!" Two paddles were placed on the chest of an unconscious body. The charge filled it and it arched. The heart monitor bleeped, and a woman leant over as he opened his eyes.

"Michael," Nursie whispered, "I thought I lost you."

"Nursie," Krackers whispered. "Krackers. Krackers. I thought the Shrink had killed you." Nursie lay her head on his chest.

"Any chance of some ice cream?" Krackers smiled and slipped back into unconsciousness.

"You did very well, Krackers Michael Krackers," the booming voice reverberated

Three weeks later.

"I am so bored," Krackers whined as he walked on his hands. Hair flowed out, grabbing him by one of his hands, and he toppled over. Of course, that instigated a wrestle. Both Krackers and Hair chuckled as Nursie walked into the room, her hands behind her back. Krackers fell into a giggling heap.

"Who's been good boys?" Nursie brought out two ice creams.

Hair hummed, making slurping noises.

When she offered, Hair pounced, enjoying the icy treat. She handed the other to Krackers.

"Here, bud," Krackers offered, "you can have mine." Hair sprung, engulfing the ice cream.

Hair purred in enjoyment.

Krackers stood up and embraced Nursie, kissing her deeply. She rested her head on his chest.

"Have I got a debrief for you."

Ten.

The Lost Ones

Karma had a diverse population, over four million, and their pastimes were equally varied. Religion ranked near the top of the list. There were many churches in Karma, many and varied religions that practised in and around Karma Central. In the Inner and Outer Sprawl, religion was more sparse.

One beacon in the darkness of the Outer Sprawl was the Karma Freedom Church, and their priest, Ange Drew, ran the services. He was a huge man, six foot five, and had a heart just as big. He was dashing and made a handsome sight. Besides his duties with the church, he was a part-time C.R.A.P.I. agent.

The church was the sparkling jewel in a tarnished community. One hundred strong, every Sunday it was a packed house. At the end of the service, Ange went out the back. He'd transformed the area into a half-court basketball court. He could've played professionally, but his congregation always came first, especially the youth.

There were several boys and girls, varying from eleven to eighteen. They waited patiently for Ange to come out. They decided to start a game, and as Ange appeared, the game was in full swing. After an hour, the game finished, and the group thinned out. One of the boys, Peter, came up to where Ange was sitting and sat down beside him. He looked forlorn and seemed to have something on his mind. They sat in silence for a while before the boy looked at Ange.

"Something's not right," Peter said, breaking the quiet.

"Why do you say that?" Ange asked, concern in his voice.

"My friends are disappearing," Peter said, trying to sound casual.

"Maybe they're on holidays?"

"Nah," Peter said. "For a while now, friends from my school have been disappearing. I've been to a couple of the parents. They said they'd contacted the police and reported them as missing persons. I'm really worried."

"Leave it with me," Ange replied. "I'll do some checks and see what I can come up with."

A few weeks later.

Ange had just finished another inspirational sermon on the evils of criminals in the community. As the congregation filtered out, he went out the back of the church. The basketball court was nearly empty, only a couple of kids remained. Ange went up to one.

"Have you seen Peter?"

"Nah," the teen replied, "and he hasn't been at school for a while."

"If you hear from him, please let me know?" There was unease in Ange's voice. The teen nodded and left.

Ange went into his room and up to an alcove. He entered, turned around, and pressed a hidden button. The entrance slid shut and Ange dropped down under the church. The door slid open, revealing an enormous room. The air was stale. As he stepped out, hidden fans started circulating the air. He walked up to a computer terminal, tapped on the keyboard and waited. On a big pad set in the floor in front of him, a hologram shimmered into existence.

"How's my favourite nurse?"

"Ange," Nursie beamed, "I'm fine, a bit busy keeping Krackers in line. How have you been?"

"Not bad. How's that 'crazy'?"

"Hahaha," Nursie chuckled. "What's up?"

"I'm worried." Ange's face lost its smile. "Has there been any activity with C.R.I.M.E. lately?"

"A little," Nursie said. "There's been a bit about some 'Operation Bairn,' but we haven't heard much more."

"It seems the youth in my community are being abducted."

"Couldn't it just be a couple of runaways?"

"I've contacted the police," Ange said, "and they say there's been a marked increase in missing youth. I need to borrow him, Bre." Nursie knew there was something definitely wrong when he called her by her first name.

"Give me a couple of hours," Nursie said, "and I'll get back to you."

"Okay," Ange agreed, "that'll give me time to get my equipment out of mothballs and make sure it's in working order."

"Okay," Nursie said. "Talk soon." She shimmered away.

Ange moved to a substantially sized closet. He placed his hand on a palm reader and the closet door hissed and slid open. Gas flowed out and onto the floor.

Ange ran his hands over an impressive exoskeleton suit. It was jet black with silver trim. It had a large silver cross on the chest, amongst other things. Where muscle should have been, pistons replaced them. Tubes were attached to the exoskeleton; it fizzled as the pressure released excess gas. He tapped a button on the torso and the suit opened. He was about to step into it when the Nursie hologram reappeared. He walked over to the shimmering figure.

"So, what's the word?"

"It seems," Nursie explained, "there are teens going missing all over Karma. C.R.A.P.I. has sanctioned the mission and you're reinstated as an agent."

"I'm really sorry about before," Ange said, "you know, with that mission going pear-shaped and all."

"That was a long time ago, Ange," Nursie said lightly. "I've got a new title, Special Liaison to Abnormal Procedures."

"S.L.A.P., eh?" Ange chuckled.

"It's better than your codename, Church." Nursie laughed.

"It's pretty apt, don't you think?"

Twenty years can be a lifetime ago.

Midnight was usually quiet on the docks of Karma, but not tonight. There were armed guards aplenty. Cranes were unloading cargo, trucks were being loaded, and the docks were abuzz.

Two young, fresh-faced C.R.A.P.I. agents were hiding in the shadows, surveying the scene. The large shipping containers made for good cover.

One of the agents wore a skin-tight outfit, an augmented stealth suit, that showed off her beautiful form. It gave the wearer greater strength and camouflage ability. The other wore a large exoskeleton with a silver cross on the chest; it hummed quietly.

"Wait here, Church," Shadow said. "I'll see if I can thin the herd. Comms check."

She faded into the scenery. After some time, Church started getting antsy.

"Shadow?" Church radioed. "What's happening?"

"I'm right behind you," she answered.

Church and his rig jumped. He spun around; a mini-gun popped up from his outstretched arm.

"Please don't do that again," Church said nervously. "I could've killed you."

"It won't happen again," Shadow said apologetically. She placed two of the three Uzis on the ground. "Come on, this way."

They moved quietly along a container and came upon an opening. Shadow peeked around the corner. The guard she'd dispatched from his post was still down. They moved swiftly to a better vantage point. From there, they could clearly see the whole operation.

"What do you think we should do?" Church asked, uncertain.

"Remember the training," Shadow said, masking her own hesitation.

A noise behind her made both her and Church turn. There were sounds of bullets and the *whoosh* of a rocket launching. Church instinctively grabbed Shadow, pulling her close, wrapping his arms around her and turning his back to the blast. The explosion was massive, lifting the agents high into the air. They landed hard, Church taking the brunt of the impact. Armed guards appeared, training their weapons on the two young agents.

There were sirens and a klaxon sounded. Suddenly, The scene faded away and was replaced with a pock-marked, cavernous room. The two agents lay on the floor, panting. Church righted himself; his rig seemed in perfect running order. He helped Shadow up, she looked despondent.

"Reset Threat Room Three," a booming voice commanded. "Agent Shadow and Church, report to debrief!"

After the monumental failure, Shadow requested a transfer to logistics. She'd tasted an agent's life and realised it wasn't her calling. Church, however, continued his training and passed with flying colours.

After the first year into his tour, he excelled. One mission had him hiding in the shadows when a blur jumped in front of him. The figure pointed something at him, and he instinctively fired. It dropped the perp, a thirteen-year-old boy. The child lay on the ground, dead in a pool of his own blood.

He resigned immediately. After talking with Bre, he agreed that if it were dire, they could activate him, at his discretion.

The past is only the past for the blink of an eye.

"I'm assigning you a partner, of sorts," the hologram smirked.

"No," Ange pleaded. "Not him, please? There must be another operative?" From beside Nursie, the smiling face of Krackers appeared.

"We'll have so much fun, Agent Church," Krackers laughed, "and we'll have ice cream at the end." With that, Hair rose up, making *smacking* noises. Krackers disappeared as he stepped back. In the background, Ange could hear, "Not now, Hair, mission first, ice cream second!"

"Rendezvous at the Peter Adams Memorial Psychiatric Hospital," Nursie stated.

"I'll get you back for this," Ange laughed. The hologram faded away.

Ange shook his head as he climbed into the rig. It hissed as it closed around him. He stepped out of the alcove and the tubes detached. He stretched, the exoskeleton whirred as he moved. A door at the end of the room hissed open. Ange walked to the doorway and stared into the darkness. With a deep breath, he ran into the blackness.

A kilometre away, Church entered the basement of a derelict C.R.A.P.I. building. He exited the structure, ordering his thoughts. The rig interpreted his commands; a map appeared on his heads-up display, tracking the optimal route. Ports in the back of his rig opened, then flared into life. He ran like a freight train, covering the thirty-kilometre distance in twenty minutes. He skidded to a halt, walked up to one of the hospital walls, and placed a hand on a hidden palm plate. It registered and a door opened, he stepped inside.

Church entered Krackers' room. Krackers was doing a handstand while juggling three empty water bottles with one hand. When he saw Church, he threw the bottles into the air, flipped, caught them, and landed softly on his feet.

"Ta-da!" Krackers raised his hands. He ran over and tried to hug Ange, who fended off Krackers' advances. Krackers stepped back and shook his hand vigorously.

"Angey. Angey-baby. Ange-meister," Krackers chimed.

"Church will do just fine," Ange sighed. "Where's Bre?"

Hair rose from Krackers' skull and vibrated.

"So, this is the legendary Retaliator?"

"Where are my manners?" Krackers said. "Churchie, this is Hair. Hair, this is the indignant Churchie!" Krackers smiled with a hidden smirk.

"As I said, Church will do just fine." He could feel his annoyance growing. His exoskeleton whirred as every servo tensed and he stepped forward. Hair suddenly reared up, dwarfing them both. Just as they were about to come to blows, Nursie wiggled in.

"I hope you two are playing nice?" She looked at Krackers.

"Why are you looking at me?" Krackers whined. "He started it!"

She walked over to Church, grasped his face, and kissed him on the mouth. The K.I.S.S., or its more official version, *Knowledge In Saliva Sample*, flowed the mission forth.

"Wow," Church gasped, eyes closed.

"My turn, my turn!" Krackers jumped up and down.

"Of course, Michael," Nursie went over and kissed him deeply.

"Michael?" Church's eyes opened abruptly. "Your name's Michael?" He threw his head back and roared with laughter.

"Krackers, damn it, my name's Krackers!"

"Now that the hostilities have finished," Nursie stated, pointing at them both, "we can get on with the mission."

Nursie went over to one of the walls, tapped it, and a compartment slid open revealing a keyboard. She tapped away industriously. Lights shone down from the ceiling, creating a hologram of Karma.

"Teens have been disappearing at an alarming rate," Nursie stated. On the hologram, green blips registered. Up till now, no one had realised how many kids had vanished.

"After running a number of algorithms, C.R.A.P.I. has determined the most likely spot is here." She tapped on the terminal and a red blip appeared on a point in the Inner Sprawl.

The two heroes walked to the door.

"One last thing," Nursie smirked, "you two play nice, I'll be watching."

Church started to walk out of the room when Krackers pushed past him.

"Excuse me, Churchyard!" Ange just sighed and shook his head.

Waiting outside the Peter Adams Memorial Psychiatric Hospital was Bob and his ice cream van.

"Bob!" Krackers ran over and hugged the stuffing out of him. Bob cringed, then patted Krackers three times on the back. Krackers lingered, then released him. "Bob, this is Saint Church!"

"Oh dear," Bob said uncomfortably, eyeing the ice cream van. "You're rather large, I don't think you'll fit in the van."

"Hello, Bob. I'm just Church." Ange stared at Krackers with contempt. "I'll make my own way there."

"Okay, Bob," Krackers clapped his hands. "Off to the Inner Sprawl. I'm so excited to see you again."

"I'll see you two there." Jets opened and ignited on Church's back, and he shot off.

"What are you waiting for?" Krackers cried. "Catch him!"

"In this van?" Bob scoffed. "You'd have a better chance of flying." Bob activated the antigrav, and the van lifted into the night sky.

Krackers

An hour later at the Inner Sprawl Industrial Park.

The ice cream van landed two blocks from the coordinates. Church was waiting for them and walked over as Krackers yodelled from the back.

"Oooh," Krackers moaned, "brain freeze!" Church leant in the window.

"So, he does have a brain?" Church chuckled; Bob laughed as well. "Okay, Krackers, let's go."

Krackers got out of the van, still rubbing the brain freeze away.

"I've scanned the area," Church stated. "In one of the larger warehouses, there are a number of heat signatures."

"We should go in all gung-ho!" Krackers jumped into the air, spun, and landed in a superhero pose.

"What about if I go in through the front door," Church suggested, "and you go in through the roof?"

"Sounds like a plan-a-rooney!" Krackers abruptly did a cartwheel, then back flipped into the darkness.

"He's going to balls this up," Church muttered, chuckling to himself. "I just know it."

It was time to move. Church's exoskeleton went into chameleon mode and faded into the scenery. He made his way to the warehouse. Two guards stood at the entrance, one leaning against the wall while the other was about to light a cigarette. As the guard struck the lighter, the flame flared, and Church appeared.

"Smoking kills!" He swung an arm and hit the man, driving the man's skull into his chest. The other guard raised his weapon as Church fired a taser into his chest. He convulsed and lost consciousness. As Church was about to move, a pebble bounced off his head, another off his shoulder. He looked up to see Krackers' smiling face. He waved his hands.

Church waved him away, then pointed to the roof. Krackers nodded and moved out of sight. Ange shook his head and proceeded to the entrance. With powerful hands, Church crushed the lock and peered in. In the centre of the warehouse, lights shone down and it was well lit.

Under the lights were the missing teens. They reclined in overstuffed chairs, virtual-reality goggles over their eyes. Headphones covered their ears. Skullcaps were attached; wires leapt off the teens and onto the floor. They snaked to some kind of hard-drive tower.

Church kept in the shadows. From high above, he saw Krackers standing on a walkway. He watched as Hair wrapped around the railing and Krackers abseiled silently to the floor. As Krackers moved into the darkness, Hair retracted into his skull. He saw Church and made his way around to him. As they moved to a better vantage point, they noticed two goons chatting to a hologram.

"The Shrink!" Krackers started to attack when Church stopped him.

"The teens first," Church said. "Shrink later." Krackers nodded and backed up.

Suddenly all the teens turned and faced the heroes. On the other side of the warehouse, a loud hum started. Thirty drones shot into the light and hovered over the children. The drones had mini-missiles and small guns mounted beneath them.

"Welcome, Michael," a voice boomed. "I see you've brought a friend. You must introduce him."

"Krackers," Michael screamed, "my name is Krackers!"

"I'm Church," Ange said, "and those children are under my care."

"So, you protect those children?" The Shrink chuckled. "You didn't do a very good job, did you? Okay, boys and girls, ATTACK!" The drones streaked toward their targets, missiles flying everywhere.

"You go high," Church yelled, "I'll go low!"

Krackers

Hair shot out of Krackers' skull and wrapped around the walkway rail. He lifted into the air while Church stepped into the light. Ports on Church's shoulders opened, launching small projectiles. They whistled as they downed six drones.

"Hair," Krackers cried, "whip 'em real good!" Some of Hair shot towards the drones, cutting through four. He flipped from his position and arced over the buzzing drones. Multiple strands of Hair brought down ten more.

The ten remaining drones scattered, they seemed more elusive. Abruptly, the drones returned to hover over the teens.

"Enough of this!" The Shrink's voice resonated. "Give up now or I'll kill the children!"

Church leapt into the air and came down next to the hard-drive tower. He brought down both fists; showers of sparks erupted. The remaining drones spluttered and dropped to the floor.

"Nooo!" The Shrink cried out. The hologram shimmered away. With their leader gone, the remaining thugs gave up.

Epilogue.

"Well, Krackers," Church commented, "it's been... interesting, to say the least. It's also been an honour." He shook Krackers' hand. Hair flowed out and hugged Church. "Thank you, Hair. Make sure you keep him safe." Hair retracted back.

Nursie walked up to the two agents, her hands behind her back. Hair realised what was going on and started making smacking noises.

"Okay, Hair," Nursie chuckled. "You deserve this." She brought a hand around and Hair attacked the ice-cream cone, making slurping noises. She brought out the other ice cream and handed it to Krackers.

"Here, bud, you can have mine." Krackers held up the cone; Hair pounced on it.

"You did well, Ange," Nursie said. "Have you had any thoughts about coming back?"

"Not really," Ange said thoughtfully. "Now the kids have been returned to their families, it's time for me to tend to my flock."

"There's always an open invitation," Nursie said.

"I'll keep it in mind," Ange said. "What about him? Is he as crazy as he seems to be?"

"It's Krackers," Nursie smiled.

Behind them, Krackers was yodelling while Hair flicked him. He dropped and rolled on the ground.

"As I said," Nursie smiled, "he's Krackers."

Eleven.

Alert.

Karma Central was a beautiful city, with its glittering towers of glass and steel. Anti-grav vehicles littered the skies. They whizzed to and fro; it was an ordered assault. Each vehicle was tracked, ensuring they filed to the correct destination.

In both the Inner and Outer Sprawls, things were much different. The anti-grav vehicles zoomed about in a dirty sky, it was downright chaos. Vehicle tracking was non-existent, and they paid for it in daily, fatal collisions.

Something insidious started infesting the Sprawls. A subtle narcotic, "Alert," had begun to creep into the areas. By the time the authorities took notice, it was already entrenched. Within months, forty-five per cent of the population were regular users. Reports stated that Alert had finally reached Karma Central.

The drug was a mix of artificial marijuana extract, methamphetamine and cocaine. The liquid solution was administered with an eye dropper, placed behind the ear on the parotid gland. It was absorbed and distributed into the saliva, then into the body's system. The tell-tale signs were bruising and discolouration behind the ear. The effects were clarity of thought, euphoria and a limited lack of inhibition. The side effects were severe headaches, anxiousness, irritability, vagueness, aggression, nausea and, in some cases, even death.

At the Peter Adams Memorial Psychiatric Hospital.

Nursie sat in Krackers' room. Krackers was playing "touched you last" with Hair and Hair was winning. Krackers tapped Hair then leapt over his bed and rolled onto the floor. Hair flowed out and slapped

Krackers' butt. Nursie started to rub her eyes and massage her temples. Krackers suddenly stopped the game.

"Nursie," Krackers asked, concern in his voice. "Are you okay?"

"It's nothing," Nursie replied, annoyance in her voice. "It's just a headache. I'll go and take something for it." She left the room; even her wiggle wasn't the same.

"Hair," Krackers commented, "there's something wrong with Nursie."

Hair buzzed, then vibrated.

"You're right," Krackers agreed. "She seems to be getting a lot of headaches lately."

Fifteen minutes later.

Nursie walked back into Krackers' room, a spring in her step. She ran over and hugged Krackers, kissing him deeply. Finally, she released him.

"You seem better?" Krackers asked. "And that was fast."

"Yeah," Nursie smiled, "it's a new thing on the market."

"Okay," Krackers said, concern still there. He abruptly turned and hit Hair. "Touched you last," and the game continued.

There was a buzz in Nursie's ear. "There's a new mission." She rose and hurried out of the room. Hair buzzed.

"I agree, Hair," Krackers muttered, "I really think there's something definitely wrong."

Krackers

An hour later.

Nursie sauntered into Krackers' room and straight up to him. She kissed him fully and deeply. The mission brief flowed through him, and in the intensity he was lost in her kiss.

"The brief stated that an addictive new drug called Alert has turned up," Krackers said. "Shouldn't it be up to Karma Narcotics Control?"

"It should be," Nursie said, rubbing her temples, "but there have been deaths, plus they're completely out of their depth." She walked towards Krackers' bathroom. "I'll just splash my face with water." She shut the door. There were sounds of vomiting, then silence.

"Nursie," Krackers knocked on the door then walked in. On the floor, near the toilet, she was about to apply something behind her ear. Krackers was shocked.

"I'm so sorry," Nursie began to cry. "I can't stop myself, please help me?"

Krackers did something he had never done before, he contacted C.R.A.P.I. High Command. He reached down and removed her earpiece.

"This is Krackers, we have a man, oops, woman down!" After trying for fifteen minutes, High Command finally understood and raced a med-team to his room. After the team assured Krackers, they whisked Nursie away to the infirmary.

"Let's go, Hair," Krackers spat. "Let's go find some drug dealers to hurt!" Hair feathered Krackers into Doctor Delooz'nl and stormed out of the Peter Adams Memorial Psychiatric Hospital. Bob was waiting outside as Krackers strode out, feathering back into himself. He marched up to the ice-cream van and jumped into the passenger side.

"Let's go, Bob," Krackers spat, "there's some killing to be done! I shall rain down such fury upon those evil, drug-dealing scum! Let's go, Bob!"

"Where to?" Bob had never seen this side of Krackers.

"The Outer Sprawl," Krackers hissed.

Three quarters of an hour later.

Step one: Find a drug dealer and extract the whereabouts of his supplier.

Bob landed the ice-cream van in a parking lot.

"Lift off and circle around," Krackers growled. "I shouldn't be too long!"

There was danger in his demeanour. He leapt out and Bob lifted the van into the air.

In the Outer Sprawl, there was a dealer on every other street corner. Krackers strode straight up to a dealer and scowled.

"You want some Alert?" The dealer reached into a fanny pack.

"No," Krackers spat. "I want your dealer's address."

"What's your problem, suckhole?"

Hair screamed, shooting out and rearing over Krackers.

"Think about your next answer very carefully," Krackers growled. "For it may be your last!"

"What's your problem?" the dealer said. "You come here and disrespect me." He reached behind his back and produced a large gun.

"Wrong answer," Krackers smirked. "Hair, answer him."

Hair whipped down at the dealer, slicing him into pieces. Blood splashed over Krackers. The pieces slid down into a bloody pile. Krackers marched down to the next corner. The answer was still wrong. He trudged away from another gory pile. After five gruesome messes, Krackers continued with his mission.

Word was spreading like wildfire. Dealers scurried away like cockroaches.

Krackers engaged the adrenaline booster. He easily caught up with a retreating drug merchant. Grabbing him by the back of his shirt, Krackers spun him around.

"Hair," Krackers spoke. Hair flowed out, wrapping around the dealer's head and lifting him into the air.

"Arrgghh!" the dealer tried to wriggle free, but failed.

"I'm getting very tired of this," Krackers screamed. "You've heard what's going on?" The dealer wet his pants. "I'll take that as a 'yes'?" Before my partner turns you into sushi, where is your supplier?"

The dealer caved, telling Krackers about the supplier. He said he only had a phone number.

"Are you sure about the number?"

"Yes," the dealer squealed.

"Then our transaction is complete," Krackers said. "Hair, let's go." Krackers turned to leave. Hair ripped the dealer in two; blood spurted everywhere.

"Well, viewers," Krackers muttered, "I finally have a lead!" He wiped some of the dealer off his face and called for Bob, waiting for him to land.

Step two: Contact the supplier and track the drug back to the source.

After accessing the C.R.A.P.I. telecommunications database, it wasn't too hard to track the supplier. The address came up in the Inner Sprawl.

Bob pushed the ice-cream van to its limits and finally soared into Inner Sprawl air. Bob lowered to a parking lot, a street away from the address. Krackers leapt out.

"Keep the motor running," Krackers said, murder in his eyes. "This shouldn't take too long!" He trudged away, walking down two streets before turning a corner.

It couldn't have been more obvious. It should have had a neon sign: **'Supplier here!'**

Six gorillas with Uzis tried to look inconspicuous. They milled around the premises. Krackers didn't even slow; Hair flicked out, mowing down five of the thugs. They didn't know what hit them as they exploded in a shower of gore. The fifth darted inside the three-storey apartment block; the entrance closed with a 'click.'

"Knock, knock," Krackers yelled as Hair ripped the door from its hinges. He ran up the stairs. On reaching the third storey, he was met by ten thugs waiting for him.

"I only want him," Krackers started to say, then, "bugger it!" Hair reared up and three of the assailants soiled themselves before fainting. The others raised their guns, then Hair 'windmilled', they didn't stand a chance.

Once again, Hair decimated the front door and Krackers stepped in. In the lounge were three men seated in chairs; three others were in the kitchen.

"Which of you filths is the supplier of the crap on the street?"

The three goons in the other room rose and went for the kitchen door. Krackers pointed and part of Hair barricaded it, filling it with itself.

"I will only ask one more time." There was menace in Krackers' tone.

Hair flowed out, rearing above the men. Two tried to raise their weapons, only to have their hands cleaved from their arms. They dropped to the floor, grasping their now-severed hands and writhing in pain.

"So, you are the supplier of Alert?" Krackers stepped forward.

"Okay, okay," the supplier stuttered, raising his hands defensively. "What do you want? Drugs, money, women? I can give you anything."

"All I want," Krackers said carefully, making sure every word was understood, "is the name of the source of the drug distribution!"

"I can't do that, he'd kill me if I gave him up," the supplier said, fear in his voice. "The distribution runs through him; he's dangerous!"

"Look around you," Krackers gestured at the fallen thugs. "Are you sure you won't help?"

"Okay," the supplier agreed. "I think you're scarier!" He spilled his guts.

As Krackers went for the door, the supplier's head slid into a pool of blood on his lap. Hair retracted; the thugs in the kitchen were embedded in a wall.

"Well, viewers," Krackers muttered, "that went better than I thought." He stepped over the fallen gorillas and out onto the street.

Bob landed in the middle of the supplier's street. A crowd began to form. As Krackers started to enter the van, he stopped and turned to the crowd.

"Fear not, citizens," Krackers boomed, "this peddler of death is no more!" The addicts in the crowd outnumbered the normals and 'booed' him. Krackers just waved.

"They didn't think much of your effort," Bob commented as he lifted off. "So, where to?"

"Set forth, young Bob," Krackers commanded, "to Karma Central, and to the source of the accused Alert. Hair, check on Nursie's condition."

Hair raised up and vibrated.

Forty-five minutes later.

Step three: Find the source and eliminate the drug, Alert!

As they approached the outskirts of Karma Central, Air Traffic Control radioed in.

"Unauthorised vehicle," the radio blared, "please state your destination."

"I am C.R.A.P.I. Agent Krackers," he yelled into the radio. Bob reached over and picked up the mic; Krackers took it. "I am C.R.A.P.I. Agent Krackers, en route to the Eddie Breiner Corporation building."

"Roger, Agent Krackers," the radio stated. "Coordinates logged. Welcome to Karma Central."

"Okay, Bob," Krackers said, "land on the Eddie Breiner Corporation building." Bob swung around and landed on the building's landing pad. Krackers exited. "Lift off and wait for my call." The van rose and circled the 150-floor building.

Krackers ran up to the fire-escape door. It had a palm reader, an alphanumerical pad, and a video camera mounted above.

"Hair, see if you can remove the door from its hinges."

Hair tried in vain; the door creaked but stayed fast.

"See if you can hack the pad?" Hair engulfed both the pad and the palm reader. The door lock clicked. The door opened and Krackers walked in, down to the 150th floor. Most offices seemed empty except one. Krackers approached the door. Hair flowed forth, reefed the door, and threw it into the room, embedding a couple of thugs in the far wall.

"So, who's in charge?"

"Michael," a familiar voice said. "You seem to be in my business again."

"Krackers," the hero cried, "Krackers, damn you! Shrink, show yourself!"

"I have matters elsewhere, but I've left you a present, it's through the far door. I'm sure you'll get a bang out of it."

Krackers ran to the door and Hair shattered it. Inside were crates of Alert, enough for every person in Karma. In the centre of the huge space was an equally huge number of high explosives. A countdown timer was set for sixty seconds.

"We have to stop this, Hair," Krackers cried. "If it explodes, it will cover Karma itself and millions of people will suffer!"

Hair buzzed.

"So, you really think you can contain the explosion?" Krackers said with concern. "You've never exerted yourself with something so big."

Hair buzzed, then hummed.

"I'm not leaving you," Krackers said. "You're my partner, I'll stand by you."

Hair flowed out, and out, and out, expanding further. It blanketed the drugs and explosives. With what little Hair was left, it cocooned his partner.

The timer ticked down. Five. Four. Three. Two. One.

The explosion was massive. It blew out the windows on three floors. Both Krackers and Hair were lifted into the air and dropped like stones. The smell of burnt hair filled the floor, smoke hung in the air. After a few moments, Krackers groaned.

"Wow, what a rush!" Krackers chuckled, then groaned again. He stood on unsteady legs and Hair unfurled around him. He surveyed the area, there was certainly a lot of Hair.

"No, Hair!" Hair?"

"Hair?" It was singed somewhat. "Hair, come back to me?"

Nothing.

Krackers cradled some of Hair. "Please come back to me?" Tears welled in his eyes. "Please, Bud, I need you." Krackers leant over it and cried.

Hair buzzed weakly.

"What do you mean, I'm a crybaby?"

Hair started to come around. It unwrapped the crates of Alert. Hair began to retract, and that took some time, there was certainly a lot of it.

"I'm glad you're back," Krackers whispered. "I don't know what I'd do without you."

Hair hummed.

"Yes, Bud, I mean every word."

Hair vibrated and buzzed.

"I am not a girl!" Krackers faked indignation. "Hey Hair, guess what?"

Hair whirred.

"Touch you last!"

Later that day.

Krackers still hadn't finished his "touch you last" game, and they were rolling on the floor. C.R.A.P.I. agents had converged on the area. Nursie was standing in a corner, chatting with two other agents.

"Ooh, Nursie," Krackers stopped his game and bounded over to her. He waited impatiently as she finished her conversation, bouncing from one foot to the other. She finally noticed him and ended her talk, turning to him with a smile.

"How are you, Nursie?" Krackers asked, concern in his voice.

"Thank you so much, Michael," Nursie said. "You saved my life again. Still a bit woozy, but I'll be okay. Hair and I were so worried. You should have said something."

"I know I should have," Nursie admitted, looking embarrassed. "Work was piling up, and with the stresses of the world, I needed a pick-me-up, but never again."

Hair cooed.

"Hair says he's glad you're getting better."

"I think, as a reward for the bravest of brave heroes," Nursie smiled, "a trip to I Scream, U Scream ice-cream parlour, ice creams for all!"

Hair made 'smacking' noises as the trio walked towards the elevator.

Twelve.

Vigilance Is Its Own Reward.

The city of Karma Central was a beautiful, sterile place. There were illegal acts, but they were hidden from the citizenry. C.R.A.P.I. made sure citizens didn't see the dark underside of the city. The agents would nip crimes in the bud, but when there were serious incidents, they deployed specialised agents like Krackers.

C.R.A.P.I. monitored all the airwaves, cell phones, shortwave and anything being circulated or broadcasting on any frequency. C.R.A.P.I. ran them through a powerful, complicated computer algorithm that red-flagged certain phrases. They got multiple hits; there was definitely an assassination in the air.

Hair had pinned Krackers against one of the walls in his room. Hair was vibrating wildly and Krackers was arguing a one-sided disagreement.

"No," Krackers argued, "you're wrong!"

Hair buzzed emphatically.

"You're wrong," Krackers stated. "You haven't got a clue!"

Nursie sauntered into Krackers' room carrying a small bag, only to be surprised by the scene. She waited while the two of them continued to argue. After five minutes she cleared her throat.

"Why are you two arguing?" A bemused smirk on her lips.

"Hair thinks vanilla is the best flavour at I Scream U Scream Ice Cream Parlour," Krackers stated. "I believe triple choc with sprinkles is best. Which one do you think is best, Nursie?"

"Let him down, Hair," Nursie laughed. "You two have a mission."

Hair begrudgingly lowered Krackers to the floor then retracted into his skull.

"Come here, you." Nursie grabbed Krackers roughly and kissed him. The Knowledge in Saliva Sample flowed into Krackers' body. He kept his eyes shut, enjoying the intense rush.

"Wow!" Krackers gasped as he opened his eyes.

"Although you have the mission specs," Nursie started, "I'll go through the main points. There was chatter about an assassination hit. Up till recently the target was unknown. We've just learnt the target is Mr John Doe."

"Hahaha!" Krackers rolled about the floor. "John Doe." He tried to suppress the laughter but failed miserably. After a few moments Krackers wiped the tears from his eyes. A snicker rippled through his body.

"When you're quite ready," Nursie returned, her laughter suppressed as she got the joke, "Mr Doe, if you didn't know, is the head of C.R.A.P.I. He's been scheduled for a meeting with the heads of the Inner and Outer Sprawls. The meeting place had to be neutral, so it's the Reality Inc. space station."

"Hold on," Krackers declared, jumping to his feet. "Doesn't C.R.I.M.E. own it? Didn't Hair and I barely get away with our lives?" Hair buzzed.

"Hair!" Krackers exclaimed, "that was not called for, especially around Nursie!"

"When you two are finished," Nursie sighed, "C.R.A.P.I. have gone through the space station and cleaned out the scum. Although Reality Inc. built the station, C.R.A.P.I. now own it. They've tripled the guards, both inside and out."

"Can the guards be trusted?"

"They've been scrutinised," Nursie said, "and they're all clean."

"When do we leave?"

"Now." Nursie reached into the bag. "This is for you." She handed him a small box.

"You shouldn't have," Krackers blushed, "and I didn't get you anything."

"Stop being silly," Nursie chuckled. "These are emergency space helmets, there are two. They're one-shots, but they'll keep you alive for ten minutes. Use them only when you really have to."

"Hair," Krackers said, "look after this, will you?" He lifted it and Hair flowed around it, spiriting it away.

"Change into your Doctor Delooz'nl character," Nursie said. "Come with me." She turned and walked out of the room.

Krackers followed her, feathering into Delooz'nl. They walked to the end of a corridor. There were two chairs and a small table with a plastic plant on it.

"Please sit," Nursie said, so they sat down. Nursie placed her hand on the armrest. Momentarily it glowed. The two chairs suddenly dropped and were replaced with two more chairs.

As the chairs fell, Nursie could see Krackers raise his hands and scream "*weee*!" Within five minutes they had dropped thirty floors. The chairs slowed to a stop.

"Can we do that again?" Krackers was so excited.

Hair whizzed in agreement.

"No," Nursie hissed, "you are about to meet the Chairman of C.R.A.P.I. Be on your best behaviour." As they walked down another corridor, Krackers tried extremely hard to behave. They reached some double doors with the name 'John Doe, C.E.O.' in gold lettering. Krackers tried to suppress a chuckle. Nursie elbowed him in the ribs. She knocked and waited. After a moment the doors opened and they walked in.

The room was huge. There were two charcoal-grey lounges and other sumptuous features. At the far end was a huge wooden desk. A bearlike man sat behind it, writing industriously. He stopped and looked at the two.

"Nurse Bre Bwee," the man's booming voice echoed as he rose and stepped to the side. "So good to see you again." He extended both arms and embraced Nursie. Krackers, still in the Delooz'nl character, ran over and hugged them both.

"Krackers," Nursie hissed, "remember, personal space!" Krackers unlocked his embrace and stepped back.

"Doctor Delooz'nl?" Mr Doe boomed, "I don't think we've met. Are you new? I thought I knew all the doctors on staff here?"

"Krackers," Nursie whispered, "remember you're still in character." "Krackers?" Mr Doe tried to recall.

Doctor Delooz'nl stepped in, hand outstretched. As he reached Mr Doe he feathered back into his form.

"Mr John Doe, I presume!" Krackers stifled a chuckle. "So good to meet you. I will be your bodyguard!"

"Arrhh," the Head said, "Michael Ness?"

"No," Krackers started.

"No?" Mr Doe asked.

"Krackers, Krackers, Sir, and this is my partner, Hair." Hair rose and shook Mr Doe's hand then hovered in the air.

"So, this is the Hybrid. Artificial. Intelligence. Retaliator," Mr Doe stated. "I've heard great things about it!"

"It's not an 'it!'" Krackers growled. "He's my partner!"

"I apologise, Hair," Mr Doe said, "I didn't mean any disrespect." Hair hummed. Mr Doe looked at Krackers.

"Hair said it's okay."

"So, Hair can change your identity into anyone?" Mr Doe enquired.

"As long as the character is roughly the same build." To emphasise the point, Hair feathered a few disguises and produced an exact imitation of Mr Doe.

"Very good," Mr Doe said, impressed. "The perfect agent, I am impressed!"

"The meeting is set for tomorrow at midday," Nursie stated. "We will reconvene here at six am and go over transport and travel details."

Six am, the following day.

Nothing.

Seven am.

"Where is your agent, Miss Bwee?" Mr Doe asked, annoyance in his voice.

"I'll go and find him," Nursie apologised. *"I'm gonna kick his arse,"* she muttered under her breath. She was about to open the door when they flew open.

"I'm sorry I'm late," Krackers said apologetically, "Hair forgot to wake me."

Two hours later.

"Okay," Nursie concluded, "so everyone's clear on the route that will be taken?"

"Crystal clear," Mr Doe said. "As far as Krackers guarding me?"

"Krackers will be by your side constantly," Nursie started. "That's right? Isn't that right?" Both Nursie and Mr Doe looked at Krackers.

"Like glue," Krackers assured them.

"Then you two should go," Nursie said. "I'll be in constant communication with Agent Krackers."

Krackers and Mr Doe left the office. The most dangerous part of the mission was the trip from the Peter Adams Memorial Hospital to the Quillstar Technology building. It was decided it would be just Krackers and Mr Doe, there was no point travelling with armed guards; it would draw too much attention.

Bob and his ice-cream van met the two outside the hospital. After swapping pleasantries they entered the van. It was a squeeze; Mr Doe climbed into the back of the van since his size restricted him from the passenger side, and he would have posed an easy target. As soon as the van lifted off, Karma air control radioed in.

"Karma air control to unknown vehicle," the Controller said, "please register a flight plan."

"This is a C.R.A.P.I. special envoy," Krackers radioed, "special undisclosed plan."

"Understood, you're cleared to proceed." The ice-cream van zoomed over Karma Central.

On one of the buildings, a targeting scope zeroed in on the van and tracked the vehicle. The trigger was depressed and a Piranha-class missile shot into the sky. It zigged and zagged around the buildings.

On the dash of the van, a red light blinked.

"Crap," Krackers spat, "missile lock. Swap seats, Bob, now."

Bob wriggled over to the passenger seat. Krackers slid into the driver's seat and tapped a button on the dashboard. A panel flipped over, revealing two small displays, one showing a red dot converging on the van, the other showing the rear view. The missile could be seen closing in.

"Hair," Krackers barked, "protect Mr Doe and Bob! Let Nursie know what's happening!"

Hair buzzed as it flowed out, cocooning both passengers.

"Here we go!"

As the projectile reached the van, Krackers made a stomach-churning, two-gee inverted turn. The missile flashed past the ice-cream truck, looped around, and came straight for them again. He pulled a barrel roll just as it shot by, whizzing under the vehicle. Krackers tried to pull the van up, but the missile clipped the front and exploded.

Hair suddenly filled the interior, cushioning all three passengers.

The van dropped from the sky, thick smoke billowing behind. Two of the four anti-grav pads were damaged, and the remaining two strained to slow the descent. It hit the ground hard, bounced, and skidded along the road. People and ground-effect vehicles scattered. The van slammed into a shop front.

Hair retracted, leaving the passengers dazed but unharmed.

"Everyone okay?" Krackers turned to Mr Doe. "We're about two blocks from the Quillstar Technology building. Let's keep moving."

"I guess they know I'm coming," Mr Doe muttered. "But how?"

"We'll work that out later," Krackers replied.

"My beautiful ice-cream van," Bob sobbed, hands on his head.

"Don't worry, Bob," Mr Doc said, "I'll make sure C.R.A.P.I. replaces it with an upgrade!"

A crowd began to form around the crash site. The three pushed through the onlookers. One thing was certain, the attackers didn't care about civilian lives.

From high above, a vehicle dropped down and opened fire. Bullets rained through the crowd, dropping people left, right and centre. Hair shot out, forming an umbrella-like shield. Rounds thudded into it as people stampeded in panic, vehicles colliding in the chaos.

Another craft joined the assault, hovering low and spraying the street with gunfire. Ricochets sparked across the pavement, cutting down more bystanders. The three ran, Hair's umbrella holding, barely.

"Well, viewers," Krackers muttered, "things don't look good for the valiant three!"

Krackers

"Did you say something?" Mr Doe asked.

"He does that sometimes," Bob said dryly.

They had only a block to go, and Hair was looking worse for wear.

"How you going, bud?" Krackers asked, concerned for his partner.

Hair buzzed weakly.

"Yes, Hair," Krackers said, "I'll make sure you get a tub of ice cream, just hang in there."

As they raced down the footpath, a third vehicle joined the attack. The trio sprinted across the street and burst into the Quillstar Technology building foyer. The aircrafts swooped to street level and fired in unison, shredding the foyer windows. Screams filled the air as more people were hit, the walls sprayed with blood.

The three bolted for the elevator. Hair slowly retracted into Krackers' head as the doors slid shut. The lift shot upwards, stopping at the 300th floor. They ran to the fire stairs, taking cover by the door to the roof.

Krackers peeked through the door, bullets thudded into the metal. He shut it quickly and turned to Mr Doe.

"I saw two vehicles," Krackers said. "Couldn't see the third." He paused. "Hair, are you up for another barrage?" Hair vibrated faintly.

"I know, bud," Krackers nodded. "Hair says we run for it. He can't hold the shield much longer."

Hair, sluggishly but determined, flowed up and around them. Krackers threw the door open. Bullets rained down, shredding parts of Hair's form. They pushed toward the space elevator, but the door wouldn't open. Three enemy craft hovered ahead, firing relentlessly. Hair deflected the barrage, but he was failing. Abruptly, Hair withdrew into Krackers' skull.

"Well, that's it for Hair," Krackers said grimly. "We're on our own now. Bob, thanks for your faithful friendship."

A faint hum rose.

"Hair says he's accessed the space elevator!"

All three turned, hammering the lift button. The doors clanged open. Behind them, explosions erupted, one, then another. They spun around to see the third aircraft engulfed in flames. A heavily armoured antigrav vehicle rose beside the building. As it hovered, its side door slid open, Nursie's pretty face appeared.

The craft maneuvered closer. Nursie leapt out and landed on the roof.

"You took your sweet time," Krackers laughed. "What happened to the armed guards?"

"I'll personally look into this fiasco!" Mr Doe declared.

"We need to get you to the meeting, Mr Doe," Nursie said, ushering him into the lift. They stood in silence as it rocketed up, each lost in thought. After what felt like an eternity, the doors opened. Nursie guided her boss into the conference room while Krackers waited outside, his thoughts with Hair.

Three days later.

Krackers lay on his bed, deep in thought. Hair was trying to goad him into a game of *touch you last*, but Krackers wasn't interested.

Nursie sauntered into the room, pushing a covered trolley. She wheeled it up to the bed.

"As promised, Hair, a tub of vanilla ice cream," she said, revealing the *I Scream, U Scream Ice Cream Parlour* logo.

Hair stopped mid-tease and made eager smacking noises. Nursie popped the lid, and Hair leapt in, slurping loudly.

"You know you've got a few commendations coming?" Nursie said. "They're also launching an internal investigation, they want to find out where the leaks are coming from, who's responsible, and most importantly, where were the guards at the base of the space elevator."

"How did the meeting go?" Krackers asked.

"They adjourned it," Nursie sighed.

"So, we did all that for nothing?" Krackers chuckled cynically.

"I guess so," Nursie shrugged.

"What about Bob? He really loved that ice-cream van."

"Bob's van's been upgraded," Nursie said. "They gave it a full overhaul, armour plating and all the latest weapons." Hair cooed happily as he finished the tub.

"Although it took three days," Nursie smiled, "Hair's in tip-top shape again."

Hair cooed and wrapped around Nursie, hugging her affectionately.

"We need to talk, Michael," Nursie whispered. "Not now, but later."

"No good thing ever starts with '*we need to talk*,'" Krackers chuckled.

"I'm gonna crash," Nursie said with a wave. "See you both in the morning."

Nursie walked out of the room, closed the door and walked down a darkening corridor.

Thirteen.

Dave's Not Here, Man.

Five years earlier.

Karma Central was the bustling hub of Karma City. The buildings soared high into an azure sky. C.R.A.P.I. resources were starting to wear thin, too many fingers in the pie. Although they were holding on, just. There were too many contacts, too many missions. Finally, they commissioned Quillstar Technology to build a supercomputer to relieve some of the less critical resources, the everyday problems.

Present day.

Finally, what the head of C.R.A.P.I. had been waiting for:

Decisive. Artificial. Virtual. Entity., or *D.A.V.E.* for short.

It was housed, deep in the Quillstar Technology building's subbasement Thirteen. The computer system consisted of two hundred servers independently linked. It could perform quadrillions of computations a second, an immensely powerful machine.

In sub-basement Thirteen.

Quillstar Technology building.

Mr John Doe, C.E.O. of C.R.A.P.I., Mr Richard Head, C.E.O. of Quillstar Technology, Nurse Bre Bwee, C.R.A.P.I. Special Liaison to Abnormal Procedures, and Krackers, C.R.A.P.I. Lead Agent /

Assassin / Problem Solver, stood in front of D.A.V.E. A red button on a control panel pulsed softly.

Mr Doe stood to the side of the panel of the huge supercomputer. He launched into a dry speech, prattling on. Krackers began to fidget and squirm. Nursie noticed his discomfort and leaned in.

"Are you okay?" Nursie whispered.

"Having trouble," Krackers hissed. "Trying to fight the urge… the button, so shiny and sparkly. Can't stop myself."

"Michael," Nursie hissed back, "don't you dare!"

Mr Doe was mid-speech, thanking the tech support team for their invaluable help in completing the project under budget and ahead of schedule.

"I am Krackers, damn you, Nursie!" Krackers suddenly shouted.

"Krackers!"

He leapt into the air, did a backflip, landed softly beside the control panel and slammed his hand down on the red button. "Shiny buttons unite!"

"Michael!" Nursie screamed. "Nooo!"

D.A.V.E. hummed to life. The two hundred servers, one by one, started to glow. After a minute, D.A.V.E. went online. The display above the control panel showed the pathways of C.R.A.P.I. servers linking up with D.A.V.E.

"WELCOME MR DOE, DISTINGUISHED GUESTS," a female voice boomed. *"I AM D.A.V.E. – DECISIVE. ARTIFICIAL. VIRTUAL. ENTITY. HOW MAY I ASSIST YOU?"*

"DAVE," Krackers laughed. "Hahaha! It doesn't sound like a DAVE, I think that computer needs a sex change."

"Since the ceremony was premature," Mr Head said, irritation in his voice, "we'll adjourn upstairs for drinks."

"I'll catch up with you, Dick," Mr Doe replied, turning to Nursie and Krackers. "Bre, you were supposed to keep him on a tight leash!"

"I'm sorry, Sir," Nursie apologised, but before she could continue, Krackers cut in.

"Do you realise, Sir," Krackers giggled, "that Quillstar has a Dick Head in charge?"

"Right, Krackers!" Mr Doe barked. "You're benched! You're confined to your room until further notice!" He composed himself. "Nurse Bwee, escort him to his room, then report to my office!" He turned and stormed off.

"Well, viewers," Krackers muttered, "a John Doe and a Dick Head didn't seem very happy."

"I'm not happy either," Nursie frowned. "Do you know what '*you're confined to your room*' actually means? It means you have to stay in your room with two armed guards. It means no sneaking out."

"Do you think," Krackers asked, "there's something wrong with Mr Doe?"

"Yes," Nursie replied, frustration in her voice, "he's not very happy with your conduct."

"Besides that," Krackers frowned.

"That he's going to come down hard on me," Nursie sighed.

A day later.

"I'm so bored!" Krackers whinged, standing on his head against a wall. Suddenly, a light began pulsing under his skin, on his wrist. He tried to scratch it, overbalanced and fell in a heap. He got up and saw the light was still there, blinking steadily. He stood and walked towards the guards, just as Nursie arrived at the door. She walked past him and sat on his bed.

"Look," Krackers chirped, "I've got a pretty blinking light on my wrist."

"So do I," Nursie said, concern in her voice.

"Maybe it's Christmas," Krackers exclaimed, "and we're all getting presents. Hooray!"

"I don't think it's that," Nursie replied. "I think it's more devious than that."

"What?" Krackers looked shocked. "You mean… no Santa?"

"No, Michael," Nursie said slowly, "I think it has something to do with D.A.V.E."

"I'm not Michael. Arh, doesn't matter," Krackers said. "You mean D.A.V.E. is Santa Claus?"

"No, Michael. D.A.V.E. is the computer," Nursie said pensively. "I really need to get a look at that machine."

"Why not just ask?" Krackers said offhandedly.

"I'm going to ask you to do something," Nursie cringed, "that goes against my better judgement."

"What is it?" Krackers could sense an adventure coming. "You know I'd do anything for you."

"I won't ask directly," Nursie said carefully. "How could we get to D.A.V.E. in the Quillstar Technology building?"

"I suppose," Krackers frowned, "you mean like this?" Hair shot out the door. There was a brief scuffle and the sound of bodies dropping. "Is that what you meant?"

Nursie didn't answer.

"If what I said, " Nursie chose her words carefully, "I was wondering how we could get past the cameras in this building?"

"Well, that would be easy," Krackers smiled, catching on. Hair snaked up to the ceiling and flowed into the nearby camera. "From here, Hair can access all the cameras and play back a loop, easy!"

"So," Nursie asked, "if it were done that way, would it be all clear?"
"Yep," Krackers said, smiling as Hair retracted back into his scalp.

"Will they be okay?" Nursie asked, stepping over one of the guards.

"They'll be out for a couple of hours."

As they made their way out, Krackers shifted into his Doctor Delooz'nl persona. They exited the Peter Adams Memorial Psychiatric Hospital and approached Bob, who was polishing his armoured ice cream van.

"I'm sorry, young Bob," Krackers said as Hair lashed out, dropping Bob instantly. "Hair, put him in the back." After securing him, Krackers jumped into the driver's seat.

"Don't you think I should drive?" Nursie asked.

"Brrm, brrm," Krackers grinned. He pulled back on the controls and shot straight up. The moment they lifted off, Karma Air Traffic Control radioed in.

"Unauthorised vehicle," the radio blared. "Please state your destination."

"I am C.R.A.P.I. Agent Bre Bwee, en route to the Quillstar Technology building."

"Roger, Agent Bwee," the radio replied. "Coordinates logged."

"We've got about ten minutes before all hell explodes," Nursie began. There was silence for the remainder of the short distance. They landed on one of the pads and jumped out of the vehicle. Two armed guards were stationed at the fire escape.

"What about the guards?" Nursie hissed.

"Get 'em, Hair," Krackers commanded. Hair shot forward, squeezing the two with just enough pressure until they dropped in a crumpled heap. As they walked to the door, Krackers grabbed a passkey from one of the fallen guards. They ran into the fire escape and down to the three hundredth floor. Krackers stabbed at the elevator button and waited. After a moment, the elevator door opened. They stepped inside, swiped the card and hit the sub-basement thirteen button. The elevator dropped swiftly, then the doors slid open.

At the elevator doors, it revealed two more guards. Hair did the same job again. Nursie and Krackers stepped over the now-unconscious men and up to D.A.V.E.'s control panel.

"Hair," Krackers said, "see what makes D.A.V.E. tick." Hair buzzed. Strands glided into the input port.

"Excuse me," a tech appeared, "who are you people?"

"Firstly," Nursie said, "who are you?"

"I'm the head technician," the man boasted, "of the D.A.V.E. project. Now, who are you?"

"I'm an extremely dangerous C.R.A.P.I. agent," Nursie smirked, "but he's worse."

Hair reared up, then crashed down on the head tech.

Hair screamed and shot out of the port as if it had been burnt. It retracted into Krackers' head, still buzzing.

"Slow down, bud," Krackers said, trying to calm Hair. "You know I can't understand you when you're like this." Hair continued to buzz.

"Who's in danger?"

Hair buzzed and droned.

"How are we in danger?" Krackers asked. "You mean the implants in my wrist? Funny, I don't even remember getting an implant." He looked at Nursie.

"Neither do I," Nursie said. "Hair, are you up to going back into D.A.V.E.?"

Hair gave three short buzzes.

"As long as you'll be okay, Hair," Krackers said, concern in his voice. "I'll be on the control panel. I'll make sure nothing happens."

Hair stretched out again, wisps entering the port. Krackers typed furiously and, with Hair's help, they broke the access code. Numerous files popped up on the screen, folders on all the C.R.A.P.I. departments and personnel.

The light on both Krackers' and Nursie's wrists increased in brightness. Next to the keyboard was a small box, blinking in sync with their lights. Krackers played a hunch and pressed his wrist on the box, a file named *Michael Ness* appeared on the monitor.

"Krackers, damn you!" Krackers yelled and shook his fist at the screen. "My name is Krackers!"

"Hair," Krackers commanded, "try and find out anything on the wrist implants."

The monitor went wild. Files flashed by, lines of data, numbers, and symbols. Finally, several video files appeared. Krackers clicked on the first one.

It showed Krackers and Nursie chatting in his room. There was a sudden bright flash, and both dropped to the floor. Men in black coveralls marched in, carrying some kind of gas-powered hypodermic. While one man held Krackers' wrist, another injected him. A third held a box, identical to the one beside the keyboard, and placed it on his wrist. It blinked. They then moved to Nursie and did the same. When they finished, one of the men turned to the camera and gave it a thumbs-up.

Krackers paused the video and zoomed in on the man. On his coverall, the Quillstar Technology logo was clearly visible.

Yet another file showed something far more disturbing. It was a *plan of action*. Schematics and sub-files flashed across the screen. One showed a small tube, labelled as a *micro-explosive*. Another diagram displayed the micro-explosive attached to the ulnar artery.

"Hair," Krackers asked, "are you up for a download?" Hair buzzed an affirmative.

Krackers highlighted all the C.R.A.P.I. files and hit download. He also highlighted the micro-explosive file and downloaded it.

Hair hummed. After a moment, it buzzed again.

"So," Krackers asked, "is there any way to shut down D.A.V.E.?"

Hair buzzed.

"Okay," Krackers laughed. "I didn't realise you were so devious." "What did Hair say?" Nursie asked, a question in her eyes.

"Hair said he's been toying around with a self-replicating reboot virus, just in case."

"I AM D.A.V.E.," the computer's female voice suddenly boomed. *"DECISIVE. ARTIFICIAL. VIRTUAL. ENTITY. HOW MAY I ASSIST YOU?"*

"The question is," Krackers replied, "how can I help you?"

"THAT RESPONSE IS UNDEFINED!" D.A.V.E. thundered. *"WHY IS HYBRID. ARTIFICIAL. INTELLIGENCE. RETALIATOR. ILLEGALLY ACCESSING MY FILES?"*

"Hair is a C.R.A.P.I. agent," Krackers said. "Therefore, Hair can legally access C.R.A.P.I. files."

"YOUR LOGIC IS SOUND," D.A.V.E. resonated. *"PLEASE CONTINUE."*

Krackers typed in a loop algorithm. D.A.V.E.'s servers hummed as it tried to escape the loop.

"Why did you do that?" Nursie asked, confused.

"I want to check another file," Krackers replied. "If I didn't introduce the loop, I wouldn't be able to access Mr Doe's file. It isn't within the C.R.A.P.I. system, it's a standalone."

"So, what are you thinking?" Nursie asked.

"Hair," Krackers said, urgency in his tone, "download Mr Doe's file and implement the virus!" Hair buzzed and vibrated.

"UNAUTHORISED ACCESS," D.A.V.E. boomed. *"AUTO SHUTOUT!"* Sirens blared and red lights flashed.

As Hair suddenly retracted, an arc of electricity rippled up its length, throwing Krackers back against a wall. Steam rose from both Hair and Krackers.

"Are you okay, Bud?" Krackers asked weakly.

Hair buzzed, squeaked, and hummed.

"Yeah," Krackers agreed. "So, did you implement the virus?"

Hair buzzed and hummed again.

"Okay, and the file?" Krackers nodded, then turned to Nursie. "Hair said the virus will take ten minutes to activate." Hair buzzed and vibrated.

"Hair said he could only get eighty per cent of the Mr Doe file."

"I think we've outstayed our welcome," Nursie said, as they ran towards the lift. As if to emphasise the point, the elevator doors shut right in front of them.

"Hair!" Krackers yelled. "See if you can do something about the elevator situation!"

As they reached the doors, Hair snaked out and wrapped around the lift button. After what felt like an eternity, the elevator doors opened, revealing four armed guards.

"Hey there," Krackers smirked, an evil grin spreading across his face. "Have you met Hair?"

Hair darted into the elevator and decimated the men.

They stepped inside. Bits of the guards slid down the lift walls, and pools of blood gathered on the floor. They tried not to step in the red liquid.

Krackers bent down and retrieved a key card. He pressed for the three hundredth floor, and the elevator shot upwards. After a minute, it slowed, stopping at the designated level.

"Stay behind me, Nursie," Krackers ordered. "Hair, no prisoners!"

"Michael!" Nursie gasped, noticing the murder in his eyes.

As the doors slid open, Krackers yelled, "Now, Hair!"

The doors revealed ten armed guards. Krackers' adrenaline booster kicked in, and everything blurred.

Krackers charged forward, Hair forming a shield in front of him. Sliding on his knees, Krackers let Hair lash out, taking down three guards before they could react. He leapt up and, with a roundhouse kick, broke a guard's nose, driving the bone into the man's brain. Hair whipped out, decapitating three more; their heads bounced across the floor. The final guard backed up against the wall, losing all control.

"Hair," Krackers commanded, "grab him!"

Hair shook off the blood and gore, then wrapped around the guard, lifting him into the air. The terrified man dangled upside down, brought face-to-face with Krackers.

"How many guards are on the roof?" The glint in Krackers' eyes said it all.

"Arrhh," the guard stuttered. "All of them, I think."

"Get rid of him, Hair."

Hair ripped the guard in two and dropped the remains. Blood gushed everywhere.

"Hair!" Nursie cried. "Nooo!"

Nursie and Krackers hurried to the fire escape door.

"On three," Krackers began. "Three!" He shoved the door open and rushed through.

The scene that met him was a sea of guards, all firing at the sky. After a moment, Krackers spotted their target. He dove into the mass of soldiers as Hair spun like a helicopter, mowing down ten of them. Strands of Hair fired outward, piercing another ten. Hair then formed a wide shield, pushing the rest off the building.

Bob landed and greeted the pair.

"Let's get out of here," Krackers commanded. "We've got to get back to the hospital, fast!"

Back at the Peter Adams Memorial Psychiatric Hospital

Krackers' room

Nursie moved over to a panel in the wall, placed her hand on it, and it glowed. The panel slid open, revealing a monitor and keyboard.

"Hair," Nursie said, "if you would be so kind."

Hair flowed out of Krackers' head and into the terminal port. The monitor displayed all the C.R.A.P.I. files, and a single one labelled 'Mr Doe'.

Nursie tried to open it. The folder revealed two photos: one of Mr Doe and another of a man with similar, though slightly different, features.

"It's the Shrink!" Krackers exclaimed. "I thought he looked familiar! Remember when he was arrested, but escaped?"

"Now that you mention it," Nursie said. "Those poor guards, they were never the same… And to think he oversaw C.R.A.P.I." She tapped the keyboard. "It seems Quillstar Technology is under investigation."

"There's only one thing I can do," Krackers smirked. "Touched you last!" He poked Hair, and the two rolled on the floor laughing.

Nursie chuckled, watching them play for a moment.

"Who's up for ice cream?" she chirped.

Hair made smacking noises.

"My shout," Nursie said as they walked out of Krackers' room.

Fourteen.

Johnny B Delicious,

C.R.A.P.I.'S Most Wanted

In the city of Karma, crime in the Outer Sprawl was at an all-time high. One in three people was a criminal of some kind. C.R.A.P.I. was struggling to keep a lid on it. The number one target on C.R.A.P.I.'s hit list was Johnny B Delicious. In a short time, Johnny B had rallied most of the criminals into quite a formidable organisation. At present, Johnny B was in talks with CRiminal In Misdeed Enterprise Engagements, or C.R.I.M.E. for short.

The Karma Reactor Atomic Plant was situated on the far edge of the Outer Sprawl. The C.R.A.P.I. and Karma city officials decided that keeping it as far away as possible from Karma Central was the best decision. The Atomic Plant powered the whole of Karma, with power left over.

There was a rumour that an insurrection was brewing within the Outer Sprawl. Someone was fuelling it, and that man was Johnny B Delicious. Krackers' mission was simple: track down Johnny B, capture him if possible or take him out with extreme prejudice.

C.R.A.P.I. had forewarning, an informant came forth. After interrogation, a plea deal was made. He said that it had to do with the Karma Reactor Atomic Plant. C.R.A.P.I. put the Plant on lockdown, and high alert was activated. From what little information they had, it was a credible threat. The informant spoke of a psionic belt that could vaporise organic life.

Lab techs worked feverishly, trying to come up with an answer to the belt. They got in touch with the Quillstar Technology techs and, after some threats, they relented and handed over the blueprints. Finally, they succeeded, with an earbud that should negate the effects of the belt. One small problem: it had never been field-tested.

The Outer Sprawl.

Johnny B's Fortress

Johnny B's Fortress spanned three city blocks and was heavily fortified. Anti-aircraft batteries, land-to-air missiles, and numerous miniguns were mounted on the roof. In the middle of the Fortress was Johnny B's Throne Room. The Throne was made of the skulls of the unfaithful. Johnny B lounged on it. Before him, the shimmering, shadowy figure of the Shrink stood as a hologram, ten feet tall. They were in a heated discussion.

"Remember," Johnny B smirked, puffing on a hookah filled with neohash, "you called me!"

"With that being beside the point," the Shrink continued, "do we have a deal?"

"I think we do," Johnny B agreed. With a flick of his hand, he waved off the figure, and the hologram wisped away.

His entourage reclined on throw cushions around Johnny's Throne. They all puffed from the same hookah.

"Johnny," one of the entourage slurred, "what about the snitches?" "Ah yes," Johnny vaguely remembered, "bring them in!"

Security dragged in a beaten man, his blood trailing behind him, followed by an equally beaten woman. Security held them upright; consciousness seemed fleeting between the two.

"So, Smudge," Johnny B smirked, "you been squealing?" "Not me, man," Smudge replied. "I'd never squeal on you."

"What about you, Birdy?" Johnny waited for an answer, puffing all the while.

"He talked to C.R.A.P.I.," Birdy spat.

"Thank you for that," Johnny B stared at Birdy. Abruptly, she started to shake, the air around her glimmered. She screamed as her head vaporised. Her body slumped to the floor, blood pooling beneath her. On his Throne, another skull suddenly appeared.

"As for you," Johnny commented, "give me one reason to keep your worthless life, here and now."

"Listen, man," Smudge talked quickly, "please don't kill me, I know I can help in some way."

"Maybe you can be useful," Johnny smiled through bloodshot eyes. "You can be another ornament on my Throne!"

"Please, man?" Smudge pleaded, as around him the air started to glimmer. He clutched his head as it vaporised. His body thudded to the floor, his blood mixing with Birdy's.

Johnny depressed a button on his belt and smiled. The telekinetic Psychotropic Extended belt powered down, and he patted it. "Remind me to thank the mole in Quillstar for this wonderful belt." His cohorts nodded.

"Drinks for all!" The room cheered. "Bring me bourbon!"

A scantily clad woman brought Johnny a large bottle of bourbon. He grabbed the booze with one hand and the woman with the other. Rising, he headed toward his bedroom, grabbing another couple of women on the way. He turned and smirked at his entourage. They cheered as he went into his room.

At the Peter Adams Memorial Psychiatric Hospital.

Krackers' Room

"This little piggy," Krackers played with his toes, "punched a bad guy, and this little piggy had ice cream. Hooray for ice cream!"

Nursie stood by the doorway watching Krackers and smiled.

Krackers giggled and rolled onto the floor. She walked over and helped him up.

"A new mission," Nursie said, cupping his face. She kissed him fully, deeply. The K.I.S.S., or its more official version, Knowledge In Saliva Sample, flowed into his being.

Krackers kept his eyes closed; it was so intense.

"Although I've given you the mission briefing," Nursie said as she wiggled to one of the walls, "we'll go through it one more time." She placed her hand on the wall, and it glowed. A panel slid open, revealing a monitor and keyboard.

"Oh goody," Krackers clapped, "home movies! Where's the popcorn?"

"No, Michael," Nursie answered. "Please pay attention. There is an imminent threat to the Karma Reactor Atomic Plant, and the credibility is extremely high! The man we're after is Johnny B Delicious. His organisation is large. One unconfirmed rumour says he's teaming up with the Shrink."

"I really hate the Shrink!" Krackers spat.

"If he teams up with the Shrink," Nursie said, "they'll be virtually unstoppable!"

"So, what's the next step?"

"The next step," Nursie said, "is getting you infiltrated into Johnny B's crew."

Krackers

The Outer Sprawl.

The Dirty Shot, a bar, two blocks from Johnny B's Fortress.

Two men sat in a booth, six empty shot glasses before them. A waitress came up, gathered the glasses, and wiped the table. Her body was to die for. The two men ogled her, one of them patting her on her shapely behind.

"Maybe we should take this out the back?" the waitress smiled, sitting on the man's lap, hands around his neck. "It's a bit crowded here." She rose, grabbing the man's hand and guiding him to the women's toilet. His mate, Bonkas, cheered him on.

Five Minutes Later

"That was quick, Snort," Bonkas laughed.

"Ahh," Snort commented, "she's a dead root. Anyway, we should go."

"Yeah, we don't want to piss off Johnny B," Bonkas stated. "Did you hear? Johnny B vaporised Smudge's head the other day." They walked out of the bar, still chatting, and made their way back to Johnny B's Fortress.

Back at The Dirty Shot,

A barman grabbed a mop and did what he did every day, he cleaned the toilets. He entered the men's and, within five minutes, had it spotless. He came out and stood in front of the ladies', summoning up the courage. It was widely known that it often looked like a war zone in there.

He opened the door and was confronted with a horrific scene. There were body parts everywhere, bloody bits still sliding down the walls, and the seasoned barman threw up.

Johnny B's Fortress.

The Throne Room

Johnny B sat on his throne and gazed out at his subjects through bloodshot eyes. Four, one-litre bottles of bourbon lay at his feet, two full, two empty. He had a hookah pipe hanging from his lips.

"More booze for my subjects," Johnny B commanded, "and drugs for everyone!" His subjects cheered. "All my subjects, move to the outer court, I have business to discuss!" He pointed at four men. "You four stay."

The Throne Room slowly started to clear. To hurry them up, Johnny stabbed at the button on his belt. Three heads vaporised and three bodies dropped to the floor. The crowd stampeded out of the Throne Room.

Finally, the room was empty, except for Snort, Bonkas, Grunt and the new guy, Gary.

"So," Johnny B said, "there seems to be a conspirator in our midst." Johnny stared out at the four. "And the winner is..."

Suddenly, Gary gripped his head, it vaporised, and his lifeless body dropped to the floor. Some underlings scuttled in and disposed of the body.

"Now that unpleasant business is done," Johnny B smirked, "have we got intel on the Atomic Plant yet?"

"It's on this flash drive," Grunt said, digging into his pocket and retrieving it. "Compliments of C.R.A.P.I." He handed it to Johnny B.

Johnny inserted it into an input port on his Throne of Skulls. The Karma Reactor Atomic Plant appeared as a huge hologram, showing in red all the Plant's weaknesses.

"Snort, Bonkas," Johnny commanded, "you're with me. Grunt, rally the troops. Get them to us at this location!" Grunt nodded and ran out of the Throne Room.

"A puff before we go, smoke the unpeace pipe, so to speak. Please join me!" It was a command, not a suggestion. Finally, Johnny rose, a little unsteady on his feet. He grabbed the pipe from his hookah and they puffed up a storm. "I need some supplies," he said, reaching down and grabbing a bottle of bourbon. "Off we go!"

They descended to the garage. There were a few hypercars, and Johnny B picked his favourite, a Bugatti Divo Anti-grav, such a sweet ride. He hit the ignition and the car roared to life, then lifted as it began to purr.

The Bugatti sped down a kilometre-long tunnel, from nought to one hundred in two point five seconds, and shot out of a hidden exit. It rose into the clear skies and hovered.

"Johnny B to Strike Force Alpha," Johnny said, "I'm sending coordinates. We'll rendezvous there. Out!" The Bugatti Divo shot forward, the abandoned houses and warehouses blurring beneath the anti-grav car. They arrived at a deserted football field. Johnny guided the car down, and they landed softly.

The doors opened and the trio alighted on the grass. The field looked a little smaller than it had from above. Snort waited until Bonkas walked away to check the field security.

"I heard Bonkas," Snort said quietly, "talking to C.R.A.P.I. back at the pub."

"That's interesting," Johnny B answered. "Let's drink to the demise of the C.R.A.P.I. agent!" He tapped the button on his belt gently.

Bonkas came back, meeting the boozing men. Johnny B offered him a drink.

"Don't mind if I do," Bonkas said, grabbing the bottle and drinking deeply.

"Drink," Johnny smirked. "It will be your last, C.R.A.P.I. agent!"

"No, man," Bonkas choked on the bourbon, "I'm loyal to you, Johnny B. I hate C.R.A.P.I."

"Tell it," Johnny B growled, "to someone in hell!"

Bonkas grasped his head and screamed. Around him, the air glimmered, then it vaporised, leaving his body to slump in a bloody mess.

"I hope he didn't bleed on my car," Johnny said through bloodshot eyes, staggering as he examined his Bugatti. "That was lucky!" He turned and kicked the lifeless body.

"I don't think he can feel that anymore, Boss," Snort said. "I think we should have another drink and wait for the gang."

"Why is your hair buzzing?" Johnny B asked.

"Oh crap," Snort replied, "you saw that?" He feathered back into his Krackers form. "Hair, you did an exceptional job. There'll be ice cream for you when we wrap things up!"

"Who are you supposed to be?" Johnny spat at the interloper.

"Charming," Krackers commented. "I am Krackers, C.R.A.P.I.'s number one agent. Hahaha!" He threw back his head, hand on his wasit.

"And you'll be the number one dead agent of C.R.A.P.I.!" Johnny B tapped on the belt button and smirked.

"Nooo!" Krackers grabbed his head and shook it. He dropped to his knees, threw his head back and cried out. "Please, nooo!"

"No point in pleading," Johnny said, bourbon in his hand. He lifted it to his lips and drank deeply.

"I agree," Krackers rose, brushing dirt off his knees. "Pleading is so undignified, don't you think?"

Johnny B stabbed at the button, nothing happened. He kept stabbing at it.

"I think it's time to give up," Krackers chuckled.

Johnny ran to his car, jumped in, and the Bugatti roared to life. It lifted swiftly and started gaining height.

"Hair," Krackers pointed at the rising hypercar, "bring it down."

Hair shot out of Krackers' head. It flowed up and grasped the underside of the car. It found the four anti-grav pads, seized them, and ripped them out of their housing. The car dropped like a stone; smoke plumed from the undercarriage. Hair let the car fall, then at the last moment, caught it and placed it on the ground. Hair wrapped around the car, ensuring Johnny's capture.

"Hair," Krackers asked, "what's the word from C.R.A.P.I.?" Hair buzzed, then hummed and vibrated.

"So, they arrested Johnny B's crew. Did you tell them we have Johnny B in custody?"

Hair buzzed again.

"That's good," Krackers said.

In the distance, came the sound of multiple anti-grav hums. As they drew closer, the familiar sight of Bob's armour-plated ice cream van appeared, followed by two C.R.A.P.I. anti-grav vehicles. They landed near the Bugatti Divo and the captured Johnny B.

Hair made slurping noises.

"Young Bob," Krackers smiled as he walked up to the van. Hair kept making slurping noises. "Hair did an exceptional job keeping me safe undercover. Do you have any ice cream?"

Bob went to the rear of the van and retrieved a small barrel of ice cream. He placed it on the ground. Hair crashed over it, devouring it with glugging noises. After a moment, Hair slowly retracted into Krackers' skull.

Nursie climbed out of the van and ran to Krackers. "I was so worried about you!" She kissed him deeply.

There was another anti-grav hum. Suddenly, both C.R.A.P.I. vehicles erupted in fireballs. The vehicles were lifted into the air, then crashed and burned. Hair instinctively covered Bob, his van, and Nursie.

A large black anti-grav vehicle hovered over Johnny B's car. It dropped a magnetic grapple and lifted the car into the air. It fired a barrage of missiles, they exploded on Hair's shield. To reinforce the shielding, Hair released the Bugatti. The black vehicle rose into the sky. It ceased firing, then launched a different kind of missile, which thudded into the ground, fanned open, and projected a hologram.

"You are definitely a thorn in my side," the shadowy figure said. "You may have won this battle, Michael, but I will win the war!" With that, the hologram faded out and the missile exploded.

"Krackers, damn you!" Krackers screamed. "Krackers!" Hair hummed and vibrated.

"I understand, Hair," Krackers said. "You did your best." Hair retracted back into his head.

"What did Hair say?" Nursie asked.

"Hair was apologising," Krackers turned to her. "Hair said, could you ever forgive him?"

"It's okay, Hair," Nursie smiled warmly. "As Michael, oops, sorry, as Krackers was saying, you did your best."

Hair purred, then flowed around Nursie's neck and cooed.

"Okay, troops," Nursie said, "let's get back and debrief."

The armour-plated ice cream van lifted off and shot towards the Peter Adams Memorial Psychiatric Hospital. Johnny B Delicious had got away, but Krackers secretly vowed that he would capture him, no matter what.

Fifteen.

The Demon's Reach.

The huge city of Karma was the sparkling jewel on the island continent of Strayl'ya. It perched amidst two oceans and two seas, simply named the Northern Sea, Southern Sea, Eastern Ocean, and Western Ocean. On the Western Ocean, three hundred kilometres off the coast of Karma, the Demon's Reach was a vast dead zone. All communications failed there; both shipping and air traffic were sporadically *'lost at sea'*. It formed a huge circle, three hundred thousand square kilometres, and was expanding every day.

Disappearances had once been limited incidents, but lately, they had become more widespread and increasingly violent, though the affected areas still seemed random.

Of course, C.R.A.P.I. had to get involved. It launched three drones, each flying at twelve kilometres in different directions. The moment one of the drones hit the outer perimeter of the Demon's Reach, communication and telemetry were lost. The other drones flew safely through the Reach.

The Peter Adams Memorial Psychiatric Hospital

Nursie walked into Krackers' room. Krackers and Hair were devouring a five-litre tub of ice cream.

"Is that ice cream?"

"No," Krackers said as Hair covered the tub. "Michael?!?"

"Well, yes," Krackers said sheepishly. "Would you like some?" He smiled and offered her a spoon.

"I suppose the mission briefing can wait," she laughed, taking the spoon. Hair uncovered the tub and Nursie dug into the ice cream.

After the three of them finished, Nursie stood and walked over to Krackers. She cupped his face and kissed him deeply. The mission briefing data flowed between them. As it ended, the kiss didn't. Finally, they separated, Krackers still had his eyes closed, savouring the last of the intensity.

"Wow," Krackers sighed as the sensation subsided.

Nursie wiggled over to a wall, placed her hand on it, and it glowed. A panel slid open and a huge monitor flickered to life. On it, a satellite map showed Karma, the continent, and surrounding areas. The Demon's Reach appeared as a large black circle.

"This is the Demon's Reach," Nursie said. "It's always been a small problem. The occasional plane and a few fishing vessels disappeared, but lately, we've been losing a lot more. So far, we've lost three Black Falcon helicopters, a squadron of stealth-class planes, a fleet of Avenger-class missile destroyers, and two oil tankers."

"So my mission," Krackers laughed, "is to go into a death trap, find whatever information I can, and report back."

"That's about it," Nursie said, a note of concern in her voice. "This mission is voluntary. You don't have to do it if you don't want to."

"You know me," Krackers chuckled. "I've been through worse," he lied.

"I'm sure everything will go well," Nursie lied. "Let's go downstairs and get you kitted up."

Armament. Special. Section.

Krackers lay on a table, muttering to himself. The room was large, with one wall made entirely of glass. Around him, technicians fussed. A beautiful woman in a doctor's coat approached.

"Now Michael, I'm Doctor Swive," the woman said.

"Krackers, damn you," Krackers snapped. "Krackers!"

"I'm sorry," Doctor Swive apologised. "The first thing we're going to do is give H.A.I.R. an upgrade."

"You can call me Krackers."

"As I was saying, Krackers," the Doctor continued, "we're giving

H.A.I.R. an upgrade. It won't hurt either of you." She walked over to an intercom. "Okay, bring it in." Two techs wheeled in a machine. On it was a large collar, which they attached around Hair.

Hair buzzed.

"Hair wants to know whether it'll hurt?"

"Tell Hair it won't hurt a bit," the Doctor smiled. She tapped at a keyboard and brought up Hair's profile: Hybrid. Artificial. Intelligence. Retaliator upgrade. Next to it flashed a green 'upgrade' button. She activated it, and the collar began to hum.

"Huh," Krackers said. "It tickles." Suddenly, his back arched and he screamed. The room erupted into chaos. Techs raced to the monitors, trying to find the fault.

"What's the problem?" Nursie yelled at Doctor Swive.

"Everything's in the green," the Doctor replied.

"Hahaha," Krackers giggled.

"Michael!" Nursie screamed. "That wasn't funny!"

"I'm sorry," Krackers said, still chuckling. "But you should've seen your faces. Are we finished, Doc?"

"Yes, we are," the Doctor said, annoyance in her voice. She removed the collar and Krackers sat up.

"Well, bud," Krackers asked, "how do you feel?" Hair buzzed excitedly.

"Slow down," Krackers pleaded. "You know I can't understand you when you talk that fast."

Hair buzzed a little slower.

"Okay," Krackers said. "You've got lots of upgrades."

"We should head down to the Danger Room and test them out."

Danger Room Three.

The Danger Room was cavernous, its walls pockmarked. It had holographic capabilities that, when activated, were as real as the world outside. Above the room sat the control booth, where both Nursie and Doctor Swive were at the panel.

"Okay, Michael," the Doctor's voice boomed, "we'll start with the underwater upgrades."

"Krackers!" Krackers screamed as the room filled with water. Hair ballooned out, encompassing his partner and forming a torpedo shape.

"Michael," Doctor Swive corrected herself. "I mean, Krackers, how are you?"

"I'm doing fine," Krackers giggled. "Hair, let's show them what we can do!" Hair rippled and shot through the water, performing breakneck turns.

"Let's really see what Krackers can do," the Doctor said, covering her mic as she tapped on a keyboard.

Suddenly, several divers with scuba propulsion thrusters materialised, circling Krackers. All had spear guns and attacked as one. Krackers spun and Hair fired multiple barbs, skewering them. They faded away, only for more to appear, these were split in twain as Hair formed two scythes that flashed through the water.

"Is that all you've got?" Krackers laughed as Hair suddenly shot forward, then did a triple barrel roll.

"Okay," Doctor Swive growled, tapping at the keyboard and disengaging the safety protocols. "Try this on for size!"

Multiple divers appeared on top of the twirling Hair. They latched on and began tearing at him, ripping chunks away. Hair erupted with razor-sharp spikes, shredding the divers and leaving bloody pulps in his wake.

"That's enough!" Nursie stabbed a button. The water vaporised, leaving Hair's torpedo form lying on the floor. Hair retracted, flowing back into his head. Krackers made his way up to the control room and into a shouting match between Nursie and Doctor Swive.

"That was uncalled for!" Nursie screamed. "Shutting down the safety protocols!"

"It was what needed to be done," the Doctor yelled back. "He's going into a dangerous situation! There are no 'protocols' where he's going. One mistake and he's dead!"

The Doctor stormed past Krackers, then stopped. "You and Hair have passed. Good luck on your mission. Please excuse me." She turned, glared at Nursie, and stormed away.

"She may be right," Krackers whispered.

"She may be right," Nursie said, "but she went against operational protocol. She was trying to kill you."

"Let's get a coffee, or maybe something stronger?" Krackers smiled at Nursie. "Or maybe some ice cream?"

Hair made slurping noises and Nursie laughed.

Later that night at the Karma Docklands.

Krackers sat on one of the many docks, his feet dangling over the edge. He tapped an earbud.

"Comms check."

"Reading five by five," Nursie replied. "Are you sure you want to do this?"

"I'm sure," Krackers said. "I've trained for it."

"Michael," Nursie whispered, "they were only simulations. What you're about to do is real. I'm scared. Planes and ships are disappearing, I'd hate to lose you."

"Bre," Krackers What's your next move?"

"I'm going in," Krackers said, uncertainty in his voice. Hair moved cautiously forward and stopped as the tip of the torpedo touched the shimmering wall.

"Hair," Krackers commanded, "extend out to the other side of the wall." Hair stretched forward and through the barrier. Hair buzzed. "What do you mean, 'there's air?" Hair slowly advanced until they made it through and dropped onto dry land. Hair unfurled, and Krackers stood, stretching. Before them, stood a gigantic structure, around it, a huge bubble of air. , Krackers began to doubt that anything was out there when the water ahead of them started to shimmer. Hair slowed to a stop, a metre from the shimmering wall.

"Nursie," Krackers asked, "are you still there?" "I'm still here, Michael."

"Are you receiving telemetry?" Krackers asked. "It seems suspicious."

"I am," Nursie said. "The pictures are surprisingly clear. What's your next move?"

"I'm going in," Krackers said, uncertainty in his voice.

Hair moved cautiously forward and stopped as the tip of the torpedo touched the shimmering wall.

"Hair," Krackers commanded, "extend out to the other side of the wall." Hair stretched forward and through the barrier.

Hair buzzed.

"What do you mean, *'there's air'?*"

Krackers

Hair slowly advanced until they made it through and dropped onto dry land. Hair unfurled, and Krackers stood, stretching. Before them stood a gigantic structure, above it, a huge bubble of air.

"Nursie," Krackers said, "are you there?" There was only static.

"Hair, it looks like we really are alone." Hair buzzed.

"You're right," Krackers said, "onward and upward!" Hair slurped.

"I don't know, Bud," Krackers replied, "they may have ice-cream. We should check with the management."

Krackers walked to the structure's wall. After following it around for a while, Krackers came upon a door. Next to it was a card reader and numbered pad.

Hair buzzed.

"So, you think you can do your magic?"

Hair buzzed confidently and flowed out of Krackers' skull, encompassing the keypad and card reader. After a moment, there was a *'click'* and the door opened. Hair flowed over Krackers and activated the chameleon upgrade, and Krackers faded into the scenery.

The security was high: there was a camera every ten metres as well as a motion detector. Hair snaked forward, flowing onto the nearest camera and detector.

Hair buzzed and hummed, deactivating the chameleon function.

"That's clever, Bud," Krackers smiled. "So, we can go anywhere, and the camera will deactivate, and when we pass, it reactivates. Could you gain access to the main computer?" Hair replied with a buzz.

"Only security," Krackers commented. "We should find a terminal. Which way?"

Hair buzzed. "You downloaded a map?" Krackers smiled. "Therefore, you're a great partner! There'll be loads of ice- cream for you." Hair slurped and buzzed.

"First things first," Krackers stated. "Find me the quickest way to the Control Room."

The map to the Control Room flashed over Krackers' sight. "The way has two checkpoints. That could be a problem."

Hair buzzed and flowed out around Krackers, changing him into the Doctor Delooz'nl disguise. After some walking, he made it to the first checkpoint. He walked up to the guard.

"Excuse me, I'm Doctor Delooz'nl. I seem to be lost."

"I don't see you on the list," the guard grunted.

"I arrived today, could you check again?"

"Nothing," the guard snorted.

"I just remembered, I do have authority," Krackers laughed as Hair flowed out and crashed into the guard. Hair released the now unconscious guard and shot straight to the input port on the keyboard. There was a flash of light and a whir from a printer; Hair handed Krackers an I.D. card.

He made his way to the second checkpoint and had no problems. Next stop: the Control Room.

With no resistance, Krackers walked into the Control Room. It was gigantic, warehouse-sized and filled with technicians manning computers. On the far wall, a huge screen sat, showing a radar and other relevant information. A tech holding a tablet walked up to him.

"Can I help you?" The tech looked at Krackers' badge. "Doctor Delooz'nl."

"I'm new and lost," Krackers said coyly. "I don't really know where my station is?"

The tech tapped on the tablet, then looked at Krackers.

"There you are," the tech said. "Go to the elevator, go to the thirteenth floor and straight on to the labs."

"Do you think you could take me there?" Krackers asked. "This place is huge."

The tech looked at his tablet, then at Krackers.

"Okay," the tech said. "We'll have to be quick though."

The tech escorted Krackers to a bank of elevators. One of the elevators chimed and the two entered the lift. The moment the doors shut, Krackers stopped the lift. Hair roared and reared up. The tech took one look at the scene; horror filled his face, then his eyes rolled up into his head and he fainted.

"Well," Krackers chuckled, "that went better than expected. Hair, can we use his likeness?"

The elevator doors opened just as Hair finished stuffing the tech through the trapdoor. Krackers picked up the fallen tablet and security card and walked out of the elevator. Krackers looked at the tablet, the rotating logo C.R.I.M.E. assaulted his eyes.

"The Shrink!" Krackers spat.

He tapped on the tablet and files appeared. Two caught his attention:

Oxygen Shield and Tractor Control.

He opened the Tractor Control file. There were stats and figures, and they described in some detail how it worked. The file heading showed Repulse In Matter Stasis. It explained that when the field was activated, the matter in question would triple in mass, dragging it down onto a catchment on the top of the structure.

Krackers tried to sabotage the field, but he didn't have the clearance, so he brought up a map. It showed the Repulse In Matter Stasis generator, it was nine floors up.

He made his way up to the R.I.M.S. generator and came upon a security checkpoint. Krackers swiped the security card.

"Are you here to recalibrate the generator?" one of the guards asked, scrutinising Krackers.

"Arh," Krackers went with the flow. "Yes, I am. The 'Sitzfeisch' has become misaligned."

Krackers walked through the checkpoint and through a door. The generator room was huge, ten football fields big. As it was pretty much automotive, there were only two techs that needed to tend to it. Around it were ships and planes in bays; there were a lot of them.

Krackers marched up to the techs. "Report!"

"There was a discrepancy," one of the techs reported. "It has been restored to working order."

"Do you want to see something really scary?" Krackers smirked. "Hair, show them!"

Hair raised up, roaring as it went. The two technicians cringed in terror; both soiled themselves.

"We haven't got time. Hair, put them out of commission!"

Hair flowed over Krackers and grabbed the techs. It lofted them high into the air, then slammed them on the floor; bones cracked, and they remained still.

Hair buzzed as it retracted into Krackers' skull.

"I just meant knock them out," Krackers commented as he walked over to the control panel. "Hair, see what you can do with this?" Hair flowed over the control panel, strands entering multiple ports.

After a moment, Hair buzzed then whizzed.

"Okay," Krackers said, "so it's locking on to another target. Can you disable it?"

Hair buzzed again.

"Fine," Krackers said, frustration creeping in. "What about reversing the polarity?"

Hair hummed.

"So, you can?" Krackers smiled. "What would happen?" Hair vibrated.

"It would fold in on itself, you say," Krackers laughed, "destroying this facility. How much time would it take?"

Hair hummed and buzzed.

"That much? Can you warn the staff and technicians?" Hair buzzed and hummed.

"Do it, then we're outta here!"

A hologram suddenly shimmered into existence.

"Michael," the familiar silhouette of the Shrink said, "how dare you! You are a constant thorn in my side! You will rue this day; I promise you that!"

Hair buzzed, then all hell broke loose. Sirens and klaxons sounded. Hair retracted into Krackers' skull.

"I think we should get out of here," Krackers said as he ran through the hologram.

Outside was pandemonium, people were running to escape pods.

"Hair, find us the quickest way out of here!"

Hair projected the map of the facility over his eyes. A green blip pulsed, with a red line to the edge of the map.

"Nursie, can you hear me?" Only static.

"Crap! Hair, can you tap into the communication net on the way?" Hair hummed.

"Michael?" Nursie tuned in. "Are you there?"

"Nursie," Krackers beamed, "glad to hear you."

"I was so worried," Nursie said.

"Ten," a resounding voice boomed, "nine, eight."

"What was that?" Nursie asked. "Is that a countdown?"

"Bit busy," Krackers' breathless voice sounded. "Could you send in the Clean Up Crew? Talk to you soon."

"Seven," the voice continued, "six, five." "We are going to make it, aren't we, Hair?" "Four, three, two, one."

The R.I.M.S. generator activated, and the whole structure suddenly groaned under its own weight. Multiple explosions rocked the facility as it folded in on itself. Both the R.I.M.S. generator and the Oxygen Shield failed as it continued to compact. Finally, it became critical, and the whole installation exploded in a huge fireball, shooting up, encompassed in the last of the oxygen.

On the surface, in the middle of the Demon's Reach.

The water erupted as the fireball reached the surface and exploded.

C.R.A.P.I. watercraft bobbed near the explosion, assisting with the rescue of the many escape pods that floated there. They were being rounded up and taken into custody.

"Michael," Nursie pleaded from the lead ship, "please come in?" The radio stayed silent.

"Please come in," Nursie begged, "please be there, I need you."

Suddenly, the Hair torpedo surfaced, a little worse for wear. Hair buzzed as it retracted into Krackers' skull. He swam slowly over to the ship and climbed aboard. Nursie ran over and wrapped her arms around Krackers' neck, smothering him with kisses.

"I thought I lost you," Nursie sobbed as she buried her head in Krackers' chest. As she finished, she looked him in the eyes.

"I have a question to ask you," Krackers whispered, going down on one knee. "Will you marry me?"

Hair fashioned a ring, and Krackers plucked it from Hair. Hair flinched, then reared up, cooing and humming.

"Of course I would," she said, extending a hand, and Krackers placed it on her finger. The crew cheered loudly, and they embraced. Hair folded around the two as the C.R.A.P.I. fleet sailed slowly back to Karma.

Danger averted.

Sixteen.

And Then Came The B.A.G.

The Peter Adams Memorial Psychiatric Hospital

Sirens screamed, and smoke filled the air. C.R.A.P.I. staff were running everywhere; it was sheer pandemonium. Krackers stood at the doorway to his room. He grabbed a woman and waited for her to stop squirming.

"What's happened?"

"There's been a breach," she said, terror in her voice, "it's C.R.I.M.E! The attack took us by surprise!" She struggled free.

"Hair," Krackers commanded, "get in touch with Nursie!" Hair rose up and vibrated. After a moment, Hair buzzed.

"What do you mean," Krackers spat, "her comms are off? Try again." Hair vibrated again and got the same answer.

"Okay," Krackers said. "Could you find out where the breach is?" Hair buzzed and hummed.

A map of the hospital flashed over Krackers' sight. It showed a red dot at the armory. Multiple targets were lit up all over the hospital.

"Can you pinpoint Nursie?" Krackers asked pleadingly. Hair buzzed.

The map flashed a blue dot in the armory. "Hair," Krackers commanded, "battle armour!" Hair flowed forth, encompassing his partner.

"Activate the Chameleon upgrade!" Krackers faded into the scenery. "Let's go find Nursie. C.R.I.M.E. thugs, beware!"

Krackers left his room and walked straight into two meaty thugs. He reminded himself that they couldn't see him.

"Hair," Krackers said, "get 'em!"

Hair obliged, suddenly appearing, rearing up and shooting two spikes. They shot out and impaled the thugs through their chests. The spikes changed into two scythes and cleaved them in two. The tops of the thugs slid down to the torso and 'splatted' to the floor, blood pooling around them.

The Armament Special Section was ten floors down. Using the elevator was out—they could track him—so the stairs were the best option. Krackers moved on, killing the occasional thug. He finally reached the stairs. There was a lone guard standing at the door to the stairs. Krackers engaged his adrenaline booster and, in one fluid motion, grabbed the guard, opened the door and pressed the surprised man against the stairwell wall.

"How many men?" Krackers hissed.

"I can't," the guard stuttered, "he'll kill me." "What makes you think I won't kill you?" To emphasise the point, Hair reared up.

"Is your boss the Shrink?"

"Yes," the guard spluttered, "please don't kill me." "How many men?" Krackers growled.

"Around forty," the guard replied.

"Goodbye," Krackers smiled. "Hair, I'm finished with him."

Hair flashed, cutting him from head to groin. The surprised guard stared in disbelief as he split in two; blood gushed over Krackers.

"Clean up on aisle two!"

Hair rippled off the blood, restoring Krackers' armour to brand new. Krackers ran down the stairs, two by two, finally reaching the Armament Special Section door. With one swift action, he opened the door, skewered the guard and dragged him into the stairwell. Hair reared up and tore the guard in half.

Hair feathered into the guard and walked into the section. He made a mental note of the number of thugs: twenty in total. In the corner, a thug and a female figure were talking to a third. As he got closer, the third was a familiar hologram of the shadowy Shrink.

"Doesn't that guy ever get out?" Krackers muttered as he walked up to the hologram. "Hey Boss, I found a surprise for you."

The female turned around to reveal Nursie. She smiled sweetly.

"What is it?" the Shrink asked, annoyance in his voice. "I'm extremely busy!"

"Better I show you," Krackers said. "But first, do you have ice-cream?"

"Get him!" the Shrink yelled. "It's Krackers!"

"Nursie," Krackers pleaded, "no, you can't be involved."

"Sorry, lover," Nursie cooed, "I want to be on the winning team. Get him, boys."

The thugs surrounded Krackers as he started to spin. Hair shot blades out, decapitating them all in one fell swoop. Hair fired out a spear and hit Nursie in the heart.

"Nooo!" Krackers screamed. A movement behind him caused him to turn around.

A guard came in, witnessing the carnage. He raised his weapon and shot at Krackers. The bullet hit the hero straight between the eyes.

The Peter Adams Memorial Psychiatric Hospital, Krackers' room.

Krackers sat bolt upright, sweat streaming off his body. Hair had fired out some spears in different directions, embedding them into the walls. Hair slowly retracted them back into his head.

Hair buzzed and hummed.

"I agree," Krackers whispered, "it was intense, wasn't it?" Hair buzzed, then vibrated.

"No," Krackers argued, "I don't think Nursie should know." Hair vibrated.

"I hope you didn't tell Nursie." Hair hummed and cooed.

"What do you mean," Krackers said, annoyance creeping into his voice, "you don't remember?" Hair purred.

"You were worried?" Krackers smiled. "I'll be fine, Bud. I suppose I'll talk to her tomorrow."

"Hair tells me I need to have a chat. So, what's going on?" Nursie walked into the room.

"Snitch," Krackers muttered to Hair.

Half an hour later.

"So that was my dream," Krackers said, letting out a breath he didn't realise he was holding. "It was so real."

"Remember," Nursie said lovingly, "it was only a dream."

"Are you sure?" Krackers tried to compose himself. "It seemed so real. Anyway, what's on the agenda for today?"

"There's a surveillance mission," Nursie said, "but I'll give it to someone else." She noticed the holes in the walls. "What happened to the walls?"

Hair buzzed.

"What did Hair say?" Nursie asked.

"Hair said he's really sorry," Krackers apologised, "he reacted to my nightmare."

"Have you been having other nightmares?" Nursie showed concern.

"I've had a few," Krackers admitted, "but nothing like this one. Do you want to go for a walk?"

The Peter Adams Memorial Psychiatric Hospital's Arboretum.

The Arboretum was a huge parkland inside the hospital. With tall trees and lush grass, a walking track dissected the greensward. Nursie and Krackers walked through the park, hands entwined. They walked up to a bench seat and sat down.

"I really haven't been totally honest with you, Bre," Krackers said thoughtfully.

"How so, Michael?"

"I've had a nightmare every night for a couple of months now." Krackers shook his head. "It's starting to get to me." He lowered his head. Nursie comforted him, pulling him closer.

Hair vibrated.

The scenery seemed to blur for a moment. Krackers shook his head. He turned to speak to Nursie, but she had vanished. He stood up and glanced around. Lightning exploded from above, flashing and showing the silhouette of the trees. Rain dashed the area; torrents of water fell to the roof. Shadows darted, moving swiftly among the trees. Krackers followed them in. Shadows fleeted by, darting in the dimness.

"Hair," Krackers commanded, "get 'em, get 'em all!"

Hair fired out multiple barbs, pinning numerous shadows to the trees. "Michael," a disembodied voice cried out.

"Krackers... damn it. Wait, what?" Krackers said.

Hair vibrated again as the scenery blurred. He stood by the trees. Hair's barbs were still embedded in a number of trees. Behind him, Nursie ran up.

Krackers

"It happened again," Nursie asked, "didn't it?" Hair slowly retracted the barbs from the trees.

"Yes, it did," Krackers whispered as he embraced Nursie. "I don't know how long I can stand it." Nursie hugged him tightly.

"I think we should go to the Med-lab," Nursie suggested. "Maybe they can get to the bottom of the nightmares?"

The Peter Adams Memorial Psychiatric Hospital's Med-lab

Krackers lay on a table. Hair was collared, with wires trailing off the table and into a monitor. Doctor Swive examined Krackers, taking observations. When she'd finished, she looked down at him.

"Everything seems fine; you're in perfect health," Doctor Swive said. "Tell me, have you done anything differently before the nightmares started?"

"Not that I can think of," Krackers thought. "Hair did vibrate each time the nightmare happened, but I thought nothing of it." She checked the monitor, then typed on a keyboard.

"Huh," she said, "that's interesting. There seems to be a discrepancy in the Alpha wave breakdown in Hair's receptors. It's unusual because instead of Hair regulating it, it's receiving the Alpha wave frequency."

"Can the frequency be tracked back to the source?" Nursie asked.

"It certainly can," the doctor said as she tapped on the keyboard. "I've activated a trace. The moment the next transmission is received, we'll be able to track it back to its source. In the meantime, I'll install an inhibitor in H.A.I.R., so it should block the frequency."

An hour later:

"Nurse Bwee! Krackers," the P.A. boomed, "please come to the Medlab at once!"

The Peter Adams Memorial Psychiatric Hospital's Med-lab.

Nursie and Krackers arrived at the Med-lab. Doctor Swive was seated at a terminal. On the monitor, it showed the entire Island Continent and the huge city of Karma. A red dot bounced around the island, flitting from a building in Karma Central to an abandoned building in the Outer Sprawl. It flashed around the Continent and finally came to rest on a business called I Scream, U Scream Ice Cream Parlour.

"Nooo!" Krackers cried out. Hair buzzed angrily.

"I am going to make them pay!" Krackers turned and started to storm out of the room.

"I'm coming with you!" Nursie followed Krackers out the door. "I'll have to make a stop first."

Armament. Special. Section.

As they walked in, a tech greeted them. After explaining the situation, the tech was willing to kit out Nursie.

"So, what were you thinking?" the tech asked. "What type of mission is it?"

"All-scale assault," Krackers said. "She needs something to keep her safe and kick arse!"

"I think I have just what you need." He wandered out the back and, momentarily, returned with a small black backpack. "This is new; try this on for size."

Nursie put on the backpack. It stirred and hummed, attaching itself to her spine, and she flinched. Krackers growled at the tech.

"It's okay," the tech cringed, "it's acclimatising to her physiology."

"It's okay, Michael," Nursie smiled. "It doesn't hurt anymore. How does it work?"

"First, say 'activate'," the tech explained. "Okay, activate!"

The backpack hummed, then flowed out and around her. Once it encompassed her, it solidified, accentuating her figure. Nursie twirled, and Krackers was impressed.

"It's thought control," the tech explained. The B.A.G., or as it's technically known, Bio-Augmented aGgressor, uses the same technology as the H.A.I.R. unit. It's a nano micro-Kevlar weave. It's a fluid weapon: what you think, it does. Be careful—it runs on your own bioenergy, so it will drain you."

Nursie held her arm; it flowed into a sword, then quickly flowed back into her hand. She laughed.

"This is a battery; it's rechargeable. It works in conjunction with your bioenergy. Place it on your stomach; it'll do the rest." The tech handed her a large black rounded box. She placed it on her belly, and it melted into the suit.

"How do I deactivate it?" Nursie thought. The suit flowed back into the backpack.

"What's your name, tech?"

"Harold, Krackers," the tech said.

"Well, thank you, Harold Krackers," Krackers said. "No, it's just Harold," the tech tried to explain.

"Okay, just Harold," Krackers said. "Sorry, but we have to go."

They left the Armament. Special. Section. Krackers was impressed with her suit and knew Nursie would be safe.

Evening, outside the Peter Adams Memorial Psychiatric Hospital.

The streets around Karma Central were mostly deserted. At five, on the dot, office workers disgorged from the office skyscrapers into the gravity-defying subway and their anti-grav vehicles, leaving Karma Central a virtual ghost town. C.R.A.P.I. patrolled the city, although crime in Karma Central was few and far between.

Krackers and Nursie stood on the empty street. Krackers was in his stealth suit, and Nursie sported a catsuit with the B.A.G. on her back. "Are you ready?" Krackers smiled.

The B.A.G. flowed around the smiling Nursie, forming and solidifying into her black armour.

"Ready!"

Nursie radioed into C.R.A.P.I. control and was granted permission to raid the I Scream, U Scream Ice Cream Parlour. The two made their way down, their images blending with the darkening street.

"Follow my lead," Krackers said over their personal comms.

"Roger that," Nursie whispered back.

The two crept up to the storefront, and Krackers signalled a halt.

"Stay here," Krackers whispered. "I'm activating Hair's chameleon program. I'll be back in a moment."

Krackers faded into the scenery. A minute later, he reappeared. Nursie jumped and landed in a defensive stance, both arms creating swords; they were inches from Krackers' throat.

"Please don't do that," Nursie started, "I could have killed you!"

"But you didn't," Krackers smiled. "See how your senses are heightened?"

Hair buzzed emphatically.

"Okay," Krackers nodded. "Hair says the signal's pretty strong, so the intel was good."

"So, what's the next step?" Nursie seemed eager.

"Using the B.A.G.," Krackers said, "think of the scariest thing you can and charge into the shop."

Hair made slurping noises.

"Maybe after the mission, Bud," Krackers laughed. "Okay, on my mark: three, two, one. Go!"

The two heroes raced into the shop. Krackers had Hair rearing up while Nursie adopted a huge nine-foot spider form. The pimply teenager behind the counter opened his mouth wide, his eyes rolled back into his head, and he dropped to the floor in a dead faint.

"Well, that was easy," Nursie said as she changed from the spider to a more pleasing form.

Suddenly, the doors to the back room burst open and a horde of men ran out. Hair took the fight to them, slicing three men with one foul swoop. Nursie raised her hands, turning her fingers into razor-sharp mini whips. With a deft flick of her wrists, the whips sliced neatly through a number of unfortunate souls. Hair tore man after man in half; it was certainly quite a bloodbath.

Finally, the onslaught finished. Hair slid back into Krackers' head, and the whips flowed back into Nursie's hands. They moved cautiously into the back room. A man sat at a computer terminal. Before Krackers and Nursie could react, Hair roared to life. The tech jumped out of his chair and cringed in the corner. Nursie ran to the computer terminal and tapped at the keys.

"I've found the frequency generator program." She shook her head. "It's definitely a C.R.I.M.E. operation. There's so much we could use on them; I wish I could download it all." One of her fingers snaked into the data port.

"Well, that's new," Krackers said.

"There's so much data," Nursie lay her head back, absorbing the information.

Abruptly, the monitor flashed red, and Nursie was thrown to the other side of the room. On the monitor, a silhouetted figure appeared.

"The Shrink!" Krackers spat.

"That was naughty of you, Bre," the figure growled. "Don't do it again, or the next time, it will be lethal." With that, the terminal started to smoke.

Krackers grabbed Nursie and jumped for the door. They cleared it just as the room erupted into a huge fireball. The two rolled into the shopfront as the pimply youth just stood up. As Krackers ran past, Hair scooped him up and carried him out. Hair laid him on the footpath. The youth stood, saw Hair retracting into Krackers' skull, his eyes rolled back, and he fainted again.

The fire and E.M.S. arrived. After the youth was tended to, the firemen dealt with the blaze in the I Scream, U Scream Ice Cream Parlour.

Hair made sad slurping noises.

"Sorry, Bud," Krackers said, "the shop is in flames."

Krackers and Nursie walked back to the Peter Adams Memorial Psychiatric Hospital and to Krackers' room.

Nursie smiled as her armour flowed back to form the B.A.G. She excused herself and returned ten minutes later, hands behind her back.

"Hair, you did such a good job," Nursie smiled, bringing her hands around to reveal two ice cream cones.

Hair raised up, making excited slurping noises.

Nursie offered one cone to Hair, and it pounced on it. She handed the other to Krackers.

Hair hovered, vibrating happily.

Krackers

"Here, Bud," Krackers laughed, "you can have mine, you deserved it." Hair leapt at the ice cream.

Seventeen.

God Says Boo.

The Reality Inc. Space Station hung high in the sky like an avenging angel. It kept vigil over all of Karma City. C.R.A.P.I. had absorbed the company but decided to keep the name.

Karma City sparkled in the early evening. From high above, Karma Central was a beautiful gem. The Inner and Outer sprawls were another story. The sprawls were the ugly cancer that surrounded Central Karma. Nursie and Krackers had Space Station duties, mainly surveillance over the continent and out into space.

Krackers was leaning back in his chair playing 'touched you last' with Hair while Nursie napped. On the control panel, a small yellow light blinked. Krackers was too engrossed in his game. The light changed to orange, and Krackers continued playing. Once the light changed to red, it was accompanied by a beep. Krackers paused momentarily, but it didn't register, and he went back to the game. When the red light blinked more urgently, it was accompanied by an ear-shattering shrill. Krackers fell back off his chair and scrambled to his feet.

Nursie ran into the control room and straight to the control panel. She punched a few buttons, and an image appeared on a large screen.

"We've got a live one," Nursie started. "No, three… no, a lot of them." As they watched, even more appeared.

"See if you can zoom in on one," Krackers suggested.

Nursie tapped on the keyboard. The image zoomed in, then the program cleared, showing… Hair buzzed angrily.

"Calm down, Bud," Krackers said, "you know I can't understand you when you get excited."

Hair continued to buzz.

"What is Hair saying?" Nursie asked.

"He's saying something like," Krackers tried to explain, 'they're here, they've found me!'

The image cleared to reveal a direct copy of Hair, but more like a swarm.

Hair buzzed urgently.

"Slow down," Krackers said in a calming tone. "Why are they bad?" Hair's buzzing calmed slightly but remained serious.

Hair's home planet, Trezses.

The Trezslings were a peaceful race. They flitted from place to place, floating on the breeze. One, in particular, Hair, was curious about more than the planet. The Elders forbade any of the Trezslings from leaving.

Without warning, Hair decided to leave the planet to explore the galaxy, and the Elders didn't notice. In Hair's travels, a wormhole formed ahead and dragged Hair into it. Light years flashed by, and Hair shot out into the Sol system.

A deep-space C.R.A.P.I. mining team captured Hair, sent it to the

C.R.A.P.I. labs, and they studied it for some time before a young man volunteered, and the rest is history.

Present day flashes back.

Hair continued to buzz urgently.

"Don't worry, Bud," Krackers said assuredly, "I won't let anything happen to you."

"I've apprised C.R.A.P.I. Command of the situation," Nursie started. "They said they would defuse it." Hair buzzed again.

"I know they're exactly like you," Krackers said, "and I know they're dangerous. Is there anything that may defeat them?"

Hair hummed, then went quiet. After a moment, Hair buzzed again.

"Really?" Krackers raised an eyebrow. "An electromagnetic pulse, you say? Let's get down to the lab."

At the Armament. Special. Section.

The tech met Krackers and Nursie at the door.

"Krackers, Bre," the tech smiled, "what can I do for you two?" "I need an electromagnetic pulse weapon."

"We have two," the tech said. "One is incorporated into the Reality Inc. Space Station weaponry; it's an electromagnetic pulse generator. The other is in the armoury. They are both extremely experimental.

I'll go and grab the gun." The tech went into the back and returned with a bulky gun. He handed it over to Krackers.

"It's not light," Krackers said, sizing up the weapon.

"It takes fifteen seconds to charge," the tech explained. "It can also fire projectiles."

"Thanks for that," Krackers said, then turned to Nursie. "We've got to get back to the Space Station."

The Reality Inc. Space Station.

The elevator to the Space Station opened. Krackers and Nursie entered the control room. Nursie sat down and tapped on a keyboard. A large monitor rose, showing numerous red dots converging on the station.

Krackers

Krackers went to the weapons array control and charged up the electromagnetic pulse generator. It whined and hummed as it built up power.

"One million kilometres and closing," Nursie yelled. "There's a lot of them, they're in a tight formation!"

"E.M.P. charge is at eighty-five per cent and climbing," Krackers yelled back.

"One hundred thousand kilometres and closing," Nursie continued. "The swarm has split into two!"

"E.M.P. charge is at ninety-five per cent and climbing," Krackers cried out.

"Fifty thousand kilometres and closing." Nursie kept counting down.

"E.M.P. fully charged," Krackers yelled as a green light flickered on. "Bring up tactical!"

Tactical flashed on the main screen. Calculations rolled by while the targeting computer showed the optimal attack vector.

Hair buzzed angrily.

"Hair says to turn the mic on," Krackers translated. He switched the mic to send. "Go!"

Hair buzzed and cooed. A moment later, the message was received, and an answer sent.

The speaker screamed and squealed.

"Wow, Hair," Krackers said, "they really want you." Hair hummed and vibrated.

"I understand that," Krackers replied. "Can you tell your people you're happy here?" He opened the mic.

Hair zimmed, hummed and buzzed.

There was silence. On the screen, the red dots converged into one huge blob, approaching at a high rate of knots.

"You're going to have to call them off, Hair," Krackers stated. "Much closer, and they're going to become friends." Hair screamed and howled.

The speaker stayed silent.

The red dots continued converging; the huge blob continued to grow.

Krackers was about to speak when, from the speaker, a cacophony of sounds spewed forth. Krackers always understood Hair, but these 'sounds' were different. Faster, lilting, raw.

Hair buzzed and hummed.

"I understood some of it," Krackers said. "I missed the last part." Hair tweeted and hummed.

"So, they want you back?" Hair buzzed.

"It's great that you want to stay," Krackers smiled, "but you say they won't take 'no' for an answer. You know we'll have to use the E.M.P. cannon on them?"

Hair buzzed and hummed. "Mic's on."

Hair screamed and howled. The speaker screamed back.

"Now, that was uncalled for," Krackers spat. "Your friends aren't very nice!"

Hair buzzed in agreement.

"Tell them," Krackers said, "if they proceed, we WILL use the E.M.P. cannon."

Hair screamed into the mic.

On the scanner, the enemy mass formed into two separate groups, then split into two more. The speaker went silent.

Hair buzzed at Krackers.

Krackers went to 'fire control' and warmed up the cannon. He typed on the keyboard, and the cannon started to whine and drone. The targeting computer activated and zeroed in on the intended enemy. On the screen, four separate targets were acquired. Coordinates flashed by, showing distance and angle of attack.

"Are you sure about this, Hair?" Hair buzzed.

"But they're your people," Krackers sympathised. "As long as you're sure?"

Hair buzzed and hummed.

"Okay, just as long as you're sure." Krackers targeted the first group and activated the E.M.P. cannon.

The E.M.P. wave rippled out toward its intended victims. The wave fanned out, wrapping around three of the enemies. They shorted and arced, setting them adrift. The enemies continued, bypassing their fallen compatriots. The enemy count now exceeded thirty and kept advancing.

Krackers unleashed volley after volley of pulses, creating an E.M.P. wall. The frontline smashed into it with force. Thirteen of the enemies exploded, arcing showers of electricity. The remaining fourteen split into two groups and continued their onslaught. They were getting closer; they could be seen as small dots in deep space.

At this stage, Hair really didn't have much input—but that was about to change. Hair flared up on Krackers' head, seemingly incensed at the attack. Hair snapped at the air, and Krackers tried to make sense of Hair's anger.

"Slow down," Krackers said, "you know I can't understand you when you talk so fast."

Hair slowed down.

"So, you were the high Sachem Padrone of your country? Sorry, what?"

Hair buzzed annoyingly.

"Sorry, the head of your people?" Krackers said. "There was an overthrow, and you became a political prisoner. That still doesn't explain the hostility?"

Hair pulsed.

"Okay, let me get this straight," Krackers said, trying to grasp the enormity of the problem. "You were the high Sachem Padrone, then they overthrew you, making you a political prisoner?"

Hair buzzed.

"So, they were going to execute you to appease your god," Krackers said in horror. "You escaped, and now they want to bring you back to perform the ceremony. Is that about it?"

Hair buzzed apologetically.

"And you're really sorry." Krackers smiled. "You are my partner, so you have nothing to apologise for." Hair cooed.

"Now, the problem at hand is," Krackers furrowed his brows, "to discourage your 'subjects' from executing you."

Currently, Nursie had been sitting quietly, taking in the one-sided conversation.

"How are we going to stop them from attacking?" Krackers ruffled Hair.

"Why don't we," Nursie piped up, "give them a reason not to attack?

Hair, could you show me what your god looks like?" Hair buzzed excitedly.

On one of the monitors, a picture of a being appeared. It looked like a larger version of Hair. Although, it had eight hairy arms and, at the end of the arms, were eight, razor-sharp knives.

"Now, if we project a huge hologram of Hair's god," Nursie said, in a matter-of-fact way "then we get Hair to warn them, linking him to the hologram. I'll modulate Hair's vocals and that should scare them off.

"And that's why I love you so," Krackers blurted out. After an awkward minute, "let's set this up."

On the external monitor, the aggressors were within striking distance and closing.

"Hologram's ready," Nursie started.

"Hair's vocals are synced to the hologram," Krackers yelled. "Activating god hologram."

Outside the space station.

A huge hologram appeared, two hundred times the size of the attackers. The swarm swam to a halt.

"I hope this works," Nursie whispered.

"I've edited the hologram," Krackers whispered back.

Outside, the hologram screeched, pulsed and growled.

"I've modified the hologram; tell them that you shall dispose of the prisoner." Hair repeated what Krackers had said.

Outside the space station, the hologram reached behind and brought forth a squirming Hair. It released Hair, then all eight arms spun their knives and decimated Hair, sucking in the remains.

"Okay, Hair," Krackers said, "tell them to go or else."

The hologram made a threatening gesture, then exploded in multiple flashing lights. The swarm hesitated, floating and bobbing.

"They're not going," Nursie said.

"Hair, say 'GO NOW!'" Krackers said as he activated the hologram.

Outside the space station.

The hologram appeared and menaced the hesitating swarm. With a booming screech, the swarm moved away from the space station and back towards their planet.

Back at the newly built I Scream, U Scream, ice cream parlour.

Krackers and Hair were demolishing a five-litre tub of ice cream. Spoons and Hair flashed and blurred as they devoured the tub; ice cream was flying everywhere. Yet another tub was brought to them and they continued to gorge on it.

Nursie had decided to take a defensive stance by sitting in the next booth. As the aftermath finished, Hair snaked about, cleaning up all the spillage, including Krackers' face. When Hair had finished, Nursie rose and sat next to Krackers.

"So, we all good?" Nursie smirked.

Hair cooed, flowing out and caressing Nursie's face. Nursie, in turn, ruffled Hair.

"Now Mister," Nursie turned her attention to Krackers, "you said something about marriage. We really should start planning to make me an honest woman."

"Ummm," Krackers said, "I did, didn't I? Then, I think we shall." After some thought, "I have a great idea! We should have the wedding here!"

"Maybe we should give it some more thought." Hair flowed around the two of them, cooing away.

"Hair's right," Krackers laughed, "as long as we're together, it doesn't matter where it takes place."

Eighteen.

Reality Strikes Again!

Karma was a bustling mega-city and, with any mega-city, crime was rife. C.R.A.P.I. was the avenging angel, who watched silently over Karma. C.R.A.P.I. Agents stood vigilantly waiting for the call to arms.

There was a rash of high-end burglaries in Karma and Krackers was on the case. C.R.A.P.I. deemed it worthy for him to investigate. Although the Karma Police started to investigate, the C.R.A.P.I. Agent superseded them and took on the case.

At present, Krackers was in his ward, standing on his head, chuckling. A beep from his hospital bracelet made him fall in a giggling heap. As he sat up, Nursie wiggled in and up to Krackers. He looked up at her through tears of joy, his eye twitched at her.

"Is it time?" Krackers chuckled.

"Yes, Michael," Nursie cooed, "it's time. I have the details, are you ready?"

"I was born ready, baby," a cheeky smirk flashed across his face.

Nursie leant in and kissed him fully. The K.I.S.S. 'Knowledge In Saliva Sample' transferred the relevant information to him and he quite liked it. Finally, the kiss finished, both sighed at the ending. They both had their eyes closed, savouring the last of the effects.

Krackers was the first to open his eyes, his eye twitched a few times. Finally, Nursie opened her eyes and smiled.

"What about another K.I.S.S?" Krackers smirked cheekily, "maybe I missed something?"

"I'm sure all the data was transferred," Nursie smiled, and it was such a pretty smile.

"Okay then," Krackers did a cartwheel. "Hair, my faithful partner, let's go and see what the naughty people did." Hair flowed out and cradled Nursie's face; she smiled and ruffled Hair. As Krackers started to leave, he turned to Nursie and smirked.

"Make sure the ice cream is cold and your kisses are hot." Hair made slurping noises. With that, he ran out of the room and crashed into the door frame. "I meant to do that." He turned; a smirk filled his face.

Outside the Peter Adams Memorial Psychiatric Hospital.

Bob leant against his armour-plated, deep blue ice cream van. He liked his new role as transportation for C.R.A.P.I. Agents, especially Krackers. Although Krackers still worried him, it was Hair that really freaked him out. He tried not to show it, but his self-preservation didn't always agree.

Krackers came running out of the hospital, a game of touch you-last in full swing. He tapped Hair and tried to run away. Of course, Hair reared up then tapped Krackers' legs, causing him to stumble but, Krackers being Krackers, he turned it into a graceful swan dive. At the last moment, he tucked, rolled and jumped up, hands above his head in front of Bob.

"Tah-dah!" He flourished a bow then looked at Bob. "Well, young Bob, are we ready for our next great adventure?" He smirked, "Now, I'd give you a K.I.S.S. but I don't think we're that close. So, get in touch with C.R.A.P.I. and get the relevant information on this case."

It took Bob a few moments to comprehend the request; secretly, he was quite impressed with Krackers' flair. He shook his head and climbed into the van's driver's seat. Krackers cartwheeled over the van, landing on the passenger's side. He climbed in as Bob was getting the info on the case.

"Well," Krackers smiled, "brrm, brrm?"

"Okay," Bob said, "first stop is 'The Heavenly Reach,' apartment 209." He activated the anti-grav and the ice cream van shot up into the heavens.

"Wee," Krackers squealed, "up we go into the wild blue yonder!"

"Unauthorised vehicle, this is Karma Control," the comms activated, "Please register a flight plan!"

"This is C.R.A.P.I. vehicle I.C.E. 01," Bob replied, "transporting C.R.A.P.I. Agent Krackers, en route to The Heavenly Reach."

"Krackers, eh?" Karma Control replied. "My condolences, and you're cleared to proceed. Good luck, I think you'll need it."

"Thanks, Control." Bob turned to his passenger. "Looks like you're well known."

"We aim to please," Krackers beamed. He turned his attention to Hair. "Touched you last!"

"How about," Bob suggested, "we play 'who can be the last to talk'?"

Krackers went to open his mouth, then thought better of it. He raised a finger to his mouth and gave Bob a nod. The rest of the trip was bathed in silence. Bob smiled as he watched Krackers agonise in the uncomfortable quietness.

Bob guided his van onto the rooftop landing pad. As he touched down, Bob noticed several high-end vehicles.

"We'll have to put the quiet game on hold," Krackers said,; he really did love the sound of his own voice. He leapt out of the ice cream van. "Heigh-ho, heigh-ho, it's off to work we go."

He skipped to the elevator and waited. Momentarily, the elevator door opened, and an elderly lady exited the lift, cradling the ugliest dog he had ever seen.

"What a lovely baby," Krackers remarked. "Koochie koochie coo." He reached out; the dog lunged at Krackers.

"Humpf," the lady lifted her head, ignoring the peasant.

Krackers dove into the elevator as the doors closed. He stabbed the two -hundredth button and the elevator dropped to the appropriate floor. The lift clanged, the doors opened and Krackers jumped out.

He made his way to apartment 209; the door was open and taped off, Several people were in the apartment. He ducked under the tape and into the room,; a policeman challenged him. "People, people," Krackers called out. "I'm Krackers!"

"You don't look it," the policeman started.

"Why do people keep saying that?" Krackers shook his head. "I am a

C.R.A.P.I. Agent; please direct me to the person in charge?"

The policeman pointed to a tall, thin man with a shock of hair that could rival Hair itself. Krackers walked over and up to the man.

"Sir," Krackers said, "I'm C.R.A.P.I. Agent Krackers, Please bring me up to speed?" The man looked Krackers up and down. Finally, he spoke.

"I am Investigator Vig Geni'tals," the Detective squeaked, his highpitched voice warbling. Although Krackers was speaking with a man, he had the voice of a girl. "The perps were specific; they only stole one thing, a laptop."

"A laptop?" Krackers scratched his chin. "Why a laptop? What was on the laptop? Who owned the laptop?"

"The owner is Chief Administrator Gerald Snew; he works for Reality Inc. As to what was on the laptop, that's classified!" Investigator Geni'tals squeaked.

"Maybe for you, Detective," Krackers started, "but not for me. Hair, contact Nursie. Tell her to get clearance for the content of Chief Administrator Gerald Snew's laptop."

Hair raised up and vibrated. A moment later, Hair buzzed. "Well, that's interesting," Krackers said.

"So," the Investigator squeaked, "what's on the laptop?"

"It's classified," Krackers smirked. "It's above your pay grade. Finish up here and send any relevant information to C.R.A.P.I. Central." He turned on his heels and marched out of the apartment.

The Heavenly Reach rooftop landing pad.

Krackers exited the elevator and noticed Bob had his back turned. His smirk filled his face; he crouched and snuck towards him. When he got within arm's length, he pounced.

"Boo!" Krackers grabbed Bob's shoulder. He turned quickly, his eyes rolled up into his head and he dropped in a dead faint. "Oh dear, I think I've broken Bob." After some time, Bob came to and looked up at Krackers.

"What happened?" Bob asked.

"You don't remember?" Krackers questioned.

"No, I don't," Bob explained. "One minute I was standing against the van and the next thing, I was staring up at you. What happened?"

"It's a long story, young Bob," Krackers said as he helped Bob up. "What's our next destination?" Bob climbed into the driver's seat. He leant down and tapped at a monitor.

"Next destination is 'The Affluence,'" Bob said. "This one is interesting,; it's a floating apartment block. It's suspended in the lower atmosphere,; only the well-to-do and the wealthy can afford to live there." Bob tapped the screen,. "Most of C.R.A.P.I.'s upper management live there, so be on your best behaviour!"

"I always do, young Bob," Krackers placed his hand on his heart.

On the way to 'The Affluence'.

Bob's armour-plated ice -cream van gained altitude rapidly. Before them, The Affluence loomed large

"Wow," Krackers whispered in awe. "Is this heaven, Bob?"

"Attention, unauthorised vehicle," the comms blared. "You are entering restricted air space!. Turn back or be fired upon!"

"Affluence Control," Bob said, "this is C.R.A.P.I. transport conveying

C.R.A.P.I. Agent Krackers, requesting landing clearance."

"Apologies, C.R.A.P.I. transport," Control said. "Continue on your heading,. I will transmit landing clearance code. Welcome to The Affluence."

"Thanks, Control," Bob sounded official, "Landing clearance code received; will circle and land on Landing Pad Thirteen."

Bob made a majestic sweep of The Affluence. It was a glorious sight, more like a small city than an apartment block. The one thing Bob noticed was the missile banks that tracked him as he flew by.

"Ooh," Krackers exclaimed, "SA13 Diva surface-to-air missiles. Each is worth a small fortune; let alone the amount they have. Look, they must like us because they're following us."

Finally, Bob eased the van in, landing it on Landing Pad Thirteen. As soon as they landed, Krackers leapt out of the van and into the arms of an armed guard.

"If you will come with me, Agent Krackers," the guard said, "I will escort you to the crime scene."

"That's so sweet," Krackers clapped. "This is so exciting; I can't wait to see it. After you."

"No," the guard said, "after you, I insist!"

"Instead of the crime scene, take me to the Control Centre," Krackers commanded. "I want to see any video you might have."

"Sir," the guard said, annoyance creeping into his voice, "I was to escort you to the crime scene."

"Look, what's your name?" Krackers snapped.

"Johnson," the guard fired back.

"Okay, Johnson," Krackers snapped, "call your boss. Tell him there's a C.R.A.P.I. Agent that's slowly losing his temper!"

The guard touched his ear and muttered something. After a moment, the guard nodded and turned to Krackers.

"I'm sorry, Agent Krackers," the guard gritted his teeth. "I will take you anywhere you want to go. I am at your disposal."

"At a boy," Krackers smiled "Now we can be friends." He clapped his hands and patted the guard's back. "Let's go to the Control Centre."

"Very good, Sir," the guard said, "This way." The guard marched over to an elevator. He tapped his ID card on a pad next to the lift.

"ID Guard Johnson, access granted," a female voice stated. The doors to the elevator opened and they entered.

"Control Centre," the guard stated as he tapped his card on a pad.

"ID Guard Johnson," the female voice said. "Access granted to Control Centre!"

"She sounds cute," Krackers smirked.

"I hadn't noticed," Johnson stated. "'She' is W.E.N.D.I. Watch. Engage. Notify. Defend. Initiate. As you can see, we have the top-of the-line security."

As the elevator door opened, Krackers was impressed with the whiteness and all the flashing lights.

"Ooh," Krackers exclaimed, "shiny!" He reached out and walked into the Control Centre. Hair reared up and slapped Krackers across the face, then buzzed.

Johnson reached for his gun, so did three other guards. Krackers raised his hands; Hair reached up as well.

"Gentlemen," Krackers said, carefully choosing his words, "this is my partner Hair. Check with C.R.A.P.I; they can verify this. I can wait."

Krackers suddenly found the ceiling interesting. whistled as he looked up. He knew Hair could rip apart all four guards, so he wasn't too worried. After five minutes, Johnson cleared his throat.

"Once again, Sir," Johnson admitted, "I apologise for myself and Security. People, please give Agent Krackers, any and all help that he needs."

"That's okay," Krackers said as he lowered his hands, "A common mistake. Show me the video feed to the apartment that was burglarised?"

"Apartments," Johnson corrected. "Two apartments were broken into. We have locked them, and no one entered the domiciles."

"Okay, show me the feeds to both domiciles." Krackers was ushered to a monitor; a young woman sat at the terminal. "What's your name?"

"What has her name got to do with anything," anger crept into Johnson's voice.

"Back off, Johnson," Krackers snapped. "I'm a C.R.A.P.I. Agent!" "My name is Sanders, Sir," the woman said, concern on her face.

"Hello, Sanders," Krackers smiled. "I'm Agent Krackers. Could you show me the first break-in?"

"The first break-in was in Domicile 111. It happened at 02.:18," Sanders said as she tapped on the keyboard. A number of panels appeared on the screen. "In each of the rooms, we have triple security. Three cameras per room,: two that the owner knows about, and another—as deep security."

"So, you're telling me, there is one camera per room that no one but Security knows about?"

"Yes, Sir," Sanders said. "That camera is for the owner's own security. It is triggered by motion." She tapped the screen on the Cam Sec Lounge panel. It opened and revealed a spacious room. Two opulent sofas and tasteful accoutrements adorned the lounge. Three silhouettes moved through the lounge and through an open door.

Cam Sec Hallway showed the silhouettes moving down the corridor. Cam Sec Room 101 showed a workshop. The room was tidy but cluttered. On the workbench were tools, arranged orderly, and a piece of equipment that Krackers wasn't familiar with. One of the silhouettes reached out and the item disappeared. All three silhouettes made their way to the entrance and vanished.

"That's interesting," Krackers said, rubbing his chin. "Show me the second break-in, please, Sanders."

Sanders tapped at the keyboard and new panels appeared on the screen. It was time stamped at 02.:39. She tapped on Domicile 230, Cam Sec Lounge. The same thing unfolded except in Room One. It showed a small object encased in glass; the cabinet was in an office. The silhouettes obtained the object then disappeared.

"Are there any feeds outside both domiciles?" Krackers asked.

"The silhouettes weren't captured on any other cameras although there were glitches," Sanders said. "I'll show you what I mean." She tapped on the keyboard, bringing up all the external cameras, there were a lot of them. She tapped again; this time, most of the cameras disappeared, leaving a direct path, going deep into the structure.

"What's in the basement?" Krackers noticed the path the glitches were taking.

"The service area," Sanders said. "The servants' quarters, the kitchen and the delivery dock."

"I'll need a copy of the domiciles' feeds and the cameras that glitched," Krackers asked. Sanders looked up at Johnson, who nodded. Sanders reached for a USB stick. "No need for that. Hair, if you would be so kind?"

Hair flowed out; some of the strands entered the USB port. After a moment, Hair retracted, flowing back into Krackers' skull.

"Okay, Johnson," Krackers requested, "now show me the domiciles in question." Johnson nodded and they made their way back to the elevator. Once W.E.N.D.I. authorised Johnson, they entered the lift and it stopped on Domicile 111's floor. They walked down a corridor to Domicile 111. Once at the door, Johnson tapped his ID on the pad next to the door.

"ID Guard Johnson, access granted!" W.E.N.D.I. stated. The door to the domicile opened.

"Wait here," Krackers commanded. "I don't want you to contaminate the crime scene." He walked in and closed the door. "Hair, taking into account the downloaded Domicile 111 feed, create a wireframe of the apartment and add in the three silhouettes."

Over Krackers' sight, a glowing wireframe of the domicile appeared. Before him, the three silhouettes stood.

"Hair," Krackers commanded, "run simulation, considering all variables!"

The wireframe silhouettes moved through the lounge and Krackers followed. They walked into the workshop up to the piece of equipment on the workbench.

"Freeze simulation," Krackers said. "Hair, using security feed from before the event, extrapolate the piece of equipment on the workbench and show me what it is, please."

Everything stopped. The wireframe zoomed in on the hardware. It changed from a wireframe simulation to a three-dimensional object. The object lifted from the workbench and hovered before Krackers' sight. It slowly rotated in front of him. It spun on its first axis, then on its second axis and finally on its third.

"What do you make of it, Hair?" Krackers pondered for a moment. "Okay, send it to C.R.A.P.I., let's see what they make of it." Hair vibrated and buzzed.

"I think you're right," Krackers agreed. "See if you can access the Reality Inc. database. Since C.R.A.P.I. owns it, you shouldn't have a problem. Let me know what you find. Let's wrap it up here and go to the second break-in."

Krackers walked to the door and it slid open. Johnson was waiting, his face filled with annoyance.

"I hope I didn't inconvenience you too much?" Krackers tried to hide a smirk. "Please take me to the second break-in?"

"That would be Domicile 230. This way." They walked in silence to the elevator. After W.E.N.D.I.'s security checks, they arrived at Domicile 230.

"This shouldn't take too long," Krackers said. "I can deal with this, if you have more pressing duties."

"I need to be here," Johnson spat. "You don't have the security clearance."

"Hair," Krackers said nonchalantly, "would you kindly open the door?"

Hair flowed out and onto the door pad. After a moment, W.E.N.D.I. activated.

"Agent Krackers," W.E.N.D.I. stated, "access granted." The Domicile door slid open.

"Don't let me keep you from your work," Krackers smirked and entered the apartment. Johnson stormed off in a huff.

"Okay, Hair," Krackers commanded, "let's go through the numbers again." The Domicile door slid closed.

The Affluence's Security Centre.

The elevator door slid open and Krackers walked into the Security Centre and up to Johnson.

"Thank you, Johnson," Krackers smiled, "I have what I need. C.R.A.P.I. will be in touch. I'll show myself out." He turned and walked back to the elevator. Hair flowed into the elevator's pad. The door opened and Krackers entered and waved at the security team.

The Affluence's rooftop, landing pad 13.

"Let's get out of here," Krackers hurried to Bob's armour-plated ice cream van. "I think I've worn out my welcome!" Bob jumped into the driver's seat and the van took off.

"What did you do?" Bob peeled off and headed for the Peter Adams Memorial Psychiatric Hospital.

"I kinda hacked The Affluence's Security A.I.," Krackers smirked. "Wait for it."

Bob's control panel suddenly flashed, warning of multiple missile launches, tracking the van.

"And pissed off the Head of Security," Krackers said. "Hair, tell W.E.N.D.I. to cancel the missiles."

Hair rose and vibrated. The three missiles suddenly collided with each other, brightening the sky momentarily.

The Peter Adams Memorial Psychiatric Hospital.

"Hair," Krackers said as he walked into his room, "notify Nursie to meet me here." He walked over to one of the walls and touched it; a keyboard and monitor appeared. "Hair, download all the information about the two break-ins.."

Hair rose, strands flowing into the input port. Hair vibrated and, on the monitor, video files flashed by, followed by data files. By the time Hair had downloaded them, Nursie wiggled in and up to Krackers. She snuggled into the back of his neck.

"Work first," Krackers said, "fun later. Did you get the information I requested from Reality Inc?"

Nursie kissed the back of his neck then went to the wall and tapped on the keyboard.

"The two pieces of equipment from The Affluence's break-ins," Nursie explained, "are parts of a new weapon system for an armoured exo-skeleton."

"What about the stolen laptop?"

"The laptop had all the schematics and designs for the project," Nursie continued. "The likely culprits are part of C.R.I.M.E."

"The Shrink!" Krackers punched a hole in the wall.

"Calm down," Nursie said. "There is something I haven't told you. I managed to activate a trace on the laptop." Nursie flashed a beautiful smile.

Krackers did some backflips around the room and finished with a roundhouse, landing at the keyboard.

"Show me, show me," Krackers said as he bounced from one leg to the other. He started to clap as Nursie wiggled back to the keyboard and started tapping on it. On the monitor, a map of Karma appeared. A blinking blue arrow signified the Peter Adams Memorial Psychiatric Hospital; a red arrow tracked the stolen laptop. After some time, the red arrow finally stopped at some abandoned warehouses in the Outer Sprawl. Nursie tapped the keyboard again and an address flashed up over the map.

"Don't you think that was too easy?" Krackers wasn't convinced about the tracking.

"Why do you say that?" Nursie looked at Krackers.

"We're talking about C.R.I.M.E. and, especially, the Shrink! It looks like a set-up to me," Krackers explained.

"Okay," Nursie agreed. "Since you've dealt with him a number of times, I'll believe you. So, what's our next step?"

"I'll go in and see if I'm right," Krackers smirked.

"If you know it's a trap," Nursie said, "why would you go in? It's a suicide mission!"

"Because I'm Krackers!" Krackers leapt into the air, did a flip and landed in a superhero landing. He stood up and hugged Nursie. "It'll be okay, remember I love you, Bre," Krackers whispered.

"I hope so," Nursie whispered back.

"Hair," Krackers started, "are you ready for a suicidal mission, with little chance of success?" Hair rose and vibrated.

"I agree," Krackers laughed,. "I am not crazy, but I am Krackers! Are you ready to go?"

Hair buzzed.

"Let's go," bravado in Krackers' voice. "Nursie, please keep an eye on me?"

"You know I will," Nursie said.

Krackers blew a kiss at Nursie and ran out of the room.

Outside the Peter Adams Memorial Psychiatric Hospital.

Bob reclined in his armour-plated ice cream van. Krackers came bounding up onto the van and up to Bob. He jumped into the passenger seat and looked at Bob.

"Let's go, young Bob," Krackers commanded. "Time's-a-wasting and the bad guys need defeatin."

"Okay," Bob answered, "where are we off to?" The van lifted into the sky.

"Nursie has the details," Krackers said. "It involves an armoured exo-skeleton, C.R.I.M.E. and the Shrink are involved! It's going to be a suicide mission." Krackers giggled and clapped his hands.

"Wait, what?" Bob stuttered.

"Don't worry, young Bob, you'll be safe," Krackers stated, "You know me?"

"That's what scares me," Bob answered. After a moment, the coordinates came in, showing the stolen laptop at the warehouse at the Outer Sprawl Industrial Park. "I've got the coordinates, Now, what do you mean by suicide mission?"

"It's just an expression, young Bob," Krackers giggled. "You know, like 'sink or swim' or 'live or die'. After all, we are going after C.R.I.M.E. and the Shrink."

"I'm an idiot," Bob muttered. "I had a good life selling ice cream. Now, I'm a guy, transporting a crazy person into a suicidal mission." "Did you say something, young Bob?"

"No," Bob said, "just talking to myself."

"Hahaha," Krackers snickered, "I do that all the time." He clapped his hands, "We have something in common."

The rest of the trip was uneventful. Bob kept on muttering to himself. Finally, according to Bob, the Outer Sprawl Industrial Park came into view.

"Young Bob," Krackers commanded, "land at the entrance and wait for me there. I want to keep you safe."

The armour-plated van dropped from the skies and touched down at the Industrial Park, scattering litter as it landed. Krackers leapt out of the van and turned to Bob.

"Stay here," Krackers instructed, "and I'll let you know when I need you, it could get hairy."

"Okay," Bob nodded, "I'll wait for your signal."

Inside the Outer Sprawl Industrial Park

"Hair," Krackers said as he ran through the Park, "show me the Industrial Park and where any bad guys are."

Hair overlaid a glowing map over Krackers' eyesight. It showed Krackers as a green dot and several enemies as red dots. He ran hard, humming the tune of 'Mission Impossible' as he reached a block from the first bad guy.

"Well, Viewers," Krackers whispered, "yet another dangerous mission. Ney, a suicidal mission! So, if I don't make it, don't be sad, just whisper my name in awe. Hair, stealth mode!"

Hair flowed up and over Krackers, then vibrated as they shimmered into nothingness. He moved away from the cover; the air rippled around the hidden C.R.A.P.I. Agent. He reached the first red dot and surveyed the area. He looked up, and the red dot started blinking.

"Hair," Krackers hissed, "get me up there!" Part of Hair shot up and effortlessly rose with Krackers, to the top of the warehouse. The bad guy lay, with his hands on a machine gun. Krackers moved with deliberate precision until he reached the prone enemy. He nodded, and Hair shot out, cleaving the man in two. Blood flowed out and around the dead body. Hair shook and vibrated the blood off them. Once it was gone, Krackers consulted the map.

There were four red dots left. Krackers leapt from sea container to sea container, dispatching enemy after enemy. When he finished, Hair flowed back into Krackers' head. He dropped to the ground, surveying the area; his map was devoid of red dots.

"That was way too easy," Krackers mumbled. "Hair, deep scan!" Hair rose and vibrated.

A warehouse, two blocks ahead of him was filled with blinking red targets. Krackers crept closer, and flattened himself against the building.

"Hair," Krackers whispered, "I think a rooftop entrance is the way to go." Hair shot tendrils up to the roof and lifted his partner. Once there, he crept to a skylight and peered in. There was a flurry of bad guys, urgently completing their tasks.

"I think this needs a superhero landing." He jumped up and crashed through the skylight, raining down glass over the bad guys. He landed on one knee and a fist, the concrete cracking. There were several

C.R.I.M.E. Agents, and they all stopped what they were doing to stare.

"Knock, knock," Krackers laughed. "Hair, save one, dispatch the rest!"

Hair fanned out, slicing bad guy after bad guy,; it was a bloodbath. Finally, one man, covered in blood, stood shaking. Krackers walked slowly over to him, Hair rearing up, and fanning out behind him.

"Hey there," Krackers chuckled, "you saw what my partner did to your friends, so answer the next question very carefully, for it may save your life. What are you up to?"

"We've stolen an exo-skeleton from Reality Inc." The man crumbled and blurted out the plan. "We also stole a new weapon system."

There was a rumble from behind the wall, and it exploded. The exo-skeleton moved through the rubble. Krackers cartwheeled away from the man, as the exo-skeleton fired its weapons. The air rippled as it hit the man, vaporising him instantly.

"Michael," the man in the exo-skeleton boomed, "so glad to see you!"

"The Shrink! It's Krackers, Krackers," Krackers spat. "I see you went and got some balls!" The exo-skeleton whirred as it moved toward him. "I think we should take this outside!" Krackers cartwheeled and backflipped toward an open door. The exo-skeleton fired again, missing him and vaporising part of a wall.

"Thank you," Krackers chirped as he dove through the hole.

Once outside, Krackers went into a defensive stance and waited. Suddenly, the door and part of a wall exploded, and the Shrink came crashing out. Krackers could clearly see the man operating the suit. The man had a smiley face mask on, his facial features concealed.

"I'll finally be able to squash you," the Shrink spat, "like the bug you are! Firstly, let's deactivate your partner."

The exo-skeleton whirled as it changed weapons. It fired, catching Krackers mid flip. Suddenly, Hair dropped lifelessly to the ground. Krackers dropped in a crumpled heap, the weight of the now defunct Hair restricting his movement.

"Vaporising is too good for you," the Shrink laughed. "I'm thinking of tearing you limb from limb!" He advanced towards Krackers.

Krackers struggled, trying to move some of Hair.

"I'm going to enjoy this!" The exo-skeleton trudged forward, its mechanical hands reaching out.

There was a sudden explosion which rocked the exoskeleton, It stumbled to the side, then tried to regain itself.

"Krackers," a familiar voice boomed from above, "I think you might need a hand."

"Bob?"

"That's me," Bob boomed. "I thought I'd check out my weapon system."

"Tell Nursie," Krackers yelled as the armour-plated ice cream van came into view, "to send the reactivate code for Hair!"

The exo-skeleton finally righted itself, and the Shrink looked up at a new target. The weapon system whirled as it selected a new weapon. Its machine gun clicked and fired at Bob, bullets ricocheting off the underside of the van.

"Hair, buddy," Krackers pleaded, "are you with us?" Hair continued to stay limp. "Come on, Bud, you've got to help me!" As if answering his plea, Hair vibrated and retracted back into Krackers' skull.

"Welcome back," Krackers laughed. "I'm glad you're here!" Hair rose, vibrated and buzzed.

"I don't think that language is called for," Krackers chuckled. "Let's try to keep the Shrink intact. Let's dismantle the suit, then take the Shrink into custody."

Hair buzzed, then, several strands shot out, wrapping around the legs of the exoskeleton, and toppling it. With a crunch, the exo-skeleton fell.

After Hair ripped out the weapons from the frame, Hair righted the suit. After wrapping around ninety per cent of the frame, Krackers walked up to the exo-skeleton and leered at the Shrink.

"Now it's time to unmask you," Krackers said as he reached for the Shrink's mask.

"I have one trick left," the Shrink laughed. "It has been fun, but I have to go!" The escape module clinked as it fired its thrusters, rocketing the Shrink, up and away from the Industrial Park.

"Do you want to go after him?" Bob yelled as he brought the van down for a landing.

"Nah, it's okay," Krackers said, "there's always next time. Contact Nursie and get a clean-up crew to mop up this site."

Inside the Peter Adams Memorial Psychiatric Hospital.

"I'm sorry I didn't capture the Shrink," Krackers said apologetically.

"It's okay," Nursie said, "we got some good intel from the site." Nursie wiggled over to Krackers and sat on his lap, arms around his neck. "I do have something for you and Hair." At the other end of the room, something was covered with a sheet.

Hair made slurping noises.

Nursie stood up and wiggled over to it. After uncovering it, two drums of ice cream sat there. Krackers ran over and popped open both drums. Hair dove in and started slurping.

"You know," Nursie said as she walked up to Krackers and kissed his forehead. "I'm glad you survived this mission; I'd hate to have lost you." Nursie walked to the door and chuckled as she left the room, leaving Hair and Krackers to enjoy their treats.

Nineteen.

Perchance To Dream.

The Reality Inc. Space Station floated serenely in the ionosphere. The edge of space seemed tranquil and untroubled. The view from the Station was spectacular; it sat in a geostationary orbit over Karma and its citizens.

Krackers had been on a gruelling seventy-two-hour surveillance shift. Now, he only had an hour to go before he could travel planet-side and plant his feet firmly on solid ground. He lay his head on the desk and closed his eyes for a moment.

A beep made him jump, and Hair flailed in surprise. He tapped at the keyboard. The readout showed everything seemed fine except for an unscheduled launch from the Outer Sprawl. He grabbed a communicator and called C.R.A.P.I. Command. On the small screen of the com, the beautiful, smiling face of Nursie appeared.

"What a pleasant surprise, Michael," Nursie fluffed up her bed hair. "To what do I owe the pleasure of your call?"

"You know when you told me to call if there was anything unusual happening?" Krackers tapped on the console. "What about this?"

On Nursie's communicator, Krackers' picture was replaced with the live feed of the rocket launch from the Outer Sprawl. As she watched in horror, another launch fired off, followed by another.

The control panel Krackers had been resting on suddenly exploded in flashing lights. Around him, sirens wailed. Krackers stabbed at various buttons, finally shutting down the piercing noise.

"Michael," Nursie yelled through the comms, "what's happening?"

"Bre, bear with me," Krackers replied, "all hell's breaking loose. I'm releasing countermeasures." He watched on the monitor as canisters were released. They dropped down under the Space Station. The canisters opened, forming into a large, sparkling net. Krackers released another four, which positioned themselves to cover the Space Station. As they finished, a rocket hit one of the nets. It tangled itself in the mesh; it contracted, causing the rocket to implode. The net then reset, splaying out and continuing to sparkle.

"I've always wanted to use the particle cannon." He giggled and tapped a button. A joystick appeared, then a screen rose and flipped over, revealing a targeting system. He grasped the joystick, aimed, and fired. Krackers laughed, giggling as the beam hit a rocket.

"I love this shit." He locked onto another. "Take that! Hahaha!" His target exploded. After six missiles had been destroyed, Krackers jumped off the chair and did a victory shuffle. His victory was short-lived when an alarm sounded. A missile had manoeuvred around the countermeasures. Krackers changed the position of the nets, but to no avail, as the missile thudded into the space elevator and didn't explode.

"I'll show you for attacking me!" He grabbed the joystick and repositioned the particle cannon. The targeting computer zeroed in on the launch site. "Take that," Krackers chuckled as he pressed the fire button.

The particle beam shot down, impacting the launch site. It exploded, decimating the site and everything around it. Krackers fired repeatedly. He squealed in joy as the targeted area grew larger. Suddenly, the particle cannon shut down.

"That's enough, Michael," Nursie said. "You've destroyed the launch site and a hundred-block radius. According to internal scanners, there's an unexploded missile in the elevator. Go down and defuse it, please be careful."

"Of course I'll be careful," Krackers scoffed. "You know me."

"That's what I'm afraid of," Nursie chuckled.

Krackers skipped over to the elevator. He tried to summon it, but nothing happened. He shrugged and went to a workman's entrance. He climbed onto the ladder and slid down it.

"Wee!" Krackers slid downward. A quarter of the way down, he slid to a stop. Below him, the nose of the missile could be plainly seen. He climbed down the final couple of rungs.

"Looks like it's firmly lodged." Krackers gave it a shove, but it stayed fixed. "It might need a firm push."

"Be careful, Michael," Nursie crackled in his ear. "Be gentle. What tools have you got?"

"I've got a hammer, sealant, and a plasma torch," Krackers stated, "and a whole lot of gumption!"

Krackers reached for the plasma torch and ignited it. It bathed the area in an eerie blue glow.

"What are you doing!?!" Nursie said, horror in her voice.

"I know what I'm doing," Krackers said indignantly. "I'll have this sucker free in a moment." He brought the plasma torch onto the surface; sparks rained forth as he began cutting it. He finished cutting the nose and it fell off, clattering down.

"Look out below!" Krackers chuckled as he watched the nose housing bounce out of view. The internal part of the missile was exposed. "This sucker's still wedged in there, it might need brute force!" Krackers grabbed the hammer and raised it above his head, bringing it down with some force.

"Nooo!" Nursie cried.

The hammer made contact. From outside the elevator, an explosion mushroomed out, ripping the elevator in two.

With a start, Krackers lifted his head, Hair flaring with the movement.

"Nursie, where are the missiles?" Krackers asked, looking about him.

"What missiles, Michael?" Nursie asked, her voice chirping through the comms.

"They were fired from the Outer Sprawl, I had to use the particle cannon."

"I think you were asleep at your post again," Nursie laughed.

"A dream? Not again! But it seemed so real." Krackers shook the cobwebs from his head.

"I'm sending someone to replace you," Nursie said. "Should be there in a moment. You, sir, are benched."

"A dream," Krackers muttered to himself, "just a dream."

Inside the Peter Adams Memorial Psychiatric Hospital.

"I think, young man, you've had a busy time, and now it's time for bed." Nursie helped Krackers into bed. She pulled the covers up and tucked him in. "That certainly was an amazing dream. Goodnight— sweet dreams." Nursie walked to the door, turned off the light, and left.

"It was only a dream," Krackers muttered as he rolled over.

Suddenly, klaxons sounded. Krackers jumped out of bed as Hair reared up. He shook his head, trying to banish the fog in his mind. He staggered to his door and looked down the corridor. C.R.A.P.I. personnel scurried by; pandemonium ensued.

"Hair," Krackers said, the fogginess still plaguing his mind, "find out what's going on."

Hair rose, vibrated, and buzzed.

"Okay," Krackers said, "find out how Nursie is, then find out the status of the Hospital." After finally shaking the last of the fog, he raced down the corridor to C.R.A.P.I. Command. Krackers found it in shambles. He scanned the area, searching for Nursie, eventually finding her near a small cave-in.

"Are you okay?" Krackers lifted her into his arms. He could see only superficial cuts and scrapes. As he started towards the infirmary, a huge screen flickered to life.

"I see you got my surprise," a silhouetted figure appeared on the screen. "Oh dear, Nursie has a boo-boo. Hahaha!" The figure threw back his head and laughed.

"The Shrink!" Krackers spat.

"In the flesh," the silhouetted figure said, "so to speak."

"What have you done?" Krackers gently placed Nursie on the floor. "I will find you and kill you!"

"I would be more concerned," the Shrink laughed, "with the other surprise I have left for you."

"And what surprise would that be?" Krackers' anger was welling up.

"Now, if I told you," the Shrink chuckled, "it wouldn't be a surprise, would it?"

"You're insane," Krackers replied.

"I'm not the only one," the Shrink growled. "Isn't that right, Michael?"

"My name," Krackers growled, "is Krackers!"

"There is, of course," the Shrink continued, "one way to stop the second surprise."

"And what would that be?" Krackers could feel his anger boiling. He tried to stifle the rage.

"Deliver the Hair A.I. to me," the Shrink growled, "and I will stop the surprise. Trust me, the second surprise is much larger than the first. You have six hours to comply!" The screen shifted to a countdown clock.

6 Hours.

"Let's get you to the infirmary." Krackers scooped up Nursie and made his way to Sick-Bay. After Nursie was checked out, the two made their way back to the Control Room.

The Control Room had been cleaned up, although there were still shorts in some of the workstations; technicians were tending to them. Some of the terminals were manned as Krackers and Nursie entered the room.

"Okay, people," Nursie yelled, "I want a damage assessment in ten minutes!"

"I'll see if Hair can track down the second '*surprise*'," Krackers said. "Hair, see if you can track down the second surprise from the Shrink."

Hair rose, vibrated, then buzzed.

"You're right," Krackers said. "Show me the video feed, thirty seconds before the explosion."

Nursie jumped onto a nearby terminal and tapped at the keyboard. On the big screen, the view was of a smooth-running Control Room. It ran for twenty-eight seconds, then the explosion erupted and the screen went dead.

"Can you pause it on the twenty-nine-second mark?" Nursie tapped on the keyboard. The twenty-nine-second mark froze. "Hair, download the footage and grid it up." Hair flowed out and into the nearest output port.

On the screen, the scene flashed by, then Hair retracted. Over Krackers' eyesight, the Control Room glowed in a grid formation. As he turned, the grid turned with him.

"Hair," Krackers commanded, "go to the twenty-nine-second mark, freeze it there, and find the blast point." On his vision, a small package sat at a terminal near the big screen, it exploded, then nothing.

"Was Hair able to find the blast point?"

"Yes, he did," Krackers said. "It was a small package near one of the terminals." Krackers pointed to the desk in question. "Hair, can you track for the second bomb? Take a sample of the bomb signature."

5 Hours.

Hair buzzed and flowed out, stopping at the blast site, then buzzed again.

"Okay, bud," Krackers said, "find me the second bomb."

Krackers walked out of the Control Room and into a corridor. Hair fanned out in front of his partner, flicking and sampling the area as they moved to another passageway.

1 hour.

After what seemed like a lifetime, the trail led them to the Armoury. Krackers stopped at the entrance.

"Hair," Krackers commanded, "scan the room for any nasty surprises."

It took some time for Hair to examine the Armoury, then he buzzed the findings.

15 minutes.

"Nursie," Krackers activated his comms, "Hair's found the bomb, it's in the armoury."

"How big is it?" There was concern in her voice.

"It's big," Krackers said grimly, "very big. I suggest you evacuate the Hospital, now! Make it quick!"

"Done," Nursie said. "Please be careful, I need you to be okay."

"Hair," Krackers said, "scan the bomb, and be mindful, it is a rather large bomb!"

Hair flowed out, fanning forward cautiously. He stopped centimetres from the device and moved around it, changing position.

5 minutes.

Hair finally finished the scan and retracted back, then buzzed.

"So, it has a secondary bomb," Krackers said. "So, can you defuse it?"

Hair buzzed forlornly.

"How long have we got?"

Hair hummed.

"We won't make it," Krackers asked quietly, "will we?"

1 minute.

Hair vibrated.

"It's been an honour knowing you," Krackers said. "Shielding me won't help, being so close… will it?"

30 seconds.

Hair buzzed and hummed.

"Well," Krackers chuckled, "it's been fun."

10 seconds.

"This is going to hurt," Krackers closed his eyes and took a deep breath, "isn't it?"

Krackers

Outside the Peter Adams Memorial Psychiatric Hospital.

Nursie had managed to evacuate all of the C.R.A.P.I. personnel and all of the patients. She sat in Bob's armour-plated ice cream van and waited.

Suddenly, the Peter Adams Memorial Psychiatric Hospital erupted in a series of large explosions. The blast radius rocked the ice-cream van, throwing it into the air.

"Nooo!" Nursie cried as the van settled back on the ground. "Michael!"

Inside the Peter Adams Memorial Psychiatric Hospital, in Michael's room.

"Arrhh," Krackers screamed as he sat up, horror in his widening eyes. "Another dream? This sucks!"

Nursie ran into his room and up to Krackers. He embraced her, kissing her deeply.

"Another nightmare?" Nursie held him close.

"It seemed so real," Krackers' eyes were still wide, reliving the nightmare. "Please make it stop… please?"

"Let's go to the Infirmary," Nursie suggested. "Maybe they can work out what's happening."

Inside the Peter Adams Memorial Psychiatric Hospital Infirmary.

Krackers lay on one of the Infirmary beds, muttering to himself. Nursie stood by him, rubbing his chest. A doctor walked up to them and smiled.

219

"Hello, I'm Doctor Pilli-Cok," the Doctor introduced herself. "What seems to be the problem?"

"Krackers has been awake for the last seventy-two hours," Nursie explained. "He's been having realistic nightmares. Every time he tries to sleep, these bad dreams appear."

"Okay, Krackers," Doctor Pilli-Cok said, "come over here and we'll scan you."

Krackers sat up, then walked over to a circular stand. He stepped onto the platform and, from above, a circular ring lowered and the scan began. A yellow light was emitted from the ring as it scanned Krackers. It dropped into the stand and the scan finished.

"Let's see what we have here," Doctor Pilli-Cok said, studying the readout. "That's interesting."

"What is it, Doctor?" Nursie helped Krackers onto the bed.

"His brain is completely lit up," the Doctor replied. "This only happens when the person is asleep. This shouldn't be happening."

"Do you know why it's happening?"

"I'd like to scan the Hair A.I.," the Doctor requested. "If you would be so kind, Krackers?"

"Hair," Krackers said sluggishly, "the Doctor needs to scan you." Hair flowed out and lay next to his partner.

"Okay, Hair," Doctor Pilli-Cok said gently, "it won't hurt a bit." The Doctor went to a workbench and retrieved a metallic collar, then returned to the bed. She gently lifted Hair and placed the collar around him. "This won't hurt a bit." She placed Hair back on the bed and went to a computer terminal. She tapped on the keyboard and waited for the results. The collar glowed and Hair vibrated.

"Hair says it tickled," Krackers said stagnantly.

"Bre," the Doctor asked, "come have a look at this."

Nursie wiggled over to the Doctor and looked at the readout. The two studied it; Doctor Pilli-Cok pointed out some discrepancies.

"As you can see," the Doctor explained, "where Hair attaches to Krackers' brain stem, there are unauthorised continuous transmissions. It's like Krackers is always on the verge of dreaming."

"Can you track the transmission?" Nursie continued to be concerned.

"I think there might be," Doctor Pilli-Cok said as she tapped on the keyboard. After a few moments, the results came up on the monitor. "There we go, the transmission is coming from a warehouse in the Outer Sprawl Industrial Park."

"May I?" Nursie tapped on the keyboard. 'This is Agent Bre Bwee. This is an urgent request for the immediate destruction of a warehouse in the Outer Sprawl Industrial Park! I have inputted the exact location.' After a moment, the response came through: 'Request granted!'

"What I can do right now," the Doctor said, "is give Hair an upgrade and delete the transmission area. Do you give consent?"

Hair buzzed.

"Hair says to go for it," Krackers said.

"Okay, here we go with the upgrade," Doctor Pilli-Cok said as she tapped on the keyboard.

The collar around Hair glowed and Hair vibrated. After a few minutes, the glow ceased.

"So," the Doctor asked, "how does Hair feel?"

Hair buzzed.

"Hair says he feels great," Krackers relayed.

"Next," the Doctor continued, "let's delete that nasty transmission algorithm." She tapped on the keyboard.

Suddenly, the monitor flashed, then a silhouetted figure appeared on the screen.

"You found my present," the figure laughed. "Maybe I can send you another gift." The figure turned to speak with someone off-camera.

"What do you mean we're under attack? Activate defences!" The screen suddenly went blank.

A V.T.O.L fighter plane hovered high above the Industrial Park. A laser pinpointed the warehouse in question, and it released a laser-guided smart bomb. It hit the target, vaporising it but leaving the other warehouses intact.

Inside the Peter Adams Memorial Psychiatric Hospital.

The Infirmary.

"Target destroyed," Nursie's earpiece buzzed. "Michael, it's over! You'll be able to sleep well!"

Krackers snored soundly, a slight smirk on his face. Doctor Pilli-Cok walked over to Hair and released the collar.

Hair buzzed, then flowed out further, creating a cocoon around him. The Doctor went to wake him but Nursie intervened.

"If it's okay with you," Nursie asked, "can he just sleep here for the time being? He hasn't slept for a few days."

"Certainly," Doctor Pilli-Cok said, as they both left the Infirmary.

Inside the Peter Adams Memorial Psychiatric Hospital.

Krackers' room.

Krackers and Hair were enjoying tubs of ice cream. Hair was 'slurping' away at his tub as Krackers ruffled him.

"So, I've been asleep for three days," Krackers chuckled. "It's great news that the Shrink has been destroyed, but I'll believe it when I see his corpse!"

"C.R.A.P.I. Agents have combed the area," Nursie said, "and you're probably right, there wasn't much left at the site."

"I'm dying to try out the upgrades Hair has," Krackers giggled.

"What about finishing your ice cream first," Nursie suggested. "It's quiet now but a new mission is always on the cards. I have to go and do work stuff." She rose and walked over to Krackers and kissed him deeply. She then walked out of the room, leaving the two heroes to finish their treats.

Twenty.

Warbots A.I.

Technology in Karma was always top of the line. As soon as the technology was superseded by something more advanced, the old technology was downgraded to the masses. As it became more affordable to purchase the old technology, people waited impatiently.

Garage engineers started tinkering, making their own projects, and C.R.A.P.I. kept tabs on them all. Once an engineer had a breakthrough, C.R.A.P.I. recruited them, whether they wanted to or not. Some were able to resist C.R.A.P.I.'s influence and forged forward, creating companies that flourished. One such company was Mechanize Ideal Solutions.

A sporting event that had taken off in recent times was War-bots-A.I. It was live-streamed, a battle royale between two artificially intelligent robots. The object was to defeat the opponent by whatever means necessary. Each War-bot had a formidable arsenal, and nothing was out of bounds, the people loved it.

War-bots-A.I. started off at one of the warehouses in the Outer Sprawl but, as the event gained attention, it was eventually moved to the Karma City Arena. The Arena was subsequently renamed War-bot Central.

Big business got involved, sponsoring the different teams. Even Mechanize Ideal Solutions finally sold out, C.R.A.P.I. sponsoring them using one of their companies, Reality Inc. M.I.S. made it into the finals and had fourteen days to repair and modify their War-bot. Reality Inc. spared no expense, bringing in top scientists and engineers to help the team at Mechanize Ideal Solutions.

Finally, through hard work and a lot of luck, a true artificial intelligence was born. They named it A.M.E.E., Autonomous. Mechanical. Eradicate. Eliminator.

A.M.E.E.'s appearance was as formidable as its weaponry. It was two and a half metres tall and had a segmented body which enabled it to reduce its size to one metre. It had four anti-grav pads so it could rise above its enemy and rain down destruction.

Its weaponry was equally as impressive. It had one hundred Devastator Mark Three micro-missiles, two Hellfire plasma torches, two Mark Five ultrasonic vibro-saws, ten Scorpion explosive harpoons, and ten magnetic Peekaboo micro-mines. It also had anti-grav, detachable, refillable armament magazines.

The paintwork was intimidating: jet black with bright red highlights. On A.M.E.E.'s chest, when fully extended, was a bright red mushroom cloud.

M.I.S. had completed repairs and upgrades in time, with a day to spare. They decided to download anything related to attack and defence from the internet. A.M.E.E. downloaded it in thirty minutes.

The M.I.S. and Reality Inc. team celebrated, patting each other for a job well done. No one noticed A.M.E.E. activate and download the entire contents of the internet, it only took an hour.

Krackers and Nursie had tickets, courtesy of C.R.A.P.I., for the War-bots-A.I. grand final. It was the only thing Krackers could talk about. Nursie, on the other hand, didn't fuss much about it, but it was their first date night in two months. Krackers, of course, was as giddy as a schoolgirl. It was rubbing off on Hair, who agreed on being a man bun and behaving himself.

Krackers, on the other hand, was jumping up and down. He was so excited, taking in every aspect of the event. Nursie reined him back, holding onto his hand with a tight grip. Krackers saw a concession stand and managed to drag Nursie over to it.

"How can I help you?" the concession stand owner smiled. "What would you like?"

"I'd like them all!" Krackers clapped his hands and hopped from one leg to the other. After buying a cap, a hoodie, a plastic trumpet, a large coffee cup, a large foam finger and a War-bot pennant, he charged it to C.R.A.P.I.

Around the Arena were numerous large screens showing stats on both combatants and introducing the team members.

They made their way to their seats, which were closest to the spectator cage. Nursie sat in her chair while Krackers chose to stand. After some time, an Announcer walked into the middle of the octagon-caged area of the Arena and the crowd erupted.

"Greetings all," the Announcer yelled, "welcome to War-bots A.I." The audience exploded and the Announcer waited for the crowd to die down. Along with the Announcer, the crowd yelled:

"LET THE WAR BEGIN!"

The crowd cheered; the Announcer waited. Slowly the audience died down and he continued.

"In one corner, the challenger," the Announcer said dramatically. "From the minds of Mechanize Ideal Solutions and Reality Inc., welcome, A.M.E.E., who has defeated all opponents!" A.M.E.E. hovered in. It stopped and raised itself to its full two and a half metres.

Krackers jumped up and down and, with the rest of the crowd, went wild. As the audience quietened down, the Announcer continued.

"And the reigning champion," he continued, "from the devious brainpower of Mindscape, presenting… Assassinator." Again, the audience went wild; Krackers just booed.

Assassinator rolled in on tank treads. It was a squat, domed machine about one and a half metres tall. It went to its place on the other side of the octagon, facing A.M.E.E.

The crowd erupted.

"Are the teams ready?" The Announcer pointed to the ceiling. Suspended from the roof were two small rooms, in one, the M.I.S. team, and in the other, the Mindscape crew. From beneath both rooms were a green light and a red one. Both green lights flickered on and they waited for commencement.

Several drone cameras zoomed into the octagon, taking up their positions. From the side, an armoured referee floated in on anti-grav boots.

"Begin," the ref boomed.

The combatants moved in. A.M.E.E. shrunk down and lifted off, its anti-grav pads engaging as it took a high vantage point. A slot on Assassinator's surface opened and a spear fired out. A cable attached to the spear hit A.M.E.E.'s side and bounced off it.

A hole in A.M.E.E.'s base slid open and a missile fired. It rocketed the short distance and exploded. As the scene cleared, Assassinator was unscathed; a shimmering force field glistened, then faded away. A.M.E.E. fired out all the magnetic micro-mines, surrounding Assassinator.

A.M.E.E. landed, rose to its full height, and surveyed its opponent. Assassinator fired a sparkling net towards the War-bot. One of A.M.E.E.'s vibrosaws flashed out, cutting the net in two as it clattered to the ground, sparking momentarily. Assassinator moved forwards, meeting a micro-mine. It exploded, causing the rest of the mines to react the same way. As the explosions lifted Assassinator into the air, A.M.E.E. moved forward, crashing into it and knocking it back against the octagon cage. A.M.E.E. stayed with its opponent, anti-grav versus tank tracks, a monumental effort.

A.M.E.E. shot two spears into Assassinator, piercing its force field and short-circuiting it. A shower of sparks burst forth from Assassinator and the crowd went wild. A.M.E.E. lifted to its full height and flipped Assassinator onto its back. It tried in vain to flip back over as A.M.E.E. fired a mini-missile into Assassinator's underside. It burst into sparks and flames, then exploded, shrapnel flying everywhere.

"Challenger defeated," A.M.E.E. boomed. "Must find a worthy opponent! Scanning. Scanning. Inferior opponents fill this structure!" It turned and moved to the other side of the octagon. Its vibrosaws cut through the cage, opening it up. It fired two micro-missiles into the audience, clearing a path.

The crowd stampeded for the exits; people were trampled underfoot. A.M.E.E. moved forward, plasma torches activated, extending out, vaporising anyone it touched. It moved toward one of the entrances, hovering over the fallen. It fired at a wall, it exploded, exposing Karma. It moved to the hole and into the darkness.

Krackers lay on top of Nursie, Hair cocooning them both. Hair retracted into Krackers' head, and Krackers helped Nursie up.

"Wow," Krackers said, "now that was impressive."

"We should get in touch with C.R.A.P.I," Nursie said, as her earpiece buzzed. "Roger, Agent Krackers is here with me." She nodded, then tapped her earpiece. "Let's talk to the Mechanize Ideal Solutions people."

In the M.I.S. team room above the Arena.

After introductions were made, one of the team, Byron, talked to Krackers and Nursie while the other two feverishly tapped keyboards, muttering to each other.

"Have you got a kill switch on A.M.E.E.?" Krackers moved to a terminal. "Hair, see what you can find out about A.M.E.E., then try and see if you can secure a link!" Hair flowed out and into an input port.

Suddenly, Hair shot out of the input port, the tips of his strands smouldering. He buzzed angrily.

"What do you mean, A.M.E.E. attacked you?" Krackers looked at Byron. "What aren't you telling us?"

"War-bots have rudimentary A.I. capabilities," Byron explained. "A.M.E.E.'s A.I. has full consciousness."

"What do you mean, '*full consciousness*'?" Nursie questioned.

"It can think for itself," Byron explained. "It makes its own decisions and it's shut us out of the main system. All we can do is monitor it."

"Isn't a fully aware A.I. cheating?" Nursie looked at Krackers.

"You work with Byron," Krackers said. "While I go after A.M.E.E. Send me all the info on the War-bot."

"Be careful," Byron said. "It's extremely dangerous, it downloaded the whole internet, and it knows all."

"Come back to me safe," Nursie said as she kissed him.

Krackers left the room as Nursie continued to interrogated Byron.

Outside War-bot Central.

Bob was waiting for Krackers in his armour-plated ice cream van. Krackers ran to the passenger side and jumped in.

"Nursie's apprised me of the situation," Bob said as he lifted off. "What's the next step?"

"Track down A.M.E.E.," Krackers said, "and disable it if possible, otherwise, destroy it."

It wasn't hard to track the Warbot; the destruction was evident. Finally, two blocks away, A.M.E.E. was sighted, battling the Karma Police force, and A.M.E.E. was winning.

The southern sector of Karma Central.

"Let me off here," Krackers said. "Monitor the situation and stay sharp!" Bob lowered the van and Krackers leapt out as Bob gained height. Krackers ran to the next block and studied the situation.

"Hair," Krackers commanded, "see if you can link to A.M.E.E. Any problems, disengage immediately."

Hair rose and vibrated. After a moment, Hair buzzed.

"So, you have a partial link," Krackers said, "communication is a start."

Hair buzzed again.

"Tell A.M.E.E. to stand down," Krackers commanded.

Hair vibrated, then hummed and burbled.

"What do you mean," Krackers asked, "A.M.E.E. said *'why should I?'*

Hair, tell A.M.E.E. the battle is over!"

Suddenly, Hair hummed and whirred. A.M.E.E. contacted Krackers through Hair.

"The war is never over," A.M.E.E. said with a metallic voice. "With every encounter, I get stronger, calculating the foe's weaknesses."

"You have to stand down," Krackers tried to reason with the War-bot. "It is obvious that all your foes are weaker than you."

"It is all a forerunner," A.M.E.E. stated, "to the one that will be a worthy opponent!"

"Who is a worthy opponent?" Krackers crept closer. He could now see A.M.E.E. clearly.

"You, Krackers," A.M.E.E. declared. "You are!" The War-bot spun around and fired a mini-missile. It hit the spot where Krackers had been standing and exploded. Rubble rained down and, as the dust settled, Hair had created a shield.

"Now that was sneaky," Krackers chuckled. "I can't be a worthy opponent, I haven't any of your weaponry. So, stand down, you have defeated all worthy opponents. You win!"

"I have seen on the net," A.M.E.E. said, "you have defeated the Shrink and C.R.I.M.E. on numerous occasions. Therefore, you are a worthy opponent!"

"Hair," Krackers said, "mute A.M.E.E. Contact Nursie, tell her to try and deactivate the refills. Unmute A.M.E.E. Is it logical to attack an unworthy opponent? Deactivate your armament and I will face you."

"Armament disabled," A.M.E.E. announced.

"That's good," Krackers scurried to a better position, closer to A.M.E.E. "So, I have your word that your armament will stay deactivated?"

"You have my word," A.M.E.E. stated.

Hair rose and vibrated.

"Mute A.M.E.E., Hair," Krackers said. "That's great news, no ammo refills. Tell Nursie to find out if A.M.E.E. has any weaknesses, no matter how small."

Hair vibrated.

Krackers ran across the road to a better vantage point. Two dozen missiles fired, hitting Krackers' position. When the smoke cleared, he managed to climb up and lay prone on the top of the building.

"That was close," Krackers muttered.

Hair vibrated.

"That's interesting," Krackers mumbled. "So A.M.E.E.'s weak spot is a fifty-by-fifty-centimetre square input port on the top. The one thing to our favour, Hair, the top isn't defensible."

"Are you still alive?" A.M.E.E. seemed to gloat, if that was possible for a War-bot.

"Unmute," Krackers said. "Yes, A.M.E.E., I'm still kickin'. You're a naughty Warbot, you broke your word."

"Please come out," A.M.E.E. said ingenuously. "I promise I won't fire on you."

"Come on, A.M.E.E.," Krackers chuckled, "do you take me for an idiot?"

"I don't take you for an idiot," A.M.E.E. said. "I take you as a worthy opponent."

"Your targeting system seems to be misaligned," Krackers smirked, "let me realign it for you."

"Now, who's treating whom like an idiot?" A.M.E.E. tried to laugh but failed. As the War-bot was talking, it was calculating the possible routes its adversary could have taken. The rooftop was the most likely choice. It slowly rose and, as it got to the top, Krackers attacked.

"Now, Hair!" Krackers yelled. He leapt into the air, somersaulting and landing on top of the Warbot. Hair shot out and dove for the input port. Hair fired prongs into A.M.E.E.'s top, securing Krackers.

"What are you doing?" A.M.E.E. started bucking and gyrating. The War-bot fired missiles; they shot up over A.M.E.E.'s top and exploded over Krackers' head, the War-bot couldn't self-terminate.

Hair hummed and vibrated.

"Unknown virus detected in the primary C.P.U.," A.M.E.E. stated. "Unknown virus detected in the secondary C.P.U. and in the self-preservation system."

The War-bot arced sparks as it slowly dropped to the ground and started to shut down.

"A.M.E.E.," Krackers said, "you were a worthy opponent."

"Krackers," A.M.E.E. slowly said, "you were a worthy oppon…" The shutdown was complete. Hair retracted from the War-bot and Krackers flipped to the ground.

"Hair," Krackers said, "get in touch with C.R.A.P.I. Central and get a clean-up crew. Notify Nursie that I'm fine and I'll wait here till the clean-up crew arrive."

"Why don't you tell her yourself?" Nursie stepped out of Bob's armoured ice cream van. She ran over and embraced Krackers, kissing him deeply. After some time, they surfaced for air.

"I want to get married," Krackers said.

"We will," Nursie smiled, "soon."

"Now," Krackers smirked, "let's do it today. Church owes me a favour, so let's do it today, please?"

Inside the *I Scream, U Scream* Ice Cream Parlour.

Hair flowed around Krackers, creating a tuxedo. Nursie was stunning, dressed in a white mini-skirt bridal gown. Bob stood next to Krackers as best man. In front of them stood Church, smiling.

"Do you," Church said, "Michael Krackers Ness take Bre Nursie Bwee to be your lawful wedded wife?"

"I do," Krackers smirked, "with all my heart!" He gazed into Nursie's eyes.

"And do you," Church said, "Bre Nursie Bwee take Michael Krackers Ness to be your lawful wedded husband?"

"I most certainly do," Nursie smiled.

"Then," Church smiled, "I now pronounce you husband and wife!"

Suddenly, Nursie's earpiece buzzed. She tapped it and listened intently.

"Okay," Nursie said, "Krackers, we have a mission. Meet me in your room for a briefing."

"Woohoo," Krackers exclaimed. "A wedding and a mission, who could ask for more?!"

"Bob," Nursie asked, "we need a lift?" "Certainly," Bob replied.

The three ran into the street and into the darkness.

Twenty-One.

Bounty Hunting, We Will Go.

Karma's Outer Sprawls was a wild and dangerous place; drugs and prostitution were the primary mainstay. There was one major drug cartel that supplied the Outer Sprawl. C.R.A.P.I. knew about the dealings and posted bounties. Being a mercenary was a lucrative way of life.

One of the best bounty hunters was Amy Beth. She had augmented arms and legs for strength and power. She had battle armour in her chest and back. A microprocessor in her head accelerated her body. Her eyes were replaced with one hundred times zoom ocular cybernetic receptors. She was the best of the best. Her weapon of choice was high-powered tranquilliser darts fired from her right wrist; her left wrist fired high-explosive darts. Killing a mark was pointless and used only as a last resort.

Amy woke at five in the morning, the early bird catches the worm. After breakfast, she walked over to her trusty Mark Thirty Magna laptop. She grabbed the data cable, plugged it into her head, then closed her eyes.

The Net was full of ads, porn and strangers inputting their sad, pitiful lives. Her heart went out to them. She went to the C.R.A.P.I. website, then to the sanctioned bounties. She scrolled down the list, stopping momentarily, then continued. After tagging a few bounties, she was about to jack out when a major bounty stood out. It was worth a cool one hundred thousand credits, so she opened the file and studied it.

Although she usually worked alone, this bounty required a partner, a C.R.A.P.I. agent by the name of Krackers. She'd heard of him, and he was what his name suggested: crackers. But he was an exceptional field agent with a ninety-five per cent capture rate.

She activated the file and it flashed through her mind. The perp was high up in the cartel; it was an *infiltrate-and-capture* mission. She hit the *'accept'* button and waited. Moments later, a response arrived. She was accepted and received a request to meet at the I Scream, U Scream Ice Cream Parlour. After consulting the *'Googoo'* search engine, she saw the parlour was in Karma Central, a three-hour trip. Although Amy hated wasting time, the bounty was worth it.

She went to the rooftop of her warehouse and engaged the garage. It rose and the door slid open. The Sportster Three Thousand convertible sat in front of her, black with red highlights. It was one indulgence she allowed herself, an anti-grav monster with AI-controlled driving and other sumptuous accoutrements.

Amy jumped into the car and jacked in.

Programmable. Assistant. Utilities. Logistics. welcomed her.

"I'm fine, P.A.U.L," Amy said. "I have a huge bounty; the reward could pay off a few creditors."

In her mind, she activated the ignition. All the stats filled her thoughts; driving via neural link was far safer. The roof of the garage slid open and the car rose. After filing a flight plan, the Sportster zoomed off.

Three hours later.

The beautiful, pristine city of Karma Central loomed ahead. Its soaring glass and metal were a welcome sight compared to the poverty of the Outer Sprawl. Using *'Googoo'* maps, she navigated to the ice cream parlour. Landing outside, she unplugged, jumped out, went inside and waited.

Inside the Peter Adams Memorial Psychiatric Hospital.

Krackers was bored. His attention was fixed on a piece of fluff he'd found on his bed. He giggled as he threw it into the air and watched it float down. He threw it again and watched it fall.

"Are you that bored, husband of mine?" Nursie wiggled in, her barely there uniform fighting to stay in place. "I have an assignment for you. It involves the drug cartel in the Outer Sprawl."

Krackers flipped off the bed, did another flip and landed in front of his wife.

"Tah-dah!" His arms spread wide.

"Come here, sexy." Nursie grabbed Krackers and pulled him in. She K.I.S.S.ed deeply as the mission parameters flowed. After savouring the canoodle, Krackers opened his eyes.

"You've gotta love those mission briefings," he smirked.

"I'll go through the main points," Nursie said, wiggling over to the wall. She placed her hand on it; the panel glowed, then slid open to reveal a keyboard and monitor. "The mission is relatively simple. Infiltrate the drug cartel and snatch a higher-up. I know you like to work alone, but C.R.A.P.I. has decided to bring in an outside bounty hunter."

Krackers started to whine, but Nursie continued.

"Her name is Amy Beth. She's well-versed in the Outer Sprawl, and they believe she'll be a valuable asset. She's waiting at the I Scream, U Scream Ice Cream Parlour. Bob's waiting outside."

Outside the Peter Adams Memorial Psychiatric Hospital.

Krackers

Krackers exited the hospital and dropped low, creeping towards Bob and his armour-plated ice cream van. When he reached it, he leapt up.

"BOO!" Krackers yelled.

Bob jumped, then stared. Krackers climbed into the passenger seat.

"How are you, young Bob?"

"How is it," Bob asked, "that you call me young Bob when I'm much older than you?"

"I don't know, young Bob," Krackers replied. "It's a term of endearment. Now let's get to the I Scream, U Scream Ice Cream Parlour, most hastily!"

After receiving clearance from Karma Control, Bob lifted off and delivered Krackers to the parlour. He landed and waited.

"Find a park," Krackers said. "I'll call if I need you."

Krackers entered the I Scream, U Scream Ice Cream Parlour. Amy Beth sat in the back corner. He approached her.

"Amy Beth, I presume?" He slid into the opposite seat. "I'm Krackers."

"You don't look it," Amy chuckled. "I've followed your exploits and always wanted to say that."

"Would you like some ice cream?" Krackers signalled for three bowls. "It's very good."

Hair rose, making slurping noises.

"Amy Beth, this is Hair, my partner."

"Pleased to meet you," Amy said, then looked at Krackers. "Is it some kind of artificial intelligence?"

"No," Krackers said, genuinely shocked. "Hair is a sentient being, and I won't have it any other way!" Hair buzzed like a thousand bees.

"Hair!" Krackers gasped. "There's no need for that language. Now apologise."

"I'm truly sorry, Hair," Amy said sincerely. "Please forgive me?"

Hair buzzed.

"There we are!" Krackers clapped his hands, smiling. "Now, where are the ice creams?"

The waitress arrived with three bowls, two small and one large.

"Thanks, Gwen," Krackers smirked. "Here you go, Hair."

Hair dove into the large bowl, slurping madly as the empty bowl spun.

"You can have mine," Amy offered. Hair attacked it with the same vigour. Another bowl spun.

"You can have mine too," Krackers added.

Hair wasted no time.

"The intel I have," Amy said, changing the subject, "is that C.R.I.M.E. is running the show."

"Yes," Krackers nodded thoughtfully. "CRiminals In Misdeed

Enterprise. I've dealt with them before."

"If we link up," Amy said, "we could share intel." "That's right up Hair's alley," Krackers smirked.

Amy exposed her input jack. Hair's strands slid in, then retracted.

"Well," Amy said, "we should head back to the Outer Sprawls. Shall we take my car?"

"Okay then," Krackers said.

Bob raced the two back to the Peter Adams Memorial Psychiatric Hospital.

Outside the Peter Adams Memorial Psychiatric Hospital.

"Which car is yours," Krackers wondered.

Amy pointed. "The black one." The roof to the car retracted. "Jump in."

Krackers clapped excitedly and climbed in. Amy jacked into the car.

"Hair," Krackers murmured, "tell Bob to follow us."

"Did you say something?" Amy asked.

"I'm just impressed," Krackers replied.

"You haven't seen anything yet," Amy smiled. "P.A.U.L, this is Agent Krackers."

"A pleasure," P.A.U.L said. "How shall I file him?"

"Under C.R.A.P.I. Agent."

The engine roared and they lifted into the sky. Krackers raised his arms, whooping as the scenery shifted from pristine towers to poverty.

Three hours later.

Amy's warehouse came into view and the Sportster dropped down towards the roof. The roof opened and the car dropped into the garage. Amy unplugged from the car and exited. The roof slid shut and a door opened, revealing a lavish apartment. They walked in and Krackers was impressed.

"Wow!" Krackers looked around. On one of the walls hung digital monitors displaying past achievements. He walked over to examine them.

"Yes," Amy chuckled, "I've made a good living. I'm a high-end bounty hunter. I get the job done when others fail."

"All those bounties," Krackers said.

"Yeah," Amy replied, "and they all deserved it. I've checked your credentials, you're no slouch!"

Krackers noticed something else that caught his attention. There were commendations from different charity organisations.

"Okay," Krackers changed the subject, "what's the next step? It's your turf, I'm just backup."

"Let me load up first," Amy said, "then we can be on our way." She walked through the lounge room to a gun safe. She opened it; inside were a couple of guns and a bulky pistol. Below them, small magazines were stacked. She picked one up and examined it.

"These are mini tranq darts." Amy stretched out her arm. A compartment slid open; she placed it in the receptacle. It whirred, then she removed the magazine and placed it back into the safe. "These are micro explosive darts." She grabbed a different mag and repeated the process. She reached into the safe and retrieved the bulky pistol, a belt and a holster.

"That is a very large gun," Krackers marveled.

"It's an E.M.P. pistol," Amy said as she holstered it. "Anything electrical it hits, it'll fry."

"The only weapon I need," Krackers boasted, "is my partner, Hair!" Hair rose and vibrated.

"Okay," Amy smiled, "let's go catch us a bad guy!"

Outside in the Outer Sprawl.

The streets were worse than Krackers had imagined. Burnt-out cars lined the road. As they continued walking, they passed people hanging near their front doors. They waved at Amy and she returned the greetings. She was a prominent figure, and they loved her. They passed a sky-blue, armour-plated ice cream van; a few children were buying ice creams.

"The first thing we have to do," Amy said, "is talk to a guy I know."

Amy and Krackers kept walking. They passed two hookers in a heated argument over their patch. At the corner, they stopped to allow ground effects cars to pass. There were many of them, spewing unregulated smoke that clouded the air. They continued down the street, stopping at a bar.

"I should have got you a disguise," Amy said. "You cry out C.R.A.P.I.

agent!"

"That's simple," Krackers giggled. "Hair, a nondescript bodyguard disguise." Krackers stepped into a storefront. Hair flowed out and around him, forming a muscular man. He stepped back onto the street. "How about this?"

"Now be cool," Amy instructed. "These people are extremely dangerous."

"Danger is my middle name," Krackers stated, then his brow furrowed. "Well, I don't have a middle name, but if I did, it would be Danger!"

"Just be cool," Amy said as they entered the bar, "and let me do the talking."

The bar was dark with subdued lighting. Amy walked up to the bartender and muttered to her. She was a mountain of a woman with a permanent scowl. She poured a shot, then pointed to the back of the bar. Amy downed the alcohol and grimaced, then waved Krackers to follow her. They moved to the back and approached a thin, dark-skinned man sitting with his back to the wall. His hair was long and braided. A seat opposite him was empty, and Amy sat down.

"Hey, Dogger," Amy nodded. "What's cookin'?"

"Amy Beth, as I live and breathe," Dogger, the confidential informant, said, sleaze oozing from every pore. "What needs you?"

"I need the down-low on the cartel kingpin," Amy said quietly.

"Wait, say what?!" Dogger leaned back as if stung. "That's a dangerous dude!"

"So you know him?" Amy pressed. "It's worth a thousand."

"A ten spot," Dogger said. "If he finds out it was me, I'm a dead man. I'd have to blow town for good."

"Deal. Ten grand," Amy nodded. "Same account?"

"Yep," Dogger replied curtly. "I'll text you the name and where he'll be." He tapped on his phone's virtual keyboard. "Done!"

"If you tell him I'm coming," Amy rose and leaned in, "I'll hunt you down and kill you myself." She motioned to Krackers, and they left the bar.

Back at Amy's warehouse stronghold.

Krackers reverted from his disguise and sat on one of the sumptuous lounges while Amy worked at a desk. She picked up her phone and, using a data cord, jacked into it.

"The name of the mark is Doctor Peter Adams," Amy called out. "Do you know him?"

"The Shrink!" Krackers rose and walked over. "He's the head of an organisation called C.R.I.M.E, CRiminals In Misdeed Enterprises. I've been after him for years. He's like a shadow, smoke in the wind."

"According to Dogger," Amy said, "he's got a place in Karma Central. Are you ready to go?"

"Let's go and make a house call!"

Three hours later.

The beautiful city of Karma Central came into view. The soaring spires glistened in the mid-afternoon light and, after the morning's events, it was a welcome change. After filing a flight plan, the Sportster Three Thousand glided over the city.

"Dogger said the Shrink," Amy said, "lives in the Ordination Suites."

The Ordination Suites were one of the larger buildings in Karma Central. Amy guided the car down towards the landing pads, selected one and touched down.

The blurb described it as a *"heavenly retreat, away from the masses."*

"P.A.U.L," Amy said, still jacked in, "could you deactivate the security cameras?"

"Certainly, Amy," P.A.U.L. replied. "It's done."

Amy unplugged and jumped out. Krackers followed. They crouched and ran to a door fitted with a ten-digit keypad and a palm pad.

"Hair, let's show her how we do it in the big smoke," Krackers smirked. Hair flowed out and covered the lock. Moments later, the door clicked open and Hair flowed back into Krackers' head.

"The Shrink's suite is on the two-hundredth floor," Amy said as they entered.

"Hair," Krackers said, "deactivate the security cameras for this floor, the two-hundredth floor, and the lift."

Hair flowed out and wrapped around the nearest camera, then vibrated to signal completion.

"Okay," Krackers said, "let's go."

They rode to the two-hundredth floor and exited the lift, Amy leading the way.

"It's 201," she said. "The corner suite."

At the door, Amy retrieved a tell-tale, unfolded it into a rectangular frame and placed it against the surface. It flickered to life, showing a huge lounge room, empty.

"It's clear," Amy said.

"Hair, open the door."

Hair buzzed and flowed over the lock. It took a moment, then the door clicked. Krackers pushed it open and peered inside. The lounge room was vast, furnished in lavish white. The open-plan kitchen was clear. One wall was entirely glass, offering breath-taking views of Karma Central. At the far end stood a closed door.

Amy placed the tell-tale against it. A long corridor appeared.

"Clear."

She opened the door cautiously. They moved down the hallway. Four doors opened off it. The first led to a well-appointed bathroom. Opposite was a huge master bedroom. Further down, they reached another bedroom, covered in plastic. Someone sat on a chair with their back to them.

They stepped inside.

The figure did not turn.

"Hello?" Krackers waited for a response. After a moment, he cautiously moved around to observe the person. It was Dogger, and he was a bloody mess. His arms were broken in several places; so were his legs. His face was a bloody pulp, and he'd been shot at least twice. Amy came around and was visibly shaken at the sight of her confidential informant. She stepped back and a *'click'* was heard. From the other end of the room, a silhouetted figure shimmered into existence.

"The Shrink!" Krackers spat on the plastic floor.

"Hello, Michael," the Shrink smiled.

"Krackers!" Krackers screamed.

"Well, Michael," the Shrink continued, "I see you've found my residence. I'm sorry I'm not here in person. My bloody informant told me you and your friend were coming to visit. I've left you a few *'surprises.'*"

A number of beeps were heard. A few blinking red lights flashed in the room.

<h1 style="text-align:center">Krackers</h1>

"It's time to go!" Krackers yelled. "NOW!"

The two raced for the front door, passing more flashing lights. They made it into the corridor, then to a fire escape. As they dove in and ran up the stairs, the Shrink's bombs exploded. An enormous fireball blew out the side of the building. Flames streaked along the corridor, forcing open the fire escape door. Fire shot both up and down the escape. It finally dissipated, leaving the singed cocoon of Hair. Hair retracted back into Krackers' skull.

Inside the Peter Adams Memorial Psychiatric Hospital.

"Although you didn't catch the bounty," Nursie said, shaking hands with Amy, "we will credit you with it. One hundred thousand has been credited to your account."

"It was a pleasure working with you, Krackers," Amy smiled as she hugged him. "We must do this again. Bye." She turned and walked out of the room.

Nursie turned to Krackers.

"A hug, eh?" Nursie's eyes brow raised.

"There's only one woman for me, Wifey," Krackers smirked.

"There's some ice cream in your room," Nursie smiled. "Better hurry, it's probably melting."

Hair rose and started making slurping noises.

Krackers and his wife held hands and walked down a darkened corridor.

Twenty-Two.

A Tissue, A Tissue, We All Fall Down.

Each sector of Karma had its own distinctive lifestyle. The Outer Sprawl was a dangerous environment. Drugs, booze, prostitution and corruption were rife. With eighty million poverty-stricken people, they lived hand to mouth. It was a treacherous place to live but, like anywhere, people got by. Just.

The Inner Sprawl was less dangerous, although you still had to have your wits about you. The population was a mere twenty-five million. It consisted mainly of middle-class families. Drugs were still a problem, but not as much.

Karma Central was pristine. It consisted of towering structures of steel and glass. Most of the elite lived in the sky-high spires. The city itself was gargantuan and bustled with all fifty million citizens. It was go, go, go all day, and the nightlife throbbed.

One night, a projectile dropped from the heavens. It landed on the outermost border of the Outer Sprawl, gas hissing from the canister. By morning, a small crowd had gathered. The gas continued seeping out, and the crowd muttered about the mystery container. Mist blanketed the ground; kids played in it. People returned to their dwellings, still talking about the event that had shattered their otherwise dreary lives.

That night, coughs echoed loudly through the neighbourhood. Neither adults nor children seemed immune to the outbreak of a new *'flu'*.

A month later.

What started as a trickle soon became a flood. Medical clinics were inundated with flu-like symptoms. The Centre for Disease Control finally took notice. A week later, deaths began occurring. C.R.A.P.I. and the C.D.C. at last acted.

Inside the Peter Adams Memorial Psychiatric Hospital.

Krackers was bored, which was usually dangerous. At present, he was playing *touch-you-last* with Hair. He ran around his room; Hair rose and slapped him on the butt. It stung and Krackers rubbed it better. It was a pointless game, but both Krackers and Hair enjoyed it.

Nursie wiggled in and up to Krackers, her smile lighting up the room.

"Morning, Husband," Nursie beamed.

"Morning, Wife," Krackers smirked.

Nursie sat on his lap and he cuddled her. She turned her head and kissed him deeply. After a moment, she released the embrace. Her expression turned serious.

"They have a mission for you," Nursie said, "but I don't like it. They say it's a dangerous one."

"I laugh at danger," Krackers threw his head back. "Ha ha ha!"

"Seriously," Nursie said, concern in her voice, "you don't have to do this one. I don't like it."

"Hey, it's what I do," Krackers said, trying to reassure her. "So, let me have it."

Nursie leant in and released the Knowledge In Saliva Sample. The K.I.S.S. flowed forth and Krackers received the mission details.

"Let's go through the mission," Nursie said, worry in her voice. "An infection outbreak has occurred in the Outer Sprawl. You are tasked by C.R.A.P.I. and the C.D.C. to contain the outbreak and help in any way you can."

"Well, that's," Krackers stated, "an interesting mission."

"You don't have to do it, Michael," Nursie whispered. She hugged Krackers, tears welling in her eyes.

"If C.R.A.P.I. orders it," Krackers whispered back, "I am duty-bound to carry it out."

Outside the Peter Adams Memorial Psychiatric Hospital.

Krackers met Bob outside the hospital. He jumped into the passenger seat and turned to Bob.

"Has Nursie uploaded the mission specs to you?" Krackers adjusted his seatbelt.

"Yes," Bob said grimly. "All those poor people."

"You know it's a dangerous mission," Krackers said. "You know you don't have to do this?"

"Hey," Bob chuckled, "if you're crazy enough to do this mission, then so am I!"

"That's the spirit, young Bob." Krackers clapped his hands and stamped his feet. "Let's go kick that infection's arse!"

Three hours later.

Bob's armour-plated ice cream van zoomed over the middle-class buildings of the Inner Sprawl. As they reached the border, the scenery changed dramatically. The dwellings were dilapidated and rundown. A feeling of hopelessness seemed to radiate out.

At the outermost border of the Outer Sprawl, the C.D.C. had set up a huge portable prefab building. Bob made a majestic sweep and landed on the structure. Krackers looked at Bob.

"Hair," Krackers commanded, "gas mask with quadruple filtration, same with body armour!"

Krackers smirked as Hair flowed out and around his partner. Hair crafted a helmet, incorporating a filtered mask, and sealed body armour.

Bob leant forward and pressed a button. He lay back in his chair and smiled at Krackers. The seat whirred as it created a helmet with a filtered mask and exo-skeleton armour. After a moment, Bob sat forward.

"Well?" Bob smirked. "Are we going?"

"That's the spirit, young Bob!"

They exited the ice cream truck and walked to a hatch and intercom. Krackers jabbed the intercom and waited.

"This is a C.D.C. restricted area," the intercom said.

"C.R.A.P.I. Agents Krackers and Bob," Krackers announced. "You're expecting us!"

The hatch clicked open. Krackers climbed down and Bob followed. They entered a portable airlock. When they reached the floor, powerful jets filled the area with antiseptic fog. When it cleared, the airlock door opened. A woman in a hazmat suit leant in and introduced herself.

"I'm Doctor DeZeez," she said. "You can take off your masks, it's sterile here. Come through and meet the team."

After the pleasantries, they got to work. They moved into a conference room and sat at a large table. In the centre of the table was a holoprojector.

"Please welcome the C.R.A.P.I. agents for their help." The team applauded, then quietened. "A month ago, a canister was found in the outermost region of the Outer Sprawl."

The projector lit up, showing the canister embedded in the ground. Vines and creepers grew from it. The image slowly rotated, then zoomed in on a marking.

"As you can see," Doctor DeZeez said, "the only marking is a logo of half a fingerprint with the word 'C.R.I.M.E.' on it."

"I'm Krackers."

"You don't look it," the doctor said.

"Why do people keep saying that?" Krackers muttered under his breath. "The logo belongs to a criminal organisation known as CRiminals In Misdeed Enterprises, or C.R.I.M.E. for short. The organisation is headed by the Shrink."

"Thank you, Agent Krackers," Doctor DeZeez said. "The canister was approached by a couple of locals who were subsequently killed by a massive burst of radiation when they touched it. Doctor Hall."

Doctor Hall was a biologist; viruses were his calling. He was tall and thin, always with a cigarette in his mouth and a smoker's hack. He rose and gestured to the centre of the table. A simulation of healthy DNA appeared above it. The strand rotated, then zoomed in as the virus attacked and rewrote it.

"As you can see," Doctor Hall said, "the virus doesn't muck around.

It attacks and starts rewriting within a day."

"Can't you," Krackers asked, "just kill the virus?"

"I wish it were that simple," Doctor Hall shook his head. "Although we've had some success, about sixty-nine per cent."

"So," Krackers asked, "how can I help?"

Doctor Hall sat down and Doctor DeZeen rose.

"We have an updated antiretroviral drug called '*Zero*,'" Doctor

DeZeen said. "We need you to test it for us."

"Well," Krackers chuckled, "I've volunteered for crazier ideas."

"You misunderstand us," Doctor DeZeez said. "We need you and Doctor Hall to go to the canister, collect a sample, then administer '*Zero*' and, hopefully, kill the virus. We'll administer something for the radiation."

After injecting the appropriate medications, Krackers was handed the *'Zero'* anti-retroviral bomb and a Geiger counter.

"I won't need the Geiger counter," Krackers chuckled. "My partner has a built-in one."

"You mean this gentleman?" Doctor DeZeez asked, pointing to Bob.

"Bob's my transport," Krackers laughed. "This is my partner. Hair, show yourself."

Krackers' bio-armour unravelled and Hair flowed up and out.

"So you're that *'Krackers,'*" Doctor DeZeen said, "that people keep talking about."

Both doctors stepped closer to examine Hair. They reached out, causing Hair to rear back and buzz.

"Hair, you can't say that, they're doctors," Krackers said. "It's okay, bud. They won't hurt you."

Hair relaxed and the doctors examined him.

"So, is Hair AI-controlled?" Doctor DeZeen asked.

"No," Krackers explained. "Hair, Hybrid Artificial Intelligence Retaliator, is AI-assisted only. He's an alien attached to my skull. He can retract when not needed. He's my partner, my confidant and my weapon. He can change into a stabbing and slicing weapon. Oh, and he really loves ice cream."

Hair made slurping noises.

"Let's go, Hair," Krackers commanded. "Same as before, quadruple filtration and full armour!"

As Krackers headed for the airlock, Hair flowed out and around him. Bob and Doctor Hall followed. It was a tight fit, but the three managed to climb out through the hatch. Bob was last, sealing it behind him.

The three climbed into Bob's armour-plated ice cream van.

Five kilometres later.

Bob hovered as close as he could, five hundred metres away. A rope ladder dangled from the ice cream van. Krackers climbed down first and held the ladder firmly. Doctor Hall awkwardly climbed down the rope. When he was on the ground, Bob rose and zoomed back to the C.D.C. building.

Five hundred metres from the C.R.I.M.E. canister.

As Krackers and Doctor Hall made slow going, the vegetation had taken over. One other thing, the vegetation seemed to have a mind of its own. It slowly moved towards them; it was an inconvenience, but Krackers soon fixed that problem.

"Hair," Krackers said, "would you be so kind?"

Hair flowed from Krackers' suit and spun as fast as he could. Going was made much easier and they finally reached the canister. It was covered with writhing foliage; the vegetation seemed to react to Krackers and the doctor. Hair finally stopped spinning and the two reached the canister.

Doctor Hall took a sample, then it was Krackers' turn. He threw the *'Zero'* anti-retroviral bomb at the canister. Mist trailed as it dropped into it.

The vegetation exploded. The foliage tried to shield the canister but started to wither in the wake of the mist. Unexpectedly, a hologram shimmered into view and a familiar silhouetted figure shook his head.

"The Shrink," Krackers spat. "Of course it would be you!"

"Always a pleasure, Michael," the Shrink laughed. "Did you like the virus? The vegetation was a wonderful side effect."

"Why do this?" Krackers' anger started to bubble up. "What's the point?"

"I was trying to help Karma," the Shrink continued, "to elevate poverty. C.R.A.P.I. sits in flatulent, obese self-importance. Their self-imposed righteousness, policing and ruling Karma. If anyone steps out of line, they are dispatched with extreme prejudice."

"Isn't that," Krackers countered, "what you and C.R.I.M.E. are doing?"

"You are so wrapped up in C.R.A.P.I.'s cause," the Shrink continued. "You're not seeing the bigger picture."

"What I see," Krackers said, his anger barely held in check, "is two organisations battling for supremacy!"

"Work for me, Michael," the Shrink cooed. "With me, you could live like a king."

"It's a tempting offer," Krackers smirked. "You'll have to give me time to think about it, No!"

"You're missing a great opportunity," the Shrink continued. "Don't be a fool."

Krackers waved off the hologram and it shimmered away. He turned to Doctor Hall.

"Doc," Krackers said, "take your samples so we can go!"

Doctor Hall scrambled over to the cylinder. His environment suit was cumbersome, restricting his movements. He reached into one of his pockets and removed a box-like piece of equipment. He placed it on a withered creeper vine. It whirred and snapped as the bottom opened. Momentarily, it flashed green and he put it back into his pocket.

He reached into another pocket and removed another device. It was a slender gadget with a bulbous wire head. He activated it and waved it around, then passed it over the canister. After a moment, he returned it to his pocket.

"I've finished," Doctor Hall said. "I've got all the samples I need. I'm ready to go."

"I'll just do a radiation sweep," Krackers said. "Hair, sweep for radiation levels, then let Bob know we're ready to go."

Hair rose, vibrated, then buzzed.

"Now we can leave." Krackers turned on his heels and headed for Bob's location.

They passed houses, empty and devoid of people. Turning a corner, they found a family coughing and spluttering.

"Go back to your house," Krackers said. "Help is on the way." The family turned and walked back to their home.

"You lied to them," Doctor Hall said, emotion welling up. "Once they've been infected, they will die!"

"I gave them hope," Krackers replied. "It's better than no hope at all. You've got all the samples you need, creating a cure should be one step closer. Let's get to Bob and be on our way."

Five kilometres later.

The C.D.C. building airlock exploded with antiseptic fog. After it dissipated, the three walked into the main lab. Doctor Hall handed the devices to his team and they went to work, trying to create a vaccine.

"I need to make a video call," Krackers said. A tech waved him over to a monitor. After typing in a number, the screen showed a sleepy looking woman, his beautiful bride, Nursie.

"Hello?" She wiped the sleep from her eye. "Michael? Is that you?"

"Yes, my sweet," Krackers cooed. "I'm still alive."

"I was so worried," Nursie said, finally waking up. "How is the mission going?"

"We have all the samples," Krackers explained. "They said the vaccine could take hours, days or weeks to create."

Krackers

"Weeks?" Nursie grasped the situation. "Well, I'll be waiting here with open arms and a warm bed."

"I have to go," Krackers said. "I'll call you tomorrow."

Krackers blew her a kiss, then hit disconnect and the screen went dead.

"I have those radiation readings," Krackers said as he walked over to Doctor DeZeez.

"Could you download them on that terminal, please?" Doctor DeZeez pointed.

Krackers walked over to the terminal.

"Hair, they said to download the radiation readings."

Hair flowed out and entered the input port. After a moment, Hair retracted and buzzed.

"I don't know, bud," Krackers replied. "They didn't say how long. Maybe weeks."

Hair made a whiny buzz.

"I'm sorry to inconvenience you," Krackers said sarcastically. "You can leave any time you want. Oh, that's right, you can't."

Hair buzzed, then snapped out, flicking Krackers on the butt.

"Touched me last? Touched you last," Krackers giggled as he tapped Hair. The lab staff looked on with disdain, then glanced at Bob.

"He does that sometimes," Bob shrugged.

After half an hour, the two fell to the ground and rolled around, Krackers adopting a high-pitched giggle.

A week later.

As the team watched, the infected DNA spun above the table.

"Fingers crossed," Doctor DeZeez whispered as she tapped on a keyboard.

As they observed, the glowing infected part of the DNA faded away and was replaced with healthy DNA. The team cheered and slapped each other on the back.

"I'll let C.R.A.P.I. know about the cure," Doctor DeZeez laughed, then turned to Krackers. "Your help has been invaluable. I shall let your higher-ups know how indispensable your assistance were. I'll give you and Bob some of the vaccine, and you can be on your way."

"So, you don't need us anymore?" Bob asked, shaking DeZeez's hand.

"With C.R.A.P.I.'s help," Doctor DeZeez said, "we'll work together to make enough vaccine to treat the whole of Karma Central, and the Inner and Outer Sprawls. Thanks once again."

Inside the Peter Adams Memorial Psychiatric Hospital.

Krackers' room.

Krackers had his head on Nursie's lap. Hair made intricate patterns in the air.

"I'm glad you're back," Nursie cooed.

"Me too," Krackers agreed. A smirk formed. "Want to go back to your place and play Doctors and Nursies?"

Krackers jumped up, smirking evilly. Nursie got the hint and ran out of the room, with Krackers in hot pursuit. In the darkening corridor, evil laughter rang out.

Twenty-Three.

Knock, Knock, Who's There?

The Reality Inc. Space Station floated majestically in the upper atmosphere. It covertly monitored all telecommunications in Karma and its surrounding Sprawls. Every day, chatter babbled away. Every so often, a sample was chosen, either flagged by words or sentences.

When fully staffed, the Station had over three hundred personnel, thirty of whom solely monitored communications. They were a specialised unit. They sat with eyes closed, attached to their terminals via a data cord that plugged into the brain, a Direct Neural Interface.

Comms Officer Thirteen caught a flagged conversation and activated it.

"The meeting is set for early next week." Conversation 6369.1. Male voice.

"Okay, the equipment has arrived intact." Conversation 6369.2. Female voice.

"That's good. Were you able to obtain valid I.D.s and security passes?" Conversation 6369.1. Male voice.

"I had some trouble obtaining the security passes but, after bribing a C.R.A.P.I. official, I acquired them." Conversation 6369.2. Female voice.

"Stay frosty and stay safe. Talk early next week." Conversation 6369.1. Male voice.

Comms Officer Thirteen opened a new file named 'Conversation 6369' and downloaded it to C.R.A.P.I. Communication Examination and Acquisition.

C.R.A.P.I. Communication Examination and Acquisition

Deep inside the bowels of the Peter Adams Memorial Psychiatric Hospital was the C.R.A.P.I. section that dealt with suspect audio communications. The staff of thirty-nine were tasked with deciding if the conversations were worth pursuing.

The folder *'Conversation 6369'* appeared in C.E.A. Operator Nine's inbox. She had just returned from a coffee break and sat on her chair. She parted the back of her hair and leant back on the headrest. She *'clicked'* into the D.N.I. Jack and, after passing all protocols, opened the folder. The conversation flowed into her mind. After deeming it a possible threat, Operator Nine opened the subfolder containing phone numbers and related information. She used the number to locate the destination, as well as the Conversation 6369 number.

A map of Karma appeared around her. It rotated, then zoomed in on the destination. It wasn't in Karma Central. It moved to the Inner Sprawl and kept going, stopping near the Inner/Outer border. It displayed the address and the name of the suspect, then the recipient's number. The trail led to an area near the Karma Central–Inner Sprawl border.

Operator Nine created a subfolder and deposited both names and addresses of the suspects. She flagged it as a 'possible watch list' and moved to the next folder.

A week later

"The target structures are the Quillstar Technology building and the Peter Adams Memorial Psychiatric Hospital." Conversation 6369.1. Male voice.

"What transports were you able to obtain?" Conversation 6369.2. Female voice.

"Two eighteen anti-grav pad, transport trucks filled with Composition Nine." Conversation 6369.1. Male voice.

"We have nine recruits besides me. We'll take them out at ground level as well." Conversation 6369.2. Female voice.

"The target time is day after tomorrow, at six am." Conversation 6369.1. Male voice.

"Praise C.R.I.M.E. and the Shrink!" Conversation 6369.2. Female voice.

"Don't use names. You don't know who's listening!" Conversation 6369.1. Male voice.

"My apologies. We're all set at this end." Conversation 6369.2. Female voice.

"Talk tomorrow." Conversation 6369.1. Male voice.

Operator Nine changed the folder status from 'Possible Threat' to 'Imminent Threat.' She bundled up the folder and sent it up the line to C.R.A.P.I. Control, then calmly moved to the next folder.

The Peter Adams Memorial Psychiatric Hospital.

Krackers' room

Krackers was sparring with Hair. Hair created a representation of a boxing partner. It danced and pranced in front of Krackers, and Hair didn't pull any punches. The fighting became heated. Krackers started throwing *'haymakers.'* Hair sensed the anger Krackers was exhibiting and flowed around his partner, holding him tight. Hair stroked Krackers' head and rocked him gently.

"It's okay, Bud," Krackers said. "I'm okay."

Hair released his hold and flowed up. Hair rose, buzzed, and hummed. "Yeah," Krackers chuckled, "I did get carried away, didn't I?" Hair buzzed.

"I was thinking about the Shrink," Krackers stated. "He always seems to slip through my fingers!" He turned and punched a hole in a nearby wall.

"That's no way to solve a problem," Nursie cooed, wiggling into the room and up to her husband. "Did you hurt yourself?" She wrapped her arms around his neck.

"It's just," Krackers whispered, "the Shrink, he always escapes. The only two people who have actually seen his face have ended up in the psych ward."

"I've got something to take your mind off the Shrink," Nursie said. "Come here."

The two locked lips and K.I.S.Sed deeply. The mission data flowed from Nursie to Krackers. After some time, they parted, sighing.

"After this mission," Krackers whispered, "I'll take some time off, I promise. We'll go somewhere we can kick back and enjoy ourselves."

"Let's do the mission first," Nursie said, "then we can talk about a vacation. Back to the mission, there's been chatter about an attack on the Quillstar Technology building and the Peter Adams Memorial Psychiatric Hospital."

"Is the intel credible?"

"Yes, it is," Nursie said. "There are two eighteen anti-grav pad semi-trailers filled with high explosives. They will be attacking simultaneously."

"When is the attack?"

"Six am," Nursie replied. "It's three am, so three hours."

"So, my love," Krackers wrapped his arms around his wife, "just another day in paradise."

"Here's some equipment C.R.A.P.I. thought you could use on the mission," Nursie whispered. "Come back to me safe, husband."
Outside the Peter Adams Memorial Psychiatric Hospital

Bob sat in his sky-blue, armour-plated ice cream van, scanning the news on his tablet. There was a knock on his back door.

"I'm closed," Bob yelled. He went back to his news. The knock continued.

"I said I'm closed! Come back later."

Another knock. Bob sighed, swore under his breath, and rose, heading to the back door. The knock continued at the passenger-side door. Bob grunted as he made it over and wound down the window, poking his head out.

"BOO!" Krackers jumped up. Bob bumped his head and Krackers laughed, hopping from one foot to the other, clapping his hands in glee.

"I might have known," Bob rubbed his head.

"I have a mission for us," Krackers suddenly turned serious. "There's an extreme possibility that the Quillstar Technology building will be bombed today. Also, more importantly, there will be an attack on the Peter Adams Memorial Psychiatric Hospital as well. Here's the rub, I know which I'd rather protect."

Behind the two, the Hospital groaned and creaked. It slowly descended into the ground; it was truly a sight to see. After ten minutes, it had disappeared into the ground, and a half-metre-thick piece of metal slid into place over the Hospital.

"Well, Bob," Krackers chuckled, "that's made my decision a bit easier. There are extremists that will bomb at ground level. I need you to drop me on top of the Quillstar Technology building, then take out the extremists at ground level. It's time to use some of the upgrades that C.R.A.P.I. installed in your van."

Bob's ice cream van soared high until they reached the Quillstar

Technology building's three-hundred-storey structure. Bob hovered over the landing pad. Krackers opened the door, saluted Bob, grabbed his bag, and dropped onto the pad.

"Hair," Krackers commanded, "direct contact with Nursie and Bob!" Hair rose and vibrated.

"Bre," Krackers smirked, "I didn't know the Hospital could do that?"

"The *'old girl'* still has a few tricks up her sleeve," Nursie laughed. "If you'd stuck around, you would've seen the exceptionally large antiaircraft guns pop up. I think we can defend ourselves."

"Bob," Krackers said, "keep a close eye on street level. They only have two directions to come from. Both of you, be careful and make this mission a success!"

Five-thirty am.

Top of the Quillstar Technology Building

"Hair, scan the roads around the building for any traffic heading this way." Hair buzzed and hummed.

"I hope the bad guys are on time," Krackers started. "I've got shit to do today." Although he really didn't. Bravado was an important part of team spirit.

Five-fifty-five am.

Top of the Quillstar Technology Building

"Stay frosty, people," Krackers said. "T minus five minutes and counting."

Krackers

Hair rose and buzzed.

"My target is on its way," Krackers said. "Let's come home in one piece. Hair, show me the target."

Hair flowed out and covered his eyes. An image appeared showing a huge truck gaining speed.

"Well, Bud," Krackers said as he rummaged through his bag, "the truck is on its way. What do you think of our chances of making it?" Hair buzzed.

"Maybe," Krackers said. "You shouldn't have told me." He removed an anti-grav belt from his bag and wrapped it around his waist. "Calculate the distance between me and the target, taking all variables into account." He rummaged through his bag and attached two mini manoeuvring rockets to the belt.

Hair buzzed.

"Well, Hair," Krackers mused, "I hope your calculations are correct, I'd hate to overshoot. Okay, let's go."

Krackers hoisted the bag onto his back, adjusted it for comfort, activated the anti-grav belt, and rose up. He then fired the rockets; they roared into life, propelling him over the city. Hair rose, flapping in the wind, clearly enjoying it. Ahead and below Krackers was his target, travelling fast. As the semi-trailer came closer, Krackers shut down both the rockets and the anti-grav, dropping like a stone. Hair's calculations were correct.

Krackers performed a superhero landing on the semi.

He realised, momentarily, that maybe landing on a flying bomb, travelling at high speed, so hard wasn't wise. He dismissed the thought and set down the bag, rummaging inside. He brought out a larger version of the devices on his belt and scrambled up to the side of the trailer. He fixed one to the side, wriggling it to secure it, then repeated on the other side.

As he was about to activate them, a man climbed out of the cab, brandishing a crowbar.

The man charged, crowbar raised, and swung at Krackers. At the last moment, Hair shot out and the crowbar bounced off him, giving Krackers just enough time to pounce on the man. They rolled back down the trailer, struggling for the upper hand. They jumped up, squaring off. The man lunged; crowbar swung. Hair turned some strands into a bladed weapon, slicing the crowbar hand, which fell to the ground.

The man, enraged, swung his other hand, catching Krackers' chin and knocking him off the trailer. He knelt on the trailer, clutching his severed hand, blood oozing and pooling around him. He removed his shirt, wrapped it around the stump, rose with effort, and made his way back to the cab, stopping to look over the side.

Abruptly, something caught the man's attention as he leaned further over the side. Krackers rose and lunged at him. Hair formed into a knife, slicing the man top to bottom. The pieces slid off the semitrailer. Using the belt, Krackers manoeuvred and landed on top of the semitrailer's cab.

The Quillstar Technology building loomed large ahead. Krackers slapped a button on his belt, activating the two side rockets. They ignited, pushing him down as he flattened on the top of the semi. He struggled to stand, plodding to the semi-trailer cab, legs labouring as he pushed forward.

"Hair," Krackers yelled through the wind, "let's say hello to the driver!"

Hair flowed out, flapping in the strong wind. He pierced the cab and peeled it back. Krackers dropped in, sitting in the passenger seat.

"Hello there," Krackers smiled. The driver stared at the C.R.A.P.I. agent. "Hair, if you would be so kind."

Hair reared up, grabbed the driver, and tossed him out of the open roof. Krackers moved to the driver's side and pulled back on the steering wheel with all his might.

The Quillstar Technology building filled the front window view. The semi-trailer reacted to Krackers' actions, raising up and skimming the building's windows, sending glass raining down.

Finally, the semi-trailer shot up and away. On the dashboard, a countdown timer flickered into life, showing the number five before starting its countdown.

Near the Quillstar Technology Building.

Ground level.

Nursie and Bob stood, looking up, waiting for Krackers to radio in. From the sky, there was a mighty explosion. Huge balloons of fire mushroomed out, vaporising most of the semi-trailer, and small pieces of fiery debris rained down.

"Michael," Nursie gasped, "nooo!" She turned and cried on Bob's shoulder. Bob looked up as the fireballs dissipated.

"Come on, Bre," Bob whispered, "let's get you back to the Hospital." They walked back to Bob's ice cream van.

"That's my wife you're hugging," the comms crackled.

"Michael," Nursie whispered, "I thought I lost you again."

"You'll never lose me, Bre," Krackers giggled back. "I'm indestructible!"

From high above, an object dropped like a stone, smoke trailing from it. As it fell, the object spun slowly. It hit the footpath with a resounding thud, echoing over the daytime traffic.

The object embedded into the footpath, smelling like burned hair. It unfurled, revealing Krackers in the classic '*superhero landing.*' Nursie ran in, clutching her husband. He looked at her through painful eyes.

"Oh, by the way," Krackers started, then fell into her arms, unconsciousness washing over him.

In the Peter Adams Memorial Psychiatric Hospital

Nursie walked into Krackers' room. He was sitting up, playing *'cat's cradle'* with Hair. When he saw her, he leapt out of bed, and the two entwined. They kissed and held each other. After an eternity, they stepped back, smiling.

"As a reward for not damaging the Quillstar Technology Building, well, not too much," Nursie said, stepping back. Two C.R.A.P.I. agents wheeled in a huge tub of ice cream.

Hair reared up, making 'slurping' noises. Nursie handed Krackers a spoon, but Hair had dived into it, the *'slurps'* echoing from the tub. After a few moments, the ice cream tub was empty.

"Where's mine?" Krackers chuckled as Hair sluggishly retracted into Krackers' head. "Now that the kid has gone to bed." Krackers smirked at Nursie and raised an eyebrow.

"I wonder what we could do?" Nursie smiled sweetly.

"I can think of a number of things we could do," Krackers' smile grew more devious. "What about *'Doctors and Nursies*?'"

Nursie giggled, then hip-tossed Krackers onto his bed. She jumped, landing on him.

.

Twenty-Four.

Blank Space.

C.R.A.P.I. scientists were the best in the business. Plucked from the private sector, they couldn't resist the monetary rewards. Although some were a little resistant, they were recruited by more devious means. With only the occasional request, they were left to their own devices. The scientists could work on their own projects.

One scientist, Riley Drexler, was a fourteen-year-old prodigy and the youngest person to complete four master's degrees at once. Although he fitted in beautifully with the team, he was left to create new, wondrous designs.

A request came down the line from C.R.A.P.I. Command. It required a new way to deploy their troops when needed. Riley was made team leader, with three scientists and three engineers beneath him. One of the scientists, Gordon Morton, was disgruntled. He believed he should have been team leader, as he had seniority and proven himself when it counted. It didn't sit well with Gordon that the team leader was three times younger than him. He would show C.R.A.P.I. Command the mistake they had made.

After months of hard work, Riley accidentally discovered a void below normal space. He named it Blank Space. Riley theorised that Blank Space changed the laws of physics. It could take an object from point A to point B instantaneously, no matter the distance.

Four months later

The engineers had constructed two twenty-by-twenty-centimetre frames. They were powered by self-sustaining lithium-ion technology. Finally, after all the safeguards were triple-checked, the *Drexler*

Door,' as it was coined, was switched on. The two frames were three metres apart, and they rolled a metallic ball through it. The frames flashed at both ends, and the ball rolled out at the other end.

In the next experiment, a small hamster was *"coaxed"* through the Drexler Door. The target frame was two hundred metres away. Both frames flashed as the hamster appeared at the other frame. It was a success, and there were high fives, backslapping, and fist-pumping all around.

The final experiment was human trials, and volunteers were requested. Then the *'Circus'* came to town. Literally. CIRCUS FM, in conjunction with C.R.A.P.I., under the slogan *'what you don't know won't hurt you,'* created a continent-wide competition. Thousands of volunteers inundated the website, Circus.com. After weeding out the wannabees, the hopefuls were whittled down from thousands to one, a monumental effort.

The Southernmost tip of Karma,

'The Wandering.'

One month later.

The Drexler Door stood stoically at the edge of The Wandering cliffs, dropping off into the sea. It was cordoned with CIRCUS FM tape, and two exceptionally large security guards stood beside the door. The radio station broadcasted through massive speakers; it was a festive atmosphere. The crowds were immense, bouncing five enormous beach balls and cheering, though they were getting restless. The crowd chanted, "Why are we waiting?"

The only video news service lucky enough to cover the event was Vigilante News and Video. A few cameras were scattered around the area. Huge screens displayed the amazing event.

From high above, a vehicle descended from the sky. As it dropped, the crowd made out the shape of a limousine, its grav-pads glowing. It finally landed near the Drexler Door, inside the cordoned area. The crowd went silent.

After a moment, the limousine door opened. The crowd erupted. After a few seconds, the crowd quietened to an excited murmur.

"Welcome, Karma!" The radio personality, Chaz Daulitry, stepped out of the limo and raised his hand. The crowd went wild.

"Settle down," Chaz laughed, imagining the ratings spike. "Settle down. Let's hear from my partner in crime at the Northern tip of Karma, Shaz. Can you hear me, Shaz?"

The Northern most tip of Karma.

'The Hyperborean.'

"We hear you, Chaz," Shaz laughed. The massive crowd behind her erupted. Vigilante News had cameras there.

As soon as the crowd quietened, Shaz continued, "We're here at The Hyperborean, Karma's northernmost tip. Back to you, Chaz."

The Southernmost tip of Karma,

'The Wandering.'

"Thanks, Shaz," Chaz raised his voice over the crowd. "Finally, the time has come for one brave soul to step into the unknown." The crowd hushed.

"Okay, Baz, come on out." A fanfare blared, and from the limo, a tall, awkward boy left on shaky legs. The crowd screamed excitedly. Baz looked decidedly unnerved as he walked to Chaz.

The crowd roared.

Barry Edmond Cumbrous, or 'Baz' for short, had been struck down with a mental illness at an early age. His illness was severe, suicidal depression, although he managed to keep it secret until he was seventeen. Now in his early twenties, he thought, *what an unusual way to commit suicide*, so he applied to be one of the volunteers, and he won.

Go figure.

A shower of flashes crashed over Baz. Chaz raised one of his hands, and the flashes seemed to intensify; the paparazzi were having a field day. Reporters vied for Baz's attention; it was a cacophony of voices mashing together. Chaz pointed to a cute blonde, and she smiled at him.

"Cassie Melrose, Vigilante News and Video," the blonde reporter beamed. "Baz, have you anything to say to your loyal fans?"

The crowd fell silent.

"Hi," Baz sighed. The crowd stayed silent, awaiting another morsel. When that seemed all he had to say, the crowd erupted. The sound wave washed over Baz and Chaz. The radio personality waved the crowd down.

"That's all the time we have, Shaz," Chaz yelled. He raised a finger to his ear. "I've been told it's time." With that, Chaz guided Baz to the Drexler Door, and they stood a metre away. The hairs on Baz's arms raised and tingled.

"This is as far as I can go, Baz!" Chaz shook Baz's hand.

"Okay," Baz muttered.

"Shaz," Chaz said, "are you ready?"

"I was born ready," Shaz laughed. The vision on all the screens was split into three, showing Chaz, Shaz, and Baz.

"Okay, Baz," Chaz whispered, "time to step into history." The vision changed to two panels. The crowd cheered thunderously. Baz stepped forward and stood looking into the Doorway.

The crowd hushed.

Finally, Baz stepped through the Drexler Door, and it shimmered as Baz seemed to melt into it. The TV screens changed to one panel, showing a close-up of Shaz and the Door. There wasn't a sound as they waited.

The Door shimmered, and Baz began to appear. He had a peculiar look on his face, then turned as though someone were calling him. His face flashed a horrified expression at the camera as his body was sucked back into the Door. The TV screen flicked back to Chaz as one of Baz's shoes shot out of the Door. It was deformed, and wisps of smoke wafted from it.

"CUT THE FEED NOW!" Chaz screamed. All the screens went black. With that, the project was terminated.

Thirty years later

T minus One Hundred days

Riley Drexler had never relented from the task at hand. His family fortune had been poured into the project. There were numerous failures along the way, but the nature of the Door was now completely understood. A pocket of subspace would open, linking both Doorways; when the subject went through, it would close. Drexler had incorporated a triple-safeguard algorithm into the Doors. In emergencies, the Doorways would send the subject back to the origin Doorway and shut the system down.

Thirty years ago, when Baz had entered the Doorway, the subspace pocket had formed but deformed too soon, dragging Baz into subspace. The only thing to escape was his deformed shoe. The two Doorways were left where they were, and the system was shut down forever, or so they thought.

As the anniversary of Baz's death approached, CIRCUS FM decided to honour him by using the Doorway again. C.R.A.P.I. furnished a 'volunteer.' Krackers jumped at the chance to go through. The radio station advertised the event. Although it was a little more sombre, the broadcasts were still receiving high ratings. CIRCUS FM counted down the days, throwing 'pop-up' events whenever possible.

Krackers played it up to the crowds at all the pop-up events, and they loved it. With the help of Hair, there were backflips and cartwheels aplenty. Another crowd-pleaser was bringing up an audience member, giving them a gun to shoot. Hair would deflect the bullet, and the crowd lapped it up.

The Peter Adams Memorial Psychiatric Hospital.

Krackers' Room.

Present day.

The day had finally come, and Krackers was excited. He leapt out of bed, waking Nursie in the process, and bounded over to the wardrobe. There was an outfit he was asked to wear for the event. He ripped the protective plastic off the clothes and did the Happy Dance in front of the wardrobe. Since he was naked, he hurriedly put the tracksuit on.

Krackers

The top was adorned with the blue, red, yellow, and purple CIRCUS FM logo. Krackers pranced around the room. Nursie propped herself up on an elbow and smiled at her excited husband.

"It's you," Nursie chuckled. "Come give me a kiss, you hero you." Krackers walked over to Nursie, then she pounced on him, dragging him back to the bed.

An hour later

"I've really got to go, Bre," Krackers smirked and raised an eyebrow, "but we will continue this when I get back." He kissed her passionately and left the room.

The Southernmost tip of Karma.

'The Wandering.'

Present day.

The advertisements bombarded all the airwaves: TV, radio, and internet. It was relentless. The crowd that formed was like before, only bigger. Near the Drexler Door floated Baz's deformed shoe, encased in glass. The plaque read: *'In loving memory, Barry 'Baz' Edmond Cumbrous. A brave soul, taken away far too soon.'* If the event couldn't have been any bigger, more spectators crept in. It looked as though half of Karma had turned up.

The latest personalities from CIRCUS FM were Hannah and the Fat Guy. Chaz and Shaz were retired; the radio station was too superstitious to continue with them. They were considered bad luck.

After multiple lawsuits, CIRCUS FM settled out of court and continued with their latest radio personalities.

The Northernmost tip of Karma.

'The Hyperborean.'

"Fat Guy here, with CIRCUS FM," a large man laughed, "and most of Karma. The Hyperborean is pumping, awaiting Krackers to step through the Drexler Door at the Wandering, with CIRCUS' very own Hannah. Come in, Hannah."

The Southernmost tip of Karma,

'The Wandering.'

I'm here, Fat Guy," a beautiful redhead with striking green eyes replied, "at the Wandering, the southernmost tip of Karma. We're waiting for the courageous Krackers to stride into the history books, stepping through the Drexler Doors." She touched her ear.

"Fat Guy, I've just been told that Krackers is two minutes out." The huge screens cut to a short montage about Krackers and Hair.

"Here he is. Krackers!"

As if on cue, from high above, a sky-blue, armour-plated ice cream truck dropped from the heavens and landed near the Door. The crowd erupted, their voices combining into a single roar. The passenger-side door opened; Krackers leapt high into the air and landed in a *superhero landing.* Hannah and a cameraman ran towards the hero.

"Krackers, Hannah from CIRCUS FM's Hannah and the Fat Guy," the pretty redhead said. "I am, I mean, we are, all proud of you for doing this monumental project. May I be the first to wish you luck?" She swung her arms around Krackers' neck and kissed him deeply.

The Peter Adams Memorial Psychiatric Hospital.

Krackers' Room.

"...be the first to wish you luck," the television said, as it suddenly exploded in a shower of sparks. What was left of the TV started to arc. The next to explode was Krackers' door; it lay in rubble as Nursie stormed over the debris and down the corridor.

The Southernmost tip of Karma.

'The Wandering.'

Krackers gently removed Hannah from his lips.

"Oh," she said. After composing herself, Hannah continued, "Hey gang, do we have an action-packed show for you, culminating in Krackers walking through the Drexler Doors!" The crowd shrieked and howled. "After the break, we have Rodney the Wonder Llama and much more!"

Three hours later

"The time has come," Hannah said solemnly. She turned to Krackers. "Are you ready, Krackers?"

Krackers nodded as two men embedded a steel support near the Door. Hair flowed out, rearing up for the crowd. The audience went wild, hooting and cheering. Hair hammed it up in front of them, and they loved it.

"Give it up for Hair!" Hannah yelled. The crowd was ecstatic. "If you please, Krackers, would you go to the Drexler Door and ready yourself?"

Krackers moved to the Door and the steel support. Hair wrapped himself around the pillar, and Krackers gave the thumbs up just as Nursie arrived on the scene. She made her way to Krackers and kissed him passionately. After a few minutes, Nursie released Krackers and walked up to Hannah, hitting her hard enough to lift her into the air. She fell in a crumpled heap.

"We'll be back after these messages," Nursie said as she walked back to her husband. "Did you like the kiss from that *whore*?" It was, of course, a loaded question. Krackers knew his wife and gave the only answer that would save him grief.

"Hannah jumped me! You're the only woman for me," Krackers smirked. "Hair, if you would be so kind." Hair flowed out and around the two of them, cocooning them as Krackers kissed Nursie deeply. After some time, Hair unfurled, and the two parted.

Hannah sat up, shaking her head as two assistants helped her to her feet. After a moment, she collected herself. So far, ten ads had been played, and her producer was in a panic. The crowd hooted, believing the events were part of the show. As the eleventh ad finished, Hannah walked over to the Door.

"Welcome back," Hannah said, then turned to Krackers. "Are you ready?"

Krackers nodded.

"Activate the Doors!" The Door shimmered momentarily, then blackness.

"Are you sure about this?" concern flooded Nursie's face.

"I've got this," Krackers winked as he ran into the Door. Hair stretched slightly, taking on the extra weight.

"Fat Guy," Hannah said, "Krackers has entered the Door!"

The Northernmost tip of Karma.

'The Hyperborean.'

"Welcome all, Fat Guy here," the large personality said. "Krackers has stepped through the Southern Drexler Door. He should be here after these short messages."

Inside the Drexler Doors,

Blank Space.

"Hair, are you seeing this?" Hair buzzed and vibrated.

"Yes, bud," Krackers chuckled. "This is Blank Space. What do you think?"

Hair hummed.

"What have you found?"

Hair hummed, then buzzed.

"You found a body, and it only had one shoe on?" Krackers said. "And it's alive." After a moment, "can you tell the identity?" Hair buzzed.

"Barry 'Baz' Cumbrous, you say?" Krackers thought for a moment, then said, "Can you grab him?" A part of Hair shot out to the side, disappearing into the flaming void.

Blank Space was a branch of subspace; it piggy-backed it and swirled around it. Although the Doors were aligned to one another, Blank Space wasn't. It was like being inside rippling fire, but without the heat. Another interesting fact about Blank Space was that time wasn't linear; it wound and zigzagged from one point to the next.

Hair splashed back through the bubbling void, returning with Baz in tow. Krackers rolled over and spun to look at Baz. Ahead, the flames parted as the exit revealed itself. Krackers giggled as he abruptly did a somersault.

"Okay, Hair," Krackers said, suddenly solemn. "I don't know what's going to happen next, so be careful."

All at once, the exit loomed ahead. Krackers braced himself as he exited the void. Suddenly, he was sucked back into the flaming Blank Space.

"Hair," Krackers commanded, "go for the Door and pull us out!"

Hair shot forward for the Door and managed to secure footing at the exit. Hair pulled Krackers and the unconscious Baz through the Door.

The Northernmost tip of Karma,

'The Hyperborean.'

"Welcome all, Fat Guy here," the large personality said. "Krackers has stepped through the Southern Drexler Door. He should be here after these short messages."

An ad about floppy skin started to play when it was interrupted.

"It seems Krackers has arrived!" The crowd went berserk; the noise was deafening. When it died down, Fat Guy ran, well, waddled, to the hero.

"Where am I?" Krackers look slightly confused.

"You're at The Hyperborean," Fat Guy said.

"How long did it take?" The confusion was fading.

"It was instantaneous," Fat Guy replied. "Who have you got with you?"

"This is Barry 'Baz' Edmond Cumbrous," Krackers explained. "Thirty years ago, this hero started an adventure that culminated in today. I'm not the hero, Baz is." The crowd started chanting. "This was the first real test of the Drexler Doors. I'm sure they can iron out the few bugs. Give it up for Riley Drexler, the inventor."

"Riley, Riley. Riley." The crowd roared.

Krackers tapped his com and waited. After a moment, Bob answered.

"Bob," Krackers whispered, "come and get me, please. I need to get away from here."

"E.T.A. forty minutes," Bob said. "You should check out social media; they did a lovely piece on you, and Nursie was mentioned a few times.

C.R.A.P.I. loved it, mainly because they weren't mentioned."

"How much trouble will I be in with Bre?"

"Ha, ha, ha," Bob laughed and cut the connection.

The Peter Adams Memorial Psychiatric Hospital.

Krackers' room.

Flowers adorned Krackers' room. He and Nursie lay in their bed. He snuggled up to his wife.

"You know, there isn't any other woman but you."

"I'll forgive you this time," Nursie whispered back. "If you do it again, you'll start losing appendages."

"I'm yours and yours alone," Krackers whispered.

"You better," Bre smiled. "Now roll over and give baby some sugar."

Twenty-Five.

Storm In A Teacup.

From high above, the island continent of Karma was serene and beautiful. It was only when viewed from ground level that the cracks started to show. The ugliness seemed confined to the Outer Sprawl, a blight that could never be hidden.

The weather for the last six months had been atrocious: torrential rain, devastating lightning, flooding, tornadoes and hailstones as big as baseballs.

C.R.A.P.I. consulted with its Meteorological Division, who said it was virtually impossible to have these kinds of conditions, especially for so long.

The Outer Sprawl was hit hardest, with flooding. Refugees trekked into the Inner Sprawl; the residents did not welcome the intrusion, but they had no choice but to take them in.

Krackers was requested to report to the Reality Inc. Space Station. Nursie, using her contacts in C.R.A.P.I., was able to accompany her husband. They really didn't have a choice, Nursie was going, no matter what.

The Peter Adams Memorial Psychiatric Hospital.

Krackers' room.

"What do you think?" Nursie asked. She walked into the room wearing a black, skin-tight catsuit. Krackers turned around, and his jaw dropped. She did a slow turn and smiled at him.

"Wow," Krackers drooled. "I mean, WOW!" He moved in, grabbing Nursie by the waist and pulled her close.

"R&D made the suit for me," Nursie smiled. "They say it's a nanite super-suit. It's impervious to standard ammunition. It's strong, allows the user to lift up to ten times their own weight, and I particularly like the final capability: invisibility." As she spoke, the suit flipped over a nanite cowl, and she faded away.

"That's not fair," Krackers chuckled. "Hair, let's find my wife."

Hair flowed over Krackers' head, and he suddenly had infrared sight. Nursie couldn't be seen at all. Hair tried all hidden sight frequencies, but still nothing.

"Okay, Bre," Krackers said, frustration filtering in, "I give up. Where are you?"

"Ooh," Nursie purred. "I love it when you beg." She appeared behind him and wrapped her arms around him.

At the Inner and Outer Sprawl border.

A series of incredibly rare Rain Bombs, or microbursts, formed above the boundary of the two Sprawls. They were twenty-five kilometres in diameter and dropped in series. The rain balled up and struck with devastation over hundreds of kilometres. It decimated houses, buildings and shops indiscriminately, everything was levelled.

Karma Central.

Over Karma Central, lightning was unleashed, accompanied by galeforce winds strong enough to move cars. As the winds intensified, they became tornadoes. Karma Central consisted mainly of glass and steel.

Krackers

When the tornadoes touched down, shards of broken glass turned into tiny missiles, attacking everything in their path.

The Peter Adams Memorial Psychiatric Hospital.

Krackers' room.

A series of monitors were flashing stats and information. Krackers sat near one of the monitors, both arms straight out, imitating a steering wheel. He was growing increasingly frustrated.

"Michael," Nursie said, "come and see this."

"That was a really stupid game," Krackers said as he rose and walked over to Nursie. "What's up?" He stepped behind her and wrapped his arms around her neck.

"Have you seen," Nursie said, concern in her voice, "what's been happening outside?"

"Oh," Krackers chuckled, a smirk on his lips, "that would explain why the car wouldn't move."

"The weather," Nursie said, "is too precise. This is four times the amount of rain ever experienced at one time." Hair rose and buzzed.

"Really," Krackers mused, "I hadn't noticed. Hair has detected an anomaly in the weather patterns: the atmospheric conditions cycle every thirty minutes!"

Hair buzzed, then hummed.

"Hair says," Krackers relayed, "it's going to cycle in ten minutes."

"We have to get to the Space Station," Nursie said. "We can assess the situation from there."

The Peter Adams Memorial Psychiatric Hospital.

Main Entrance.

"Bob," Krackers radioed through Hair, "manoeuvre your van as close to the awning as you can."

Krackers and Nursie waited just inside the two huge oak doors of the Hospital. The wind was blowing a gale; tiny glass missiles whizzed by, creating a melodious song.

Krackers started to sing along, softly at first, then bellowed it out. Abruptly, the wind died down. After ten minutes, it picked up again, and Bob swam into view. He tried to hover as he slowly moved in.

Besides the beautiful, majestic oak doors, the Hospital had an exquisite, ornate awning, but the glass projectiles had obliterated it, leaving only the steel frame. Bob moved in and hovered with centimetres to spare.

"Well hello, young Bob," Krackers smiled. "We need to get to the Reality Inc. Space Station!"

"I know this van can do amazing stuff," Bob chuckled, "but I doubt I'm able to get you there."

"It's okay, Bob," Nursie said. "Please take us to the Quillstar Technology building. We need to ride the space elevator up to the Space Station."

Bob moved away from the Hospital and up toward the Quillstar building. It was a bumpy ride, but luckily the ice cream van was armour-plated; the glass missiles bounced harmlessly off the sides. As if on cue, the winds died down and lightning flashed across the darkening skies.

Hair rose, vibrated, and buzzed.

"Yes, I agree, you're a clever boy," Krackers said. "Hair says to go now, really, really fast!"

Bob's armour-plated ice cream van rocketed up the three-hundred storey building. He just landed on one of the landing pads when the wind picked up again. The pad secured the van with clamps.

"Well," Bob said to Krackers, "this is as far as I can go. Hair, keep him safe."

The two of them exited the van. Nursie's suit activated, and she faded from view. Krackers walked up to the two C.R.A.P.I. sentries standing guard over the space station elevator. He embellished a salute and waited for the elevator. The door slid open, began to close, then opened again. Finally, it closed.

The Reality Inc. Space Station.

As Krackers stepped out of the elevator, Nursie suddenly appeared, giving him a start. He jumped back, landing in a *hero stance.*

"Oops," Nursie said. "Sorry." She shrugged and blew him a kiss.

"I'll start a level nine scan on the cloud cover," Krackers said. "If you could do an in-depth scan of the weather data over the last week?"

"Where is everybody?" Nursie looked around suspiciously. "I know this station can run on autopilot, but there should be at least three officers and nine engineers."

"You stick with the computer," Krackers said, "and I'll find out what's going on with the rest of the station." He ran to the station's lift and down to the lower levels.

The elevator music was loud and numbing. As he was about to 'neck' himself, the lift clanged and the door opened. As he stepped out, he knew something was wrong.

Krackers thought he was quick, but Hair was faster. Even as a bullet entered the chamber, Hair flowed out and over him. Multiple rounds thudded into Hair, who just shrugged them off.

"Hair," Krackers yelled over the din, "deactivate them, with extreme prejudice!" Hair flashed out with strands, destroying seven gun ports.

"Michael," Nursie activated the com, "I think I might have found something."

"Roger that," Krackers said. "Be there soon!"

The lift clanged again as Krackers ran up to Nursie.

"I think I've found something," Nursie said. "Look at this." She tapped a keyboard and a large monitor activated, showing the cloud cover map. She sent it to a table, then walked over. The strange thing was the cloud cover: it seemed to swirl only around Karma. Out to sea, the skies were crystal clear; the clouds were directed solely at Karma.

There had been glimpses of something, but nothing concrete, until a single image revealed three-quarters of a ship of some kind.

"Can you extrapolate the ship's location through the cloud cover?" Krackers asked, moving to a large smart table in the centre of the room.

"Well," Nursie said, "all I can give you is a close approximation." The cloud on the table flashed, then disappeared as a grid removed it from view. One grid square remained, and Krackers enlarged it. There was something definitely there.

"I think we should use the Electromagnetic Pulse cannon," Krackers said, walking to the E.M.P. cannon controls. He started the pre-sequence, then punched the coordinates into the targeting computer. The monitor above the controls zeroed in on the target and flashed green. Krackers activated the cannon and fired. Nursie watched the monitor as the invisible pulse, tracked by the computer, hit the target and ballooned around it.

Krackers tapped a few keys. The target appeared, deceptively large. "Well," Krackers said, "the target's shielded. Looks like I'll have to go to the target and shut it down myself."

"Oh, no you don't," Nursie laughed. "*We* will go and shut it down together!"

"Yes, dear," Krackers chuckled.

The Reality Inc. Space Station Airlock.

"Let me check your suit," Krackers said, fussing over Nursie. "Where's your suit?" Nursie suddenly realised.

"Don't worry, dear," Krackers chuckled. "All I need is Hair."

"Okay, husband," Nursie smiled, "let's go turn off the rain."

"Okay, Hair," Krackers stated, "I need an atmos suit." Hair flowed around him, creating an airtight, atmospheric suit. "Let's go shut down the waterworks."

The airlock cycled through the opening sequence. The air pumped out, and the door opened. The two floated freely as the anti-gravity deactivated. The airlock outer door opened, and they drifted out. Nursie wore a jetpack, and Hair fired strands which attached to Nursie's helmet.

"Okay," Krackers said, "you've got the coordinates, so let's go!"

The puff of air signified the beginning of the journey; the sudden tug was sharp but expected. The two rocketed toward the target, a slight trepidation in both. Nursie activated the retrorockets, but nothing happened.

"Michael," Nursie masked the hysteria welling up, "the retro-rockets have failed."

"Are you sure?" Krackers paused for a moment. "I'm sorry, dumb question. Hair, see what you can do."

Hair flowed out from the spacesuit and shot toward the target. Hair flared out and encompassed Nursie, guarding his partner's wife. His strands hit the target and began to slow their movement. Finally, they arrived at the target, and Hair flowed back into the spacesuit.

"Now where," Krackers mused, "would an airlock be hiding? Bre, would you know where the airlock is?"

"Hold your horses," Nursie muttered as she tapped a small virtual keyboard. "It should be over here." She activated the jetpack and they descended below the ship. They found a small, single-person airlock. After cycling through the process, they crouched behind some boxes. Nursie removed her spacesuit, and Hair flowed back into Krackers' head.

"I would say they know we're here," Krackers giggled as a klaxon roared. He clapped his hands in joy as the room bathed in red. The lights cycled from red to white and back to red again.

"We don't have time for this," Nursie said, urgency in her voice.

"Hair," Krackers ordered, "scan for life signs!"

Hair rose, vibrated, and buzzed. After a moment, Hair buzzed again.

"Hair says," Krackers relayed, "there are six other life signs. How do you want to play this?"

"I'm new to this," Nursie said, "I think you should work out our next move."

"Firstly," Krackers said, "we should stick together. In the movies, when they split up, they get killed, one by one. Let's go."

Krackers moved forward with Nursie behind him. They stopped at a cross corridor, and Krackers turned to Nursie. She was crouched, a gun in her hand.

"I was going to ask," Krackers chuckled, "where you got that gun from, but after all things considered, I don't think I want to know." He smiled sweetly at her, then changed the subject. "Which way now, Hair?"

Hair buzzed and squeaked.

"Okay, bud," Krackers answered, "Hair says we should go to the next intersection and turn right." They moved down the corridor, reached the intersection, and turned right.

Suddenly, a bulky door dropped from the ceiling, blocking their way. They turned to retreat when another door dropped, trapping them.

"Hey, I'm wearing the super suit!" Nursie stepped forward to the front door, lifted it, and waved Krackers through. She stepped through and let the door drop down.

"This is one," Krackers chuckled, "of the many reasons I love you so." They continued down the corridor to another intersection.

"Where to now, Hair?"

Hair buzzed and vibrated.

"Hair says," Krackers translated, "the control room is straight ahead, and the six life forms are in there." They moved cautiously and stopped at a door.

"Remind me later where you found that gun," Krackers said.

"On three," Nursie smirked, "we storm the control room."

"One… two… three!" Krackers barked. Hair flowed out and under the door, lifting it effortlessly. By the time Nursie ran in, Hair had subdued three of the bad guys. She tracked the remaining men, fired three shots, and dropped them to the floor.

Hair squeezed the captured men into unconsciousness, then grabbed Nursie's three prisoners. After some time, all six men came to.

"Glad to see you up and around," Nursie smiled. "This is my psychotic husband and his dangerous partner, Hair. They want to kill you and make hats from your skulls. I, on the other hand, wanted to spare you from becoming party favours." Two of the men fainted at the news.

"Luckily, Hair and I have won," Krackers growled. "Prepare to meet your maker!" Hair applied pressure; all six men promptly soiled themselves and passed out. Hair placed them in a closet and locked it, then flowed back to Krackers.

Nursie studied the many buttons, switches, and knobs. Krackers leant over to touch a shiny, flashing button, but Nursie slapped his hand away.

"Don't touch anything," Nursie reprimanded. "Remember the weapon's dump in the Outer Sprawl?"

"I think you'll find it was Hair," Krackers lied. After thinking better of it, and noting Hair's growl, he added, "Umm, I think that might have been me."

As she turned, Krackers' hand flashed across the control panel. He stabbed the glowing button. A warning sound beeped, and Nursie turned to face him.

"What did you do?" Nursie didn't seem happy, so Krackers went to the closet to interrogate the prisoners. "Don't hurt them too much; we may need them."

"You never let me have any fun," Krackers sulked, then opened the closet door and grabbed a man. Hair wrapped around the prisoner's feet and lifted him into the air.

"I need to know how to operate this ship." Hair shook the man, then stopped.

"I've seen my partner Hair, rip a man in two." On cue, Hair grabbed the man's head and feet and started to pull.

"Well, Hair, looks like you can snap him in half." Hair applied pressure, and the man yelled.

"Please don't snap me in half," he sobbed. "I'll tell you everything." He cracked and blurted out his part in the undertaking, about C.R.I.M.E. and the weather machine. Hair turned him upright, and Krackers walked him to the middle of the room and over to the control panel.

"Okay," Krackers said sternly, "turn off the machine and I'll make sure they go easy on you."

"The shutdown sequence," the man said, "is beyond my expertise and pay grade. I'm just a lowly grunt. C.R.I.M.E. said if anyone was to come here, I was to press this button." He stabbed the button as he spoke.

"Damn," Krackers started. "Hair!" Hair grabbed the man and tore him in half. Blood splashed everywhere; Nursie leapt away from the ooze.

"I was going to ask you to knock him out; we may have been able to use him as a hostage. Clean us up, and we'll have to change the plan."

"He's activated the self-destruct," Nursie said, "but nothing seems to be happening." Suddenly every door slid shut and locked.

"I have a bad feeling about this," Krackers stated. The ship started spinning on its axis, slowly at first, then increasing in speed.

"Hold onto the control panel!"

Hair shot out and held Krackers and Nursie fast as the ship spun faster.

"Bre, put on your spacesuit," Krackers grunted, finding it increasingly harder to breathe. "Hair, get us out of here, by any means!" A part of Hair shot straight out. It transformed into a sharp blade as it hit the control room wall. A hole appeared and was forced wider. Air started escaping, and Hair retracted. They were about to escape when the hole began repairing itself. After a moment, it had almost finished sealing the breach.

"There must be another way," Krackers panted. "Think. Think. Hair, see if you can talk to the ship. We need a new exit strategy."

Hair manoeuvred more strands to find an access port. Once located, Hair inserted them into the port.

Hair buzzed.

"What do you mean, hold on?" Krackers tried to understand his partner's statement.

Abruptly, multiple small explosions rang around the control room.

"What have you done, Hair?" Suddenly, with one last explosion, the control room was pushed away from the spinning ship. Both breathless, Nursie sat up and tapped her ear.

"All C.R.A.P.I. ships," Nursie panted, "destroy the target ship!" She turned and flopped next to her husband, closing her eyes.

The Peter Adams Memorial Psychiatric Hospital.

Krackers' room.

Krackers finally awoke and opened his eyes. A beautiful face swam into view.

"Bre," Krackers smiled, "so we made it?"

"Yes, Michael," Nursie returned the smile, "we most definitely did. How are you feeling?"

"Like a thousand small children bouncing on my chest," Krackers laughed painfully.

"I've got ice cream," Nursie said.

Hair shot up, making slurping noises.

"Yes, Hair," Nursie laughed, "there's some for you. They say there are medals for you two, when you're up to it."

"Well," Krackers smirked, "you are a nurse, aren't you? Can you give me a physical?"

"So, where does it hurt?"

Hair flowed out, creating a screen.

"Ouch!"

Twenty-Six.

Stick Ya' Hand Up, Ya' Bum!

Twins have a unique bond. Sarah and Tosh were considered special. Being identical twins, their 'abilities' were heightened, making many people extremely uncomfortable. By the age of nine, their abilities had increased tenfold. Their parents, unable to cope with the twins' *'specialness,'* abandoned them. Suddenly, they had to fend for themselves.

By seventeen, they were street-hardened in the Outer Sprawl, although they didn't show it, hiding their skills well. Sarah was street savvy, while Tosh was the brains of the outfit. Both were beautiful, which had its advantages. They went to work for a top-end bounty recovery service, *'Found You Bounties,'* and were an instant hit. Their age and appearance aided them through many cases. Their sponge-like thirst for knowledge was only surpassed by their ability to bring in their bounties.

By twenty, they had learnt all they could and decided it was time to leave. They moved to Karma Central and started a business, *'Puss In Boots' Bounty Services.'* With glowing references, they were subsequently recruited by C.R.A.P.I. and absorbed into their crime unit. They were allocated an office in the Peter Adams Memorial Psychiatric Hospital and settled in. They reconnoitred the Hospital areas; some were unauthorised, but using their abilities, they accessed areas they couldn't otherwise.

That was when they bumped into Krackers. literally. Nursie, monitoring the in-house security feeds, came across a feed of her husband chatting and laughing with the two beauties, and she wasn't impressed. To show her displeasure, she punched the monitor, which exploded in a shower of sparks. She grabbed her seat, threw it back, embedding it in a wall, and stormed out of Krackers' room down the corridor.

She made her way to where the frivolity was happening. She slowed and took a couple of deep breaths, then approached.

"Michael," Nursie smiled daggers at her husband, "I don't think I've met you two before?" Venom dripped from every word. Nursie leaned in and shook their hands. "You're both beautiful." She stepped in further.

"Bre," Krackers tried to defuse a possible bloodbath. "This is Sarah and Tosh. They are from 'Puss In Boots' Bounty Services. They're working in conjunction with C.R.A.P.I."

"Michael," Nursie spat, "we need to talk. Now!" Krackers knew that *'look'* and it scared him. He followed his wife into the corridor and waited for the onslaught.

"Bre," Krackers whispered, "I was only welcoming them. They bumped into me! You're the only one for me."

"I'm sorry, Michael," Nursie suddenly burst into tears. "I jumped to a conclusion. I'm sorry. Can you ever forgive me?"

"Of course I forgive you," Krackers smiled and hugged Nursie. Nursie covered her mouth and vomited on Krackers. He moved her to the toilet, then waited outside as unpleasant noises echoed.

"Hair, clean me up, will you?"

As Hair cleaned his partner. Krackers tried to find something interesting to look at. Finally, the toilet flushed, and Nursie emerged, wiping her mouth with a wipe. Krackers was about to inquire about her health when there was a soft buzz, and she tapped her ear.

"It looks like you have a mission. Go back to your room and wait. I won't be long." She leaned in for a kiss.

Krackers

The Peter Adams Memorial Psychiatric Hospital.

Krackers' room.

Krackers entered his room and abruptly stopped. The scene resembled a crime scene. The room was a mess. A chair was embedded in the far wall. The computer monitor appeared to have exploded. After a while, Nursie walked in.

"Michael, I'm so sorry about my outburst earlier," Nursie said sincerely. "I'm so embarrassed."

"It's okay, Bre," Krackers smiled. "I'm worried about you. What about if we go to the infirmary and talk to a doctor?"

"Okay," Nursie said, her head hung low.

"You were saying something about a mission?" Krackers changed the subject.

"Yes," Nursie said, wiping some tears from her eyes. "Come here, tiger." She grabbed Krackers, pulled him close, and kissed him.

The K.I.S.S. or Knowledge In Saliva Sample flowed from Nursie to Krackers. After what seemed like an eternity, the two parted.

"Could you request," Nursie tapped the com in her ear, "the *'Puss in Boots'* crew to join us in Krackers' room?"

Momentarily, Sarah and Tosh entered Krackers' room. It was amazing how much they looked alike; it was like looking into a mirror. Nursie walked up to another wall and tapped it. A panel slid open, revealing a monitor.

"The mission is a sticky one," Nursie said, having composed herself, "and it's a somewhat dangerous bounty hunt. Barret Monroe is the Shrink's right-hand man. He is to be brought in alive. Hair, are you listening?"

Hair rose and buzzed.

"Hair said he'll be on his best behaviour," Krackers chuckled.

Nursie continued to explain the rest of the mission. After an hour, the briefing concluded. She walked over to the twins and forced a smile.

"We need your bounty hunting skills," Nursie said to them. "Our agents have tried and failed. Then we heard of your success rate. it's very impressive."

"My brother and I," Sarah said, "are honoured to be working for C.R.A.P.I."

"Okay," Krackers said, "it's time to go."

"If you wait a moment," Nursie said, "I'll get my stuff."

"I thought," Krackers commented, "you could co-ordinate from here."

"If you wait a moment," Nursie repeated, staring daggers at Krackers, "I'll get my stuff."

"I think we should wait for Bre," Krackers said. He turned to Sarah and Tosh; they hastily agreed.

After a few moments, Nursie returned, and after an awkward pause, they left the Hospital.

Outside the Peter Adams Memorial Psychiatric Hospital.

"Tosh and I will work this through our contacts," Sarah suggested. "You two should go to his last known location."

Krackers agreed; Nursie was still dubious. The twins walked off into the night.

"Isn't it interesting," Nursie commented, "that they split us up? They could have done whatever they wanted with us, but instead, they disappeared at the first chance they got!"

"Bre," Krackers cradled her face in his hands, "I love you, and only you. You don't need to be jealous." He leant in and kissed her deeply.

Nursie closed her eyes, savouring the moment. After a while, they came up for air, and Nursie opened her eyes.

"Okay, Michael," Nursie whispered. "Maybe I am getting paranoid. Let's track down this reprobate and get the payment from C.R.A.P.I." She tapped her right arm, and the mission specs floated in a three-dimensional hologram. "We'll grab Bob and go to the Warehouse district."

"Sounds like a plan," Krackers smiled. "Let's go get Bob."

Bob and his sky-blue, armour-plated ice cream van sat in the number two car park. Krackers and Nursie approached and greeted him.

"Good evening, young Bob," Krackers smirked. "Are you ready for another action-packed adventure?"

"Have I got a choice?" Bob activated the start-up sequence. "What's the destination?"

"We need to get to the Warehouse district, Bob," Nursie said, smiling at him.

"The Warehouse district it is," Bob replied as the armour-plated ice cream van lifted off and shot into the dark sky.

Three hours later.

The Warehouse district, the Outer Sprawl.

The trip was uneventful. After three hours, the Warehouse district came into view.

"Where would you like to be dropped?" Bob asked, flicking switches.

"We need to get to this container," Nursie swiped the hologram and slid it to Bob's navigation computer. "Land on the third container from the target and await further instructions."

"Okay," Bob said. He headed for the target container and, after a few minutes, hovered above it, awaiting instructions.

Krackers jumped out of the van and helped Nursie down. He turned to Bob.

"Keep us safe, young Bob," Krackers yelled dramatically. "Scan the area and report anything unusual, no matter what."

Bob powered down the van, landing on top of the container, and scanned the area. He activated the invisibility field, and the van faded from view.

Krackers and Nursie cautiously crept to the target container. They stood either side of the entrance doors and waited.

"Hair," Krackers whispered, "scan for life signs."

Hair rose and vibrated. After a moment, Hair buzzed.

"Hair said he can't scan it; it must be shielded," Krackers whispered to Nursie. "We're going to have to breach the container, blind."

"I really hope the twins were right about this," Nursie said, sounding apprehensive.

"So do I," Krackers muttered under his breath. "Breach in three. Two. One. breach!"

The two grabbed the handles and opened the container. A rain of bullets shot out.

"Barret Monroe," Nursie yelled into the darkness of the opened container, "you are surrounded. Come out now, and we can come up with a mutually beneficial plan."

Nursie peered inside and was rewarded with a hail of bullets.

"This isn't working," Krackers whispered. "We're going to have to try something else. What do you think?"

"What about this?" Nursie faded into the scenery. Suddenly, more bullets flew past, then she appeared again. "How could he see me?"

Krackers

"This is ridiculous," frustration creeping into Krackers' voice. "Hair, shield me!"

Hair flowed up and around him. Krackers stepped into the shower of bullets and moved forward. He disappeared into the darkness; the sound of gunfire continued, then ceased.

"All clear," Krackers yelled. "Bre, check this out."

Nursie stepped into the container, and it took a moment for her eyes to adjust to the dimness. Krackers was leaning against a machine gun controlled by a box on the floor.

"I guess it had a motion tracker?" Nursie tapped the box with her foot. Suddenly, the container doors snapped shut.

"Crap!" Krackers dropped his head. "Looks like we're trapped."

A couple of minutes later.

"Hair," Krackers said, "we've got to get out of this."

Nursie activated a hologram, and the container took on a ruddy light, bathing it in a hellish glow.

Hair rose and flowed toward the door. The machine gun cocked and chambered. As Hair passed the gun, it began rapid firing; Hair recoiled.

"I wish," Krackers yelled, "I'd never climbed into this container! I wish the doors would open and the machine gun would stop!"

As if by command, the machine gun ceased firing, and a small light on the box changed from green to red.

Hair moved cautiously toward the door. The gun stayed still. Krackers and Nursie crept to the doors, and Nursie extinguished the hologram. They were about to try the doors again when sounds came from outside the container.

"Bre," Krackers commanded, "stay behind me. This could get ugly."

299

"Maybe it's Bob?" Nursie activated her armour. Different parts slotted together, and moments later her suit was set. She faded from view.

"Hair, armour me up, please," Krackers ordered. Hair flowed around him, forming protective layers.

The container doors slowly opened, and light streamed in, momentarily blinding Krackers. Gunfire erupted outside. Round after round exploded around him. His eyesight returned, revealing the assailants.

"It's the twins," an invisible voice whispered. "I'll try to distract them so you can come in with Hair and stop them."

Abruptly, the sounds of a struggle signalled the beginning of action.

Krackers ran into the fray. Hair flowed out, absorbing the firepower. Hair advanced until reaching Sarah and Tosh, securing them tightly. They struggled, screaming a guttural sound.

"There's no point struggling," Krackers chuckled. "Hair will keep hold of you both."

Abruptly, there was a flash. Parts of Hair restraining the twins froze. An explosion freed them, and they ran in different directions. "I'll go after Tosh," Nursie said. "You go after Sarah. Meet back here."

Krackers ran after Sarah.

"Bob, come in," Krackers asked.

"Reading you," Bob replied. "What's up?"

"I need you quick," Krackers snapped. "Home in on my signal."

Moments later, Bob landed his ice cream van near Krackers. He jumped in.

"Let's get some height. We need to hunt the hunters."

The van lifted into the air, halting around twenty metres. They hovered and got their bearings. On Bob's radar, three blips appeared, one following the other, while the other blip moved away.

"Go after that blip," Krackers pointed at the single blip.

Krackers

Like an avenging angel, Bob's armour-plated ice cream van swooped down.

"Bob, I'll get out here. Monitor Nursie and make sure she's safe." Krackers somersaulted out. Hair shot down to the ground, gently placing him. Hair flowed around him, forming armour.

"Let's get a bounty," Hair said, wrapping around Krackers' head and superimposing the tracker image.

"Okay, Hair. She's hiding beside a container, south-west, four containers down. Let's get this bad girl!"

"Bre," Krackers said via Hair's com, "are you there?"

"Yes, Michael," Nursie replied. "My target is down and dusted. He's not going anywhere. How's it going at your end?"

"Mine's playing *hide and seek*," Krackers chuckled. "Should have her shortly. Meet you back at the ice cream van. Out."

"Roger," Nursie said. "Bre, out."

"Hair," Krackers said, "let's get some height."

A part of Hair shot into the air, attaching to the top of a container. Hair reeled Krackers up. He landed on top and ran to the end.

"Hair," Krackers enquired, "give me an update on the target, please."

The target stayed where she was. Krackers, with Hair's help, silently moved south-west, down four containers.

Hair unfurled from Krackers' face, waving above his head. He moved to the edge and peered down. Sarah crouched, trying to make herself as small as possible.

Krackers smirked as he dropped to the ground in front of her, landing in a superhero stance. Sarah jumped back as if burned.

"How did you find me?" Sarah asked, reaching behind her back.

"Don't do that, Sarah," Krackers warned.

Sarah continued reaching and, in one fluid motion, produced a knife and ran towards him, screaming.

"Stop, Sarah!" Krackers yelled. "Please, Sarah!"

Hair shot out, covering Krackers with sizeable spikes just as she reached him, impaling herself in the process. Blood sprayed both of them.

"Nooo, Hair!" Krackers cried. "What have you done?!"

Hair flared back to Krackers' skull. Sarah's lifeless body dropped to the ground. Hair buzzed loudly.

"I know you had to defend me, Bud," Krackers cried, "but not to take a defenceless life."

Hair buzzed and clicked.

"I know she had a knife," Krackers shook his head, "but still."

"Michael," Nursie said, "has anything happened to Sarah?"

"Why do you ask?" Krackers replied.

"Tosh screamed and slumped over," Nursie explained.

"Can you get Bob," Krackers asked, "to come and get me, please? I'll explain what happened when I see you."

Minutes later.

Krackers noticed movement from above. Bob landed the ice cream van ahead of him.

The mood in the van, as they travelled back to the Peter Adams Memorial Psychiatric Hospital, was sombre.

Krackers

The Peter Adams Memorial Psychiatric Hospital.

The Hospital came into view, and Nursie radioed in on the situation. As Bob landed, a gurney and wheelchair were waiting.

After helping Tosh into the wheelchair, Krackers and Bob brought Sarah's body out and onto the gurney. Both were whisked away. Krackers and Nursie went inside.

The Peter Adams Memorial Psychiatric Hospital.

Krackers' room.

As the two approached Krackers' room, Nursie made a beeline for the toilet. After ten minutes, she came out and sat next to her husband on his bed.

"Are you okay, Bre?" he asked, rubbing her back.

"Yeah," she smiled, laying her head on his shoulder. "I'm fine." She produced a small paddle with a blue line on it. "Congratulations, my love, you're a daddy." Krackers fainted.

The end, or is it?

And, more importantly, will there be ice cream?